Spells of Tarot & Tragedy

HARLEY JANE ROSE

Stay up to date on all the latest writings by Harley
Jane Rose by following on socials:
@HarleyJaneRose (TikTok, Instagram, Twitter)

SPELLS OF TAROT & TRAGEDY

HARLEY JANE ROSE

ISBN: 978-0-6486445-1-4

Cataloguing-in-Publication Data

Summary: Mackenzie stumbles upon an underground world of
magic and tarot while she searches for her lost family.

First Edition: February 2023

Cover design © Jaqueline Kropmanns

*To all those still looking for
their place to belong…*

1: THE ANNIVERSARY

The old pickup truck gurgled its way to the side of the road, parking beside the emerald-green expanse of the forest. Mackenzie sat in the car, arms braced against the steering wheel despite its now-dead engine as the smell of pine intruded upon the cabin, attempting to lull her into a daze that refused to linger. Mackenzie's heart threatened to crack ribs as it tried to break free. The ball of lead in her stomach pulled her organs tighter as the cold flowed through her veins. Her lungs barely seemed to function, as though they'd lost the memory of how.

Opening the creaking door of the pickup, she eased herself out of the seat she'd taken comfort in for years. As her hiking boots touched the gravel, she tried to breathe deeply to focus on the way her body connected to the ground and reminded herself to relax… at least a little. Convincing her body to do the same was a different battle.

The pine forest—despite the dangers it held within— welcomed her. The scent of pine invaded her nose and made her mouth taste like she'd drunk perfume with cooking spices in it. The mountains climbed in the near distance, overseeing all, reaching above the clouds with alpine secrets they would never tell Mackenzie. After the number of times she'd visited this section of the woods, the tree line that greeted the road was memorized and predictable. She waded into the forest, the noise from the road disappearing as the new sounds assaulted her ears. This natural world, generally ignored by the nearby small town, had its own thriving life: wind played with the trees, testing the strengths of their branches; old pines needles rained down from above, keeping only the strongest attached; and birds twittered in their games of hide-and-seek.

All of it was a daily constant for Mackenzie during her walks, including the eyes that watched from an unknown place. She couldn't quite ever find them, no matter the number of times she searched for the source of her prickling neck. It had been a recent development but had been reoccurring for weeks now with no explanation she could find.

The silver heart-shaped pendant hung from the branch ahead of her, glistening at her eye height. Sometimes the angle with the light hitting it just right made it look like a faerie was using it as a swing. But she knew it hung alone and untouched as it had since she'd left it there. It was almost luminous against the lush greenery and moist, dark-colored bark that surrounded it, letting Mackenzie know she was on the correct bearing.

The corners of her eyes swam with tears as she fought the surge of emotion from her gut that threatened to have her sobbing against the tree with no control. She lifted her fingertips to brush the cold metal of her necklace, filled with so much history she didn't know, that it made her mind swim with questions. There was no one left to ask for the answers, and at the thought of her loneliness, the tears managed to escape. Dropping her hand quickly, she dug her fingernails into her hand, focusing on the pain as it bit into her palm rather than the overwhelming pressure of her repressed emotions in her head. *Don't lose it now*, she told herself, *not after this long.*

With a last glance at the name of her mother Anne engraved on the pendant, she moved past it, pushing forward on her journey in determination. She became more aware of the cool morning air that blew against the tears that crept down her cheeks, chilling her face. Wiping them away quickly, she pushed her body faster, feeling the beginnings of sniffles she wanted to avoid. Her eyes darted around, searching through the pine trees the way she was supposed to, looking for any movement or foreign items. She tried to be methodical, checking the area around her as though it were a grid, sweeping each box before moving on. Nothing presented itself in increasing monotony, and her heart, which had raced so frantically when she entered, slowed in disappointment.

The moist air lingered in her nose as she stepped sure-footedly towards the lake, the noise of cracking twigs underfoot sounding out through the forest. She seemed to be on her own, but she still felt the gaze of someone or something following her, and—despite the discomfort—it gave her a twisted sense of hope. If there were people or things here that she couldn't find, maybe her mother was too.

Mackenzie cleared the pine tree line, finding the freshwater lake she'd set as her first destination marker for the day and paused at its edge. The bright, ice-blue water glittered with the approaching morning sun, crystal clear in its depths. The mountain climbed into view, towering over the opposite side of the lake, imposing its' might upon the forest. At the base were many caves that had not been seen by human eyes for fear of the dangers that lurked inside. Until today, Mackenzie had made note of these caves on her previous walks and had decided that on her final day of the search, she would muster the courage to check them all. She didn't care if being out all day looking through them would put her in a world of trouble with her surrogate family when she got home, she just wanted answers. One way or another.

She climbed through the shrubbery on the shore that clung to the water like a lifeline and stepped up on the rock she knew well. It jutted out over the lake's edge, offering a good vantage point where she could rake her eyes over its surface, searching. The clearness of the water allowed her to search nearby depths, looking for deathly white in amongst the dark colors of the water plants and fish.

Nothing still.

She kept her eyes on the surface, hoping for new signs that her mother had been here or even that she had found her last rest in the bowels of this lake. Still no evidence, same as *almost* every other day before.

She remembered the day the search parties had come out here—with her in tow—and she'd spotted that heart-shaped necklace in this spot. That piece of jewelry was the only hint that had ever presented itself to her as proof her mother had been here. Once again, the tears of loss threatened to overtake her, even after so many years.

Her only solution was to pull herself back up to her feet and begin the new search she had dreaded undertaking—the caves at the base of her mountains.

Mackenzie had barely glanced across the lake toward her destination when she caught a gaze that made the air around her feel like ice. Two large glowing red eyes caught hers. The creature they belonged to was a large, black-furred mass that looked like a mix of bear and giant wolf but somehow unlike anything she'd ever seen or imagined. She kept its gaze, afraid to break it and lose sight of the creature that she could see breathing heavily. It reminded her of a salivating dog, excited for a piece of meat brought out for dinner. Her heartbeat stopped for a long moment that strung out enough for her to panic that it might not start again.

She wouldn't be going over to the caves with that *thing* there. Could she run faster than the creature could get to her? The muscles in her legs tightened harshly, readying. The beast stepped forward, stalking closer to the edge of the lake curiously. Time to leave.

She leapt off the rock, feeling the wobble in her limbs as they landed on the hard ground. Her knees buckled on impact, and the flash of pain made her hiss through her teeth. Bracing her hands out in front, she pushed off the ground as it came in reach. Her complaining body would make it through this.

Her neck prickled as the eyes watched her. She sprinted towards the car and the direction of the necklace, frantically whipping her head around to check her sides. Everything in her readied for the moment the nightmare of a creature could pop out of the dense woodland.

Her eyes slipped from the path as the ground flew towards her, colliding with her forehead before her hand could stop her fall.

Black spots spun in her vision, her ears and head ringing with the impact as she rolled herself onto her back and tried to refocus her eyes. Her heart was frantic as she rushed her body to a state of function it was not ready to accept. All of which, still felt too slow compared to what pursued her. Fighting the urge to vomit, Mackenzie forced herself to her feet as quickly as her body would allow and continued to run on shaky legs. Lightheadedness fell away from her focus as she kept her eyes on the path ahead. She couldn't afford another slip-up. She didn't know how close the creature was.

Bolting past the necklace in the tree, the car finally coming into view did nothing to quell Mackenzie's panic. She tried to act quickly as she reached the door, fumbling for the keys and unsteadily jimmying one into the lock. It wasn't until she made it into the driver's seat with the door locked behind her and the engine on that she took a quick, deep breath. Everything in her buzzed as though she had ten cups of coffee in her system and her head ached with dizziness she couldn't shake. Staring into the dense pines, she kept expecting the red glowing eyes to appear—feeling them watching her. Before they could show, she gunned the pickup into reverse, pulling back from the boulder she'd parked behind and quickly tearing out onto the road, her eyes never leaving the pines.

The loud horn of the car that almost ran up the back of her had her jumping in her seat like a frightened rabbit and cursing her stupidity. The Chevy driver begun to overtake her with obvious gestures, yelling out of his window. She tried to ignore it in her periphery, focusing on taking deep breaths and watching the road properly this time. She was staring intently ahead—not meeting the other driver's face—until he finally pulled in front of her and drove off. She relaxed a little.

The eyes of the forest followed Mackenzie and she was no longer sure if she was being watched or if she was utterly paranoid. The road broke from the pines, heading into town, and the prickling weight left her spine. Her breathing and heart rate returned to normal, despite her discomfort with the city. A heavy sensation settled through her muscles as the adrenaline began to subside and her head demanded to be acknowledged as the throbbing grew worse. The weight of her limbs helped push the accelerator and get her home as she slowly lost the will to be anywhere but in her bed lying down.

When the pineapple-yellow house with white trim and white picket fence came into view, she lost the final tension that her forest adventure had created. The house had never felt more welcoming in her life; usually, it caused the eternal ball of lead in her stomach to expand and consume her lower organs. A reminder that she had no real family left in this world but a friend of her mother's who had been shouldered with her as a burden.

Swinging the car quickly and tearing towards the house, she knew she was coming in too fast the moment she stomped on the brake. The car scraped on the gravel drive, trying its hardest not to slip on the loose stones and dirt. Mackenzie could only brace her arms tightly on the steering wheel and look over the dash as the pickup scraped to a halt an inch from the metal garage door. A "phew" escaped her lips once she felt it all still. Pulling the car slowly and carefully into park mode, and yanking the parking brake as hard as it would go, she released her foot from the pedal and waited nervously for it to roll. The vehicle stayed still and she sunk back into the seat, letting her eyelids fall shut and her hands cover her face, defeatedly.

Even though tiredness pulled on every muscle and her head wanted to fall into the oblivion of sleep, the memory of the red eyes bored through her skull as though they still watched her. There was a ferocity in those eyes, she'd noticed, that might never let her sleep again.

Thunk. Thunk. Thunk.

The knocking on the window made Mackenzie jump so hard she thought her heart might explode. Her wide, frightened eyes met those of her best friend Lucy's.

With natural golden-blonde hair that fell in perfect waves, kind hazel eyes currently filled with worry, full lips, and fair skin, Mackenzie had always been envious of Lucy's beauty. She'd spent so many years seeing how plump Lucy's lips were without any product and resented her own thin top lip; had seen how easily Lucy could maintain her nearly hairdresser-perfect curls while Mackenzie struggled daily with her tight auburn ringlets that would knot together in an unattractive mess all too often. But despite all their physical differences, Lucy was Mackenzie's best friend and had always been supportive of her.

"KZ! What are you doing? Get inside before my mom comes home and finds you!" Lucy called through the window.

Using the residual buzzing energy still in her body, Mackenzie sprinted for the house. Lucy jumped back to give the swinging car door room before she followed. As both made it inside, they leaned against the front door, backs pressed against it like it was a lifeline, breathing hard.

Mackenzie pushed forward, leaning to brace her hands on her knees as she let her body try and regain some normalcy. Lucy tapped her twice on the back of her arm as she moved past, ushering her friend up the stairs to the landing and into Mackenzie's room.

"Any luck on the last day?" Lucy inquired with a hopeful glint in her voice, despite knowing the real answer before she'd even asked.

Mackenzie opened her mouth to retort, but bit it down and considered the truth. With her back to Lucy, her friend couldn't see the indecisive turmoil she was in. If she told her, what would the knowledge of that creature being out there do to her? At the same time, could she spend her life telling no one and fearing the memory?

"There was… *something* out there…" she replied, turning around. On a day like today, she didn't want to feel any more alone.

Lucy's eyebrows and forehead pulled together in confusion.

"Something? What kind of something are we talking about here?" she questioned, her usual bubbly tone replaced by a heavy weight of worry.

"The kind that had me returning here the second I saw it." Mackenzie admitted, meeting Lucy's eyes and allowing her to see how shaken the experience had left her. "I'd fully planned to spend the entire day investigating those caves today. All of them."

Lucy's eyes searched her best friend's, a frown pulling at her lips as Mackenzie's voice wavered.

Moving across the room, both sank to sit on the edge

of the bed, feeling the weight of the day spread over their shoulders.

"What did it look like?" Lucy asked cautiously, fidgeting with her perfect blonde hair.

Mackenzie stared at the carpet as though it could help her manifest the memory more vividly.

"It was massive. It was as big as a bear but it wasn't one! It was like a lion, a bear, and a wolf mixed into one animal with black fur and glowing red eyes. I know I didn't imagine it and I know it was real, but I don't know how else to explain what I saw. It was… terrifying!" she said, unloading her fear and confusion, feeling her heart rate increase again at the mere thought of it.

"Where did you see it?" Lucy squeaked nervously, not questioning a single word she'd heard.

"Out on the other side of the lake near the mountain base. I spotted it near the water's edge watching me, so I ran."

"Did it chase you?"

"I didn't see it behind me but I'm certain it did! I could feel it watching me until I left the highway."

"Oh my goodness! Are you okay? Please tell me you're not going back to that forest any time soon!" Lucy gushed, drawing Mackenzie short of words.

Even though it wasn't a question, she couldn't assure her friend she wouldn't go back. She couldn't lie to Lucy. She wouldn't even try.

"I don't know! I know it's there now and I could avoid the forest for the rest of my life because of it. But I've been there nearly every day for years and never seen it before. What if I never see it again? I don't know what to tell you! Is there even any point?"

"Any point? What do you mean?"

"Well… I mean… Today was the last day and I failed to find her… Tomorrow it's legally official… My mom is dead." As the words slowly climbed their way out of her throat, she braced her hands on her knees, feeling like a

500-pound weight was slowly being pressed onto her shoulders. Her words hung in the air, silent and crushing, enveloping any hope of further conversation as the reality set into both girls' hearts.

Bringing her knees up to her chest, Mackenzie felt the welling tears she'd been holding back come loose from their hiding place. She knew she couldn't stop them this time. Her body felt like it was going to fall apart and as she fell further into her sorrow, the distance between her body and mind grew. Like she was underwater, slowly losing control as her body crumbled.

Her body wasn't hers anymore. It had been claimed by the void.

The loss that had been waiting so long to take over finally asserted its ownership.

"Aw…" Lucy breathed, flinging her arms around her mourning friend without hesitancy.

Knowing how much she needed it, Mackenzie welcomed the embrace, placing her hand over Lucy's and breathing in the sweet-smelling perfume she wore that had always reminded Mackenzie of candy.

"I know…"

Mackenzie knew well before Lucy had uttered those words that she understood what she was going through. Lucy had seen the agony her best friend had been in over the last ten years.

The two girls had been having a sleepover together while Mackenzie's mom went camping in the pine forest near the town. That had been a routine once a month that no one had questioned or worried about—until she didn't come to collect her eight-year-old daughter at the usual time at the end of the weekend.

Both children—despite their love of spending time together—were panicked for good reason. Lucy's mother, Mary, had driven the girls to Mackenzie's house in the hopes of finding Anne there, busy or sick. But the house had been empty.

Lucy had been there as search parties were sent out

in search of Anne, the entirety of their small town turning up to assist.

It wasn't enough to find her though. For months the town had run search parties continuously; each time Mackenzie and Lucy insisted on coming along, until the town gave up hope.

Lucy had seen the damage and loneliness that had taken over her best friend. The town had settled on the belief that Anne must have been attacked and taken by a wolf or bear, despite her vast knowledge of the woods At first, Mackenzie had spent her time curled up in bed, falling numb and hopeless.

Until she started going to the forest on her own to search, fighting the looming depression off with determination.

After years of searching, Mackenzie had made a promise to Lucy and herself: on the tenth anniversary of her mother's disappearance, she'd finally move on from the forest and accept her mother as dead. She was sure in that time she would have found another clue, but nothing had presented itself.

"Did you manage to bring the necklace back?" Lucy whispered, her mind also lingering—same as Mackenzie's—on the only item found in that forest.

Mackenzie couldn't bring herself to speak through her emotions, only shaking her head as the tears fell faster. They saturated her cheeks, snot dripping like a tap from her nose onto the arm of Lucy's shirt, as her limbs lost their capacity to function. Her back sagged out of the hug, not able to hold her body up anymore as her arms slipped from her knees.

Lucy went with her, lying back on the bed and rolling Mackenzie's body into her, ignoring the fluids that now leaked on her. She didn't care about any of that, she never had.

The bed called Mackenzie to climb inside its blankets and never leave, as it had done before. She knew the next day would be the hardest and could already feel how drained her first real day as an orphan would be. The bed looked more and more like the comfortable sanctuary she needed. The place she could lose her will to get up and nothing would happen. It was predictable. It was safe.

The noise of all her destructive thoughts and feelings was a weight that pressed her deeper into the bed. She didn't know how to make it stop. She didn't know if she could. Squeezing her eyes shut as though she could hold off the world and reality, she let Lucy just hold her for a moment.

Before long, Mary called from her place at the bottom of the stairs, needing her daughter's assistance. Mackenzie let Lucy shuffle out from under her, unperturbed by the disappearance of her friend's embrace.

"I'll just check what she wants and then come right back," Lucy said quietly from the doorway, waiting for Mackenzie to acknowledge her before she left.

Mackenzie managed a nod, letting her body sink into the bed, as though it was always supposed to be there.

The words sank into Lucy, pulling her lips tight and creasing her normally smooth forehead.

"Okay…but I'm coming back at ten a.m. and you're getting up then," she said sternly, making it clear to Mackenzie that her sympathy only went so far. She'd learned to be wary when Mackenzie enjoyed the company of her bed more than her best friend.

Lucy didn't wait for a response. Mackenzie knew that it wasn't optional.

The room was immensely silent, but Mackenzie barely noticed. She slid the duvet from under her until it was free and able to cover her in its warm embrace. She knew the room wasn't cold but her arms were coated in shivering goosebumps, and she was sure the tears had leeched all the remaining heat from her body. The pain in her gut was sharp, numbing her to the rest of the body. It reminded her she was still connected to it and that time would never heal the hole in her life where her family had once been.

She'd been an orphan for ten years, convinced that she wasn't. The moment of truth she'd avoided was finally here, unable to be ignored. Searching the woods had kept her occupied, giving her a purpose. A tunnel-vision.

She wished she could return to that time when she could hide behind her hope.

Mackenzie lay in her bed, staring at the blank ceiling, letting her thoughts overwhelm her, too tired to fight them.

Could someone please walk through this door and tell me this is all a mistake or a nightmare?

Something that will explain away my pain after all this time.

Maybe even just an answer.

Something definitive.

No one came, and the only voices she could hear were the muffled ones of Lucy and her mother downstairs. She supposed they were probably talking about her backsliding into a depression that she'd struggled hard to get out of two years prior.

2: THE STRANGER

"This is me telling you it's time to get up, KZ." Lucy's quiet but stern voice called from the doorway. Mackenzie hadn't slept or rested her eyes, getting too lost in her thoughts as she stared at the blank wall next to her bed. The tears just fell silently down her cheeks and nose, dripping onto the pillow.

Mackenzie heard the words but couldn't move her body to respond with enough gusto to make any sort of progress. All her remaining energy would be needed just to get her out of bed. She'd want to retreat instantly but knew Lucy wouldn't let her.

Lucy wouldn't take 'no' for an answer.

She walked over to the bed, pushing lightly on Mackenzie's shoulder until she rolled onto her back. Taking her hands carefully, she pulled, lifting her upper body off the bed. Mackenzie didn't fight. She knew it was useless to argue with her best friend about this.

"I know," Lucy said clearly. "Believe me, *I know.* And I'm well aware you hate hearing this, but she wouldn't have wanted this for you. That was exactly why you applied to college in her hometown, far away from here, remember?"

Lucy waited, even though both girls knew the answer to the rhetorical question. Mackenzie's mouth dried as she met her best friend's soft gaze. Tears spilled quietly as memories of their tough past conversations overwhelmed her, still as potent and bitter in her mouth as though she were having them again.

"Take your time, KZ. Feel your pain, that's fine and understandable. But when it comes time to go to that college—I know you got in and haven't told me—go and live your life. Don't look back. You need adventure. You don't have to forget your life here, but enjoy being in a new place and find out where you came from," Lucy continued, her hazel eyes glistening with tears that refused to fall. Mackenzie could see the sadness Lucy tried to hide for her sake.

"How do I do this without you, Luce?" Mackenzie said, her voice cracking at the thought of being without her best friend. She leaned forward and pulled her in, stroking her blonde waves softly as her friend burst into tears too.

"I don't know, I'm pretty amazing!" she said confidently against her shoulder, laughing through the tears. Mackenzie joined in.

"You are," Mackenzie whispered in her ear, pulling her tighter in a squeeze. She closed her eyes, wishing for that moment she could just forget what was coming, feeling Lucy return the embrace. The giggle died on both of their lips, the quiet settling in as they both came to the same conclusion that they needed to breathe deeply and push the tears back for the moment. The time for goodbyes would come, but there was no point in dreading it now.

Lucy pulled back, staring into Mackenzie's eyes carefully. The light brown in Lucy's eyes ringed so carefully by olive green was almost hypnotic. Those eyes had never let Mackenzie hide anything from her best friend. It worked both ways though. *At least it had always been fair*, Mackenzie thought.

"You're amazing too, and you're going to be okay," Lucy said. "I know it. You don't have to do it without me completely though. We'll video chat all the time! I promise. Now, can you tell me that you got into that college already, because you suck at hiding things from me."

"I got in… on a scholarship," Mackenzie whispered, letting the full truth out with a half-smile and hearing Lucy's squeal of excitement in return.

"That's amazing! I knew you would!" she said. Despite knowing they wouldn't be together in the same place, Mackenzie knew that Luc was genuinely happy with her accomplishment. "And New York isn't too far away! We'll visit each other all the time!"

"That better be a promise!" Mackenzie laughed, watching the way her best friend's smile grew even more. Mackenzie couldn't help the relieved smile that overtook her face and hurt her cheeks—having finally told her friend what she'd avoided telling her for months. "You better be coming to Salem all the time!"

Mackenzie's stomach groaned loudly, her hand reflexively hovering over it as her eyes widened and her cheeks flushed pink.

"I guess running through the forest works up an appetite!" Lucy said, smiling as she got up from the bed and extended her hand for Mackenzie to join.

"We're joking about this now, are we?" Mackenzie said, only half unsure as to whether she should be talking so flippantly about it.

Lucy just shrugged, watching her friend carefully.

"Let's go get some food, I'm starving too!"

Mackenzie surrendered, giving her hand to Lucy who tugged her to follow. She slid her feet off the bed without a second thought. Lucy skipped off to the doorway, allowing Mackenzie to trail behind the childish exit. She watched her friend ahead in amusement, enjoying the silliness rather than letting her thoughts linger on the bed. If she thought about it too much, she was sure she'd climb back in and never get out.

Lucy eagerly led the way to the front door. Mary,

Lucy's mother, moved into their walkway, making a point of crossing her arms and watching Mackenzie with a disapproving expression. Her dyed brown eyebrows were raised. Her fingers held her forearms in her cross, massaging the muscle in frustration, trying to soothe some tension. Both girls halted in their tracks, waiting for the lecture they knew was to come.

Mackenzie chewed her lip, knowing exactly what this was about.

"Did you think I wouldn't find out, Mackenzie?" Mary said sternly, her voice still raspy from the cigarette she'd just had on the front porch.

Dropping her eyes to the floor, Mackenzie mumbled her apology and hoped that would be enough. It wasn't.

"You could have killed someone or yourself, do you understand that?"

Mackenzie's eyes snapped up quickly in confusion, looking at Lucy to see if she understood why her mother was rousing on her. Lucy raised her eyebrows and subtly shrugged her shoulders.

Mary spotted the gesture.

"Mr. Walcourt called today to complain about your reckless driving... Something about you pulling out in front of him and almost causing an accident in front of the forest hiking trail?" she said.

Mackenzie cursed herself for not checking her rearview mirror again, knowing her stupidity had not only almost killed her but had now unveiled her adventure of the day to Mary. If she hadn't accidentally done that, would Mary have found out about her morning excursion?

"We have talked about you being out there before, it's dangerous with bears around, surely you realize that by now. And now endangering others while driving? I thought you were better than that, Mackenzie Anne Harris."

Mackenzie flinched, her breath catching in her throat as the sting of Mary's words hit her. She knew that Lucy's mother was sure Anne had died because of a bear—she had fallen in step with the beliefs of the town—but hearing the two names she shared with her mother injured her in a way she couldn't tell anyone. The pangs of guilt overtook her and the more she thought about what her mother would have said, the worse the taste in her mouth became. It was threatening to suffocate all inklings of positivity left in her.

"I know I can't stop you from going into that forest on your own," she continued, and the acrid taste slid into Mackenzie's lungs threatening to drown her in her guilt. "And I know my daughter probably knew of your whereabouts, but Mackenzie, I thought you at least knew better than dangerous driving. I didn't see you as someone who had a death wish."

Mary was exasperated—and at that moment Mackenzie needed to be anywhere but at the end of the punishment spear that was wounding her more than Mary could have known. The discussion was a python constricting the air from her lungs.

"I don't have a death wish, Mary," she said abruptly, feeling Lucy suck in a breath next to her. She needed this conversation to be over. "I appreciate everything you've done for me, I do. Taking me in, looking out for me, it's all more than I can ever thank you for. Not checking when I pulled out this morning was a stupid mistake that I'm already sorry for. I was emotional about my mother. I won't apologize for looking for her in the forest though. It's the last day before her legal death. What happened with the car shouldn't have happened. It is unfortunately too late to change my mistakes now. I'm sorry."

Mackenzie couldn't lift her gaze as she finally took a deep breath, having let some of the tension go from her body. She didn't want anyone to see the agony in the depths of her eyes.

Mary was content with the response though, surrendering her anger and moving from her place in front of the door, letting them pass before she cleared her throat to speak again.

"Oh, Mackenzie," she started again, disappointment lost from her voice. "Mrs. Tresle called to say the appointment for your mother's will reading is at noon tomorrow at her office."

Mackenzie stepped through the entryway to the outside porch and faltered as the ground rushed towards her. Lucy grabbed under her arm, stopping the collision as Mackenzie waited for her legs to recover their strength. She wasn't sure how to respond to Mary—or if she even could—as her mouth flopped open, not making any sound, the breath not entering her lungs.

"She'll be there, Mom. We have somewhere to be right now though," Lucy said, smiling over her shoulder before flicking the front door shut behind them with her foot.

Mackenzie didn't look back, worried that her face was so pale Mary would ask questions. She let Lucy lead her numb body to the car, unsure how her legs held her up at all. The keys were in Lucy's hand before she registered that they'd ever left her jacket pocket. She climbed into the passenger seat, letting Lucy take over the responsibility of driving.

"Seatbelt," Lucy commanded, glancing at her friend as she reversed the car.

Mackenzie complied, letting her body work free of her, only obeying commands as she struggled with what Mary had told her. Her mother's will reading… She had a will? There were things to give up? *Your mother had possessions,* she reasoned with herself, *she didn't die with zero items to her name.*

It was still hard to wrap her head around.

She was dead.

The word continued to ring through her with just as much potency as it had hours ago. *Dead.* Nothing else mattered. She was now officially alone. She knew Lucy would always try to be there, but this was different, this was a tangible loneliness that no one could fix.

Lucy pulled out onto the road before Mackenzie could climb out of the car and crawl back to her bed.

Mackenzie barely paid any mind to the drive. The world outside the car felt like it was miles away, the air conditioning felt too cold, and she had lost the ability to process any more information. Surely, this was the point she'd finally had too much of the crap life had to offer. Surely this was the point where it all stopped and the world cracked into pieces and swallowed her whole.

Yet the car kept driving along the smooth, newly repaved road, and the radio quietly worked its way through the solemn country song as though nothing was wrong. The world around her continued to move—to her dismay—and all she could do was watch in shock, half expecting that everything would just stop for her pain.

It didn't.

"Hey, come back to me! We knew this day was coming, I know you didn't want it to, but it did," Lucy said, sighing slowly and taking one hand off the wheel to squeeze Mackenzie's knee. "I wish it wasn't here either but for the hundredth time, you need to live, KZ. You can't spend your entire life pining for your mom like you have been the last ten years. You just can't."

Mackenzie stared at the dash, listening to the words, and knowing they were right. She just didn't know how to snap out of it like they wanted her to. Her body felt like it was seven feet underwater and couldn't find the surface.

Lucy glanced at her sporadically while she drove, the green in her eyes catching the sunlight as they made their way to the small town roads that somehow always felt too crowded to Mackenzie. Too many people gave her eyes of pity, glances that said she was deluded in believing she might find something more about her mother. That she'd been holding on to her hope too long. She heard the whispers about the "poor girl" when they thought she was out of earshot, believing her mother to be long dead.

She knew where they were headed but wasn't sure she was prepared for it as they pulled up in front of the diner. She knew Lucy had intended that though—pushing her into functioning for her own good.

Her friend had parked the car and gotten out before Mackenzie could even register her movements. Sliding herself reluctantly out of the car, she caught up with Lucy.

With boots crunching on the gravel car park, Mackenzie shut the door, breathing in the smell of deep-fried potato, and trekked up to the store door, following Lucy. Her friend pushed the door open and the smell of warm fried food welcomed her while the jingle of the bell rang.

The woman behind the counter gave them a warm smile and let them find a comfortable spot.

Mackenzie took the lead, moving past Lucy and deciding on a table away from most of the people already occupying the diner. Being alone in the back corner wouldn't be for long—this was the only place to get a decent meal in town—but for the moment, while she came back to herself, she needed the space.

It was the usual crowds sitting around the diner as they entered. The older couple, Maggie and Jo, sat with coffee and a serving of waffle fries between them, doing their separate newspaper crosswords as always, only speaking occasionally as they asked each other for hints. The single mom, Loretta, with her young son, Tyler, who never seemed to be able to do anything but sleep on her lap as she worked through messages or finances on her phone, always seeming stressed.

Mackenzie breathed a sigh of relief as she flopped into the booth in the far-left corner, facing the door to keep an eye on any newcomers. She didn't want to be surprised by anyone belonging to the pity-party brigade.

Lucy sat opposite her, pulling the menu out from its

holder at the end of the table and opening it, deciding with a glance what she wanted.

"You get the same thing every time, I don't know why you bother checking the menu," Mackenzie said quietly, knowing what she'd also order without having to look. She gave the woman behind the counter a small smile and let her get her items ready to come over and take their order.

"One day it might change," Lucy replied confidently.

Mackenzie rolled her eyes, her frown pulling up slightly at the ends before it disappeared and she averted her eyes from her friend's.

"You can't just do things to appease me as you do with my mom," Lucy said. "I know the job you got was just so she would stop telling you to get out of the house, and I know you don't really care about Josh, sleeping with him is just leading him on. You're leaving soon and he cares about you. You need to check in to your life and stop letting your body live on autopilot, and I want you to promise you will when you leave. None of this 'just saying it to make me happy' crap. A *proper* promise." Lucy's voice turned harsh.

Mackenzie could feel the vile taste of guilt in her mouth again.

"It's hard, Luce. You're right. I made you that promise long ago that today was the last day. I won't go back to the forest, I'm done looking. She's gone and I can't bring her back. Tomorrow I will go to the reading and collect the last pieces of her and then it's over. I promise," Mackenzie said quietly, her eyes never leaving Lucy's as she tried to show the truth in her gaze.

"I believe you," Lucy whispered, letting her sympathies show through her hazel eyes. Both shared a small smile, sitting silently until the waitress appeared to take their order.

"What can I get you, girls?" Carol asked, holding her pad lazily, seemingly already knowing what they were going to order but asking all the same.

"Can I get some waffle fries with extra salt and a vanilla malt shake, please?" Lucy said quickly, getting a thin-lipped jealous 'mm-hmm' from Carol in response. Lucy just continued to smile at Carol as Mackenzie looked up to order.

"Just cobb salad and an iced tea for me, thanks." Mackenzie smiled, watching the look of approval from her waitress in response.

Carol moved off to give the order to the kitchen, while the girls shared a knowing grin about Carol's judgmental looks.

The bell on the door jingled.

Mackenzie and Lucy watched as someone they'd never seen before sauntered into the diner. Glancing at each other in a moment of confusion as to why anyone would visit their small town, even as a tourist, they tried to size him up. He was taller than the average man and muscled in a way that said he was fit but not obsessed with the gym. With sandy blonde hair, a basic V-neck, and cargo pants, he reminded Mackenzie of someone who had belonged to the military and preferred the regimented lifestyle. She observed him as he walked in alone, moving through the diner and smiling tightly at Carol behind the counter, who batted her eyelashes in return and lost all animosity about her. He ignored it, uninterested in her attempts to flirt while he searched the diner for a table, catching eyes with Mackenzie.

She averted hers quickly, feeling her cheeks flush under the gaze of his gray-blue eyes.

Lucy, who had also turned around to investigate, whipped back to her friend with a knowing grin as the man continued to a table in the middle of the room, claiming it as his own.

"You're going to go talk to him," Lucy commanded, leaning forward to prop her hands on her elbows as she grinned at Mackenzie.

"Why would I do that?" Mackenzie asked incredulously, trying to figure out her friend's angle.

"Because you just promised me you'd live your life and I saw the way you two looked at each other!" she responded, quietly enough that he couldn't hear.

Mackenzie reeled for some answer that could refute her reasoning.

"You also pointed out that I'm leaving soon and shouldn't be hurting anyone!" she tried, watching Lucy's amusement only grow at her reddening face.

"He's not in love with you! I somehow don't think you'll be hurting him, besides he's probably leaving soon too. He's not exactly one of our townies. It's perfect. Now go, just practice talking to a real person that isn't me."

"I talk to plenty of real people."

"Stop arguing over semantics and get." Lucy tapped her foot, the final sign she wasn't taking no for an answer again.

Mackenzie climbed out of the booth, taking a deep breath and giving her friend the tight smile and lifted eyebrow that said '*I can't believe you're making me do this.*'

Lucy gave her a wave with a knowing grin.

Mackenzie walked over to where he sat, finishing up his food order with Carol, who looked confused at Mackenzie's presence at the table. Carol wandered off and she braced herself.

"Hi, um… sorry. I've been sent over here by my friend," she started, drawing his attention. He leaned back in his seat, his brow pulling together in confusion even though his mouth pulled into an amused smile. He glanced at Lucy for barely a second.

"If she sent you over for my number, I'm afraid I don't use messengers and I'm not interested," he said slowly, watching her carefully for her response.

"She sent me over because she reckons I need to be more social," Mackenzie admitted, feeling the shy smile on her lips and heat in her cheeks as she pulled her eyes up from the table to meet his gray-blue ones. They pulled her in—in a way she didn't know how to explain—holding her in place as she waited for him to tell her again that he wasn't interested or that he was busy, so she could be free.

"Well, by all means then… sit," he said, gesturing to the chair with a glance that finally broke the hypnotic spell his eyes were casting.

She pulled the chair out and sat before she could turn and bolt, feeling the nervous fluttering in her stomach, and then held her hand out in greeting.

Nothing is going to happen. I'm not going to let it. It's just a conversation with a very attractive man and even if it did, Josh and I aren't exclusive, he can deal.

"Mackenzie, but most people call me Kenzie," she said, waiting as he reached out to shake her hand. His hand was warm against hers, squeezing just tight enough for her to feel and see the muscles through his hand and up his arm flex. He held her hand a moment longer than what should have been customary, and it wasn't until she retracted her arm that he let her go. The butterflies made an impact against her ribs, trying to rescue her heart beating wildly in her chest. She made her best effort to seem unfazed.

"Kai. So why does your friend think you need to be more social? Or is she just trying to set us up?" He let a mischievous smile linger on his lips.

The reminder of her past caused Mackenzie to flatten slightly, and she took a moment to compose what she was going to say—she couldn't tell him about her damage in the first conversation. That was a road to judgment she didn't want or need.

"Probably a bit of both. But I've been living in the past and have struggled to move on from some life drama."

"Boy or family drama?" he asked, his smile turning to a curious frown as he tilted his head and watched her face carefully.

"Family," she clarified, hoping he wouldn't push to

find out more. He seemed to sense her hesitancy to share though and instead dragged her brain out of the lingering trauma.

"I figured… You didn't seem like the type to get yourself caught up over a guy."

She snapped her eyes up from the table in confusion, getting caught in his gaze.

"Thank you? Was that supposed to be a compliment?" she said, bewildered by his statement.

"Yes, it was. You seem like a genuine, grounded person, that's all. Not the kind to get caught up by that at all," he explained, his eyes never leaving hers, as though they were daring her to be the first to look away.

"You barely know me…" she said, stunned by his declarations.

"And you haven't observed anything about me?" he said, sitting back in his chair, the sexy, daring smile never leaving his lips as her mouth popped open, attempting to figure out what to say.

After a few moments, she shut it and tried a different approach.

"Fair. Well, thank you, then, I guess. You have an interesting accent. East Coast?"

"Boston."

"What's it like?" she asked, excited to know about the city she'd be moving near soon, but his smile faded slightly and turned to an expression of disinterest.

"Boring when you've lived there your whole life. You long for the adventure, to meet interesting people, and make it worthwhile," he said with a wink, returning to his carefree, mischievous attitude he used to hide something she couldn't quite place—self-doubt maybe? His own trauma? She wasn't sure.

"Smooth," she said, acknowledging his obvious attempt at flirting and feeling a bite in her throat at just being a notch on his belt. "Do you say that to all the other girls?"

"Who says there are any other girls?" he drawled,

looking her up and down, knowing exactly where her mind went, but undeterred by her accusation.

Mackenzie opened her mouth, ready to spout a witty response that never came, trying to hide her loss of words before he could notice, but she saw the way his face softened quickly.

"I'm just messing with you," he said, careful of her. "But in the spirit of adventure, would you be interested in showing me around town?"

"I did come here with my friend. I can't just leave her." But despite her words, the excitement in her stomach intensified. The urge to disappear on an adventure with him was too enticing and her brain was telling her to run away. Find Lucy and get out.

The table she'd been sitting at with Lucy was empty. Eyes wide, she felt the panicked flutter of her heart as she checked around the diner. She found Lucy by the counter in her faded blue skinny jeans and pale pink shirt—grabbing her food and drink in takeout containers. The girls caught eyes before Lucy waved goodbye with the car keys in one hand and the food in the other, grinning as she left.

"Turns out I could tour you around," Mackenzie said, "although she's currently leaving with my car…"

The way her skin heated around Kai made her stomach twist in ways she'd never felt before, and it unnerved her. Everything felt heightened, as her nerves awakened from the numbness and her organs let the butterflies run wild. She wanted him to say it was too bad she couldn't tour him around because he didn't have a mode of transport, so she could escape how everything in her felt magnified.

Instead, he fumbled in his pocket and carefully put a set of car keys on the table in front of her, watching her as though he knew of her conflict about escaping this conversation.

"I've got a rental we can use." He smiled, his eyes back to holding hers.

"You'd trust a stranger with your rental car?" she asked, not sure how else to escape this interaction, but still not sure she wanted to.

"As I said, I like the adventure," he responded with a mischievous smile and a glint in his eyes that made her skin crawl with excited goosebumps. "You in?"

She didn't want to give herself time to think about it. She knew with enough thought she'd pull out of it and Lucy was right, she needed to live, and this was one way to start. And it was only for one day.

"I guess I am."

3: THE ADVENTURE

Mackenzie and Kai wandered down the main street. She chewed on fries she'd taken away from the diner, and he held on to his shake that she was sure he'd finished a while ago. Her excited mood still lingered, her stomach fluttering and clenching at his closeness to her as they walked side by side, and her heart beating so loud she was sure he could hear it. But her jittering was muted by the town around her. People wandered down the streets past her, trying to be subtle and failing miserably as they whispered about her.

Kai had started to sense how the town was reacting to her, glancing at her and whispering about her.

She tried to ignore it, pushing the thoughts aside—how was she supposed to move on with her life when the town was always reminding her how broken she'd been for so long? Despite her best efforts, the food began to feel stale in her mouth and hard to swallow, and she threw the fries in the nearest bin as they walked past, defeated. The chewing in her gut was slowly consuming the butterflies of excitement.

Kai threw his cup away at the same time, taking her hand lightly, much to Mackenzie's surprise. It made her smile, though, and she felt slightly lighter as they moved down the main street.

"I don't know what about this town you really thought would be an adventure, we're pretty basic," she said finally, breaking the silence that had been between them since they'd started down the street. "We're sort of a small town…"

"Sort of?"

"Okay, we are. Not even a fast-food joint around here for miles. This is pretty much it!" She smiled, honest but chuckling softly.

He chuckled along with her and playfully changed the subject.

"So, if this is a small town—then that would explain why all these people know you. But my question is, what do they know about you that I don't?" He nudged his shoulders into hers. "You're not a murderer or something, are you?"

The idea made her giggle, but it died on her lips quickly.

"I'm not *that* interesting, it's just a town that's bored and in need of gossip. Sorry, I'm not comfortable talking about it with a complete stranger," she said, glancing up at him expecting to see judgment or annoyance at being left in the dark.

His hand tightened on hers for a moment, squeezing lightly as he gave her a reassuring smile and the anxiety quieted in her stomach slightly.

"Well, I'm a Leo," he started. "I'm from Boston and I've lived around there my whole life, as have my family. I'm an only child although sometimes I wish I'd had siblings, but I'm also not sure I could have handled anyone else in my family having the attention, so maybe not. I like hiking and the great outdoors, live for adventure, love traveling, and I have this thing for a certain auburn-haired girl who I think might be a secret murderer," he said quietly, watching the unrestrained grin break out over her face.

She giggled, catching his eye, unafraid to hold his gaze.

"I'm not a secret murderer!" She laughed, continuing their walk down the street, enjoying the warmth of the sun's rays.

"If you want to be alone, we can be. I think you're the one person I'd let murder me. It must be those killer good looks!" he said, running with their joking tone, watching her lips intently every time she smiled and laughed.

She wasn't sure if he was just enjoying that she was smiling or if he was ready to kiss her, but her heart smashed her ribs assuming the latter. Her cheeks grew hot as she continued smiling and soon they began to ache, but it couldn't stop her.

"Maybe you're the real murderer. I don't think I'd let you murder me, I have too much of my life to live." She chuckled.

He pretended to be offended, holding his hand over his heart as though it were breaking, making her grin wider and her eyes crease at the corners.

"So to avoid either of us being murdered, we'll stay out here then," he said, before adding with a cheeky smile. "But you'd definitely enjoy being alone with me, only pleasurable pain allowed, I promise."

Her jaw dropped before she could stop it, her breath catching. She didn't want to admit how tightly everything clenched at his words or how fast her heart raced at the notion. She was surprised at how much she wanted to be alone with him, but her rational brain was the one running the show and while meeting him and touring him was one thing, going somewhere to be alone with him was an entirely different matter. And reckless. She reeled herself back in, containing her surprise—but not before she saw his enjoyment at her shock.

She cleared her throat, getting her voice under control before she spoke.

"I'm not the girl who goes to a stranger's motel with him," she said seriously, but trying not to be too abrasive. She braced, expecting some negative attitude in response.

He turned to her, his face serious, squeezed her hand, and walked towards her.

She stepped away until her back pressed into the shop window as he moved in.

"I never thought you were, it was just a joke. I did, however, mean that if you wanted to get away from the gossip-fueled town, we could. We can go somewhere else… There's a beautiful forest nearby that has none of these people there. I also understand if you don't want to be alone with… Well, a stranger," he said candidly, no hint of the mischievousness or cheekiness in his voice or face.

His gray-blue eyes stared into hers, not breaking the gaze as she thought about what he said, feeling his breath against her face. She couldn't help breaking the connection, glancing at how close his lips were to hers. She wanted to kiss him but she also knew that her brain was telling her not to. If she kissed him, surely it would all be over and she would care. Then, after today, she'd never see him again.

This was only going to hurt her if she followed her instincts.

A roguish smile pulled his serious frown up—making her stomach lurch as he noticed her gaze and train of thought.

He leaned closer, threading his other hand with hers, slowly closing the distance between their faces, their breathing mirroring each other…

"Mom, why doesn't Kenzie have any parents?" a young, high-pitched voice said, just loud enough for them to hear as it passed. Mackenzie's stomach bottomed out, falling into the depths of her body—as far as it could go. Her eyes dropped as she pulled her chin down and away from the closing kiss.

Kai also hesitated, having heard the child's words and seeing Mackenzie's shame. He rocked back on his heels slightly, giving her space as she felt the pink shame take over her cheeks.

She looked over his shoulder, spotting the five-year-old she'd babysat being towed away by his mother who was looking back apologetically.

She tried to manage a smile at the mother, faltering quickly the second she glanced away, her gaze returning to Kai.

He looked concerned and she could see the pity in his eyes that he didn't speak aloud.

She was done with the town for the day.

"Can we go somewhere else?" she said quietly, her voice cracking slightly, but she was determined not to let any more than that emotion show. She waited for some sort of resistance from him but none came.

He nodded, released one of her hands—still holding on to the other—and walked back to the car.

He drove silently, pulling out on the road, letting the rock song resonate through the speakers. She waited for him to speak, to say something about what he'd heard, but he drove on in silence, letting the quiet chew a hole of worry in her stomach. What if he didn't like her anymore? Was he just getting her away now because he felt sorry for her and was no longer interested? She couldn't begin to know what was going through his mind, and the silence let her question and make assumptions too dark to ask.

He pulled the car out to the same shoulder of the road she had been on that morning, and her whole body froze up. The memory of the creature haunted her as she waited to feel the eyes watching her from the forest, expecting to see the mass of black fur in the tree line waiting.

Her heart climbed her throat, as though it could escape her body and make a run for it. She could feel the heat leech from her face. She was a pale, scared sight when Kai turned the engine off and glanced over at her.

"Hey!" he said quietly, placing his hand on her arm

and making her look up into his eyes. "I'm not going to hurt you, it's okay."

She looked into his concerned face and realized what he must have thought of her, trying to remove the fear from her eyes as she looked at him.

"That's not it," she said hurriedly, knowing the truth was the only way to reverse the confusion. "I was here this morning and I saw a creature."

"A creature?" he questioned, noting her word choice.

She was willing to tell the truth for the most part but didn't fancy letting Kai think she was insane.

"A bear," she clarified, lying.

"That's odd for these parts, isn't it? Maybe you disturbed it?" he reasoned, curious rather than worried. He looked at her, and she knew he wasn't believing her words, as though he could read the lie in them.

"Probably."

"We don't have to go in if you don't want to."

"No, it's okay! I'll be fine, you're probably right and it was just a rarity," she said, putting her brave face on and opening the car door, watching him follow suit.

Climbing out of the car, they quietly set off into the tree line. The weight lifted from Mackenzie's shoulders, and the longer they wandered without anyone watching her, the more confident she grew about being around him in this place.

"Sorry about back there," she said, breaking the renewed silence.

"Guess now I know why they talk about you," he said with a sad smile. "You don't have to tell me anything more about it if you don't want to. Whatever it is, it sounds like it would be difficult to deal with, and I'm happy to just be the person you choose to be social with today."

Her lips turned up slightly at the mention of Lucy's demands, touched by his level of understanding.

"My dad died just after I was born and my mom and I moved here. When I was eight, she went out on a camping trip in these woods and disappeared. The town was sure a bear got her, but I never stopped looking... Until today." It was a simplified version, but it would do. She held his gaze as they both slowed to a stop.

"Because of the bear?" he asked, his head tilting as he tried to put the pieces together.

"No. It's the tenth anniversary of the day she went missing, and I made myself a promise that I would find a way to move on. Tomorrow she's legally dead."

Silence followed her words as he thought about it, coming in close and taking her hand again, his thumb tracing the back of it.

"I'm sorry to hear. That must be tough—not knowing."

"It is, but Lucy has been a really good friend and she's good at pushing me into new situations." She smiled.

"Like talking to me?" He moved in closer again, reciprocating her smile.

"Yeah, like that," she said as he slid his arm around her waist and looked deep into her eyes, holding her in a moment of anticipating silence.

"No one to interrupt here," he said quietly, leaning into her, his eyes glancing down at her lips.

"So you can murder me here without any witnesses?" She smiled as his lips touched hers gently at first.

His chuckle against her lips was ecstasy. She giggled in return, proud of her joke as she slipped her hand from his. Both arms came up and around his well-muscled shoulders, pushing herself up onto her toes, bringing their bodies closer.

His arm tightened around her waist, lifting her until her toes were off the ground, giving her a rush as she felt weightless.

He pulled her closer, his lips more insistent as they worked hers apart, his tongue sliding past her lips. His free hand cupped her butt cheek, as she hooked her legs up and around his waist, needing to be closer. They worked in perfect sync, able to sense the movements of the other effortlessly as they drew their bodies closer and closer.

Mackenzie could feel him hard underneath her as she took his bottom lip in hers and sucked it, feeling his muscles clench at the movement.

She returned his lip to him. His kisses and tongue became more insistent as he pushed her back against a tree trunk, and she let his mouth claim her neck.

Everywhere he kissed, blood rushed eagerly, letting her nerves buzz to the skin in response and boiling the muscles underneath where his touch had lingered. He slowly traced a line along the middle seam of her jeans with his forefinger, pressing just hard enough to feel but light enough that she found herself moaning in response, trying to adjust to the sensation again.

His lips returned to hers and she fought to free the edge of his shirt from the top of his jeans, pulling harder to try and slide it from where it was caught between her legs and his torso.

Mackenzie loosened her legs slightly too much and found herself slipping from his waist. She cursed herself for losing her grip but his arm caught each of her knees, lowering her legs carefully to the ground.

She finally pushed his shirt up, and he let her pull it over his head, breaking their contact for barely a moment before he pressed himself up against her again, his hot bare skin making the intensity of their passion flare brighter. He undid the zipper on her windbreaker, sliding it down and off her shoulders.

Mackenzie dropped her arms and let the jacket fall to the ground, keeping contact with his hypnotic, mesmerizing eyes as he pulled her shirt up over her head, searching for any hesitancy in her eyes.

She had left her second thoughts somewhere back on the path and she didn't mind. The way he desired her, the passion and need she could see in his eyes, gave her no question that in this fleeting moment, there was a connection between them.

Kai's lips were on her again as he slid his arm behind her back and found the bra clasp, unfastening it with one hand. She felt the pop of the elastic letting her upper body loose, but she was too pressed up against his body to feel the freedom in her chest. He leaned down, sliding an arm under her knees and cradling her in his arms. She felt the cool air against her body, goosebumps rising on her skin. On his face was a lascivious smile that made places within her curl and tighten that she wasn't aware could do so.

He moved their clothing piles together with his foot and dropped carefully to the ground, laying her on the clothes as he moved over her. His muscles bulged as he held himself above, pressing just enough to feel the raw heat of their bare torsos against each other, but mindful not to crush her.

As he slipped himself between her legs, pushing them apart, she could feel his desire pressing hard against her jeans. Reaching down, she undid the top button of his cargo pants and then slowly pulled the fly down, feeling how she freed the size it contained. She couldn't help the small gasp that escaped between kisses, making him pull back for a moment just enough to study her wide eyes and surprised face.

"You want to do this?" he whispered, less sexy, more concerned. At his small moment of care, she felt her heart squeeze and knew her answer without any doubt.

"Oh, yes…" she breathed, letting him help her out of her remaining clothing and assisting him with his. As he trailed kisses down her body and finally claimed her with his mouth, her back arched, and pleasure overcame her, the rest of the world fading away until all that remained was his tongue between her legs and the ecstasy that overwhelmed her.

4: THE LETTER

This is the last will and testament of Anne Elizabeth Harris.

To my darling daughter Mackenzie Anne Harris,
If you are reading this, I've passed on from this world to the next. I'm sorry that I've left you alone.

I leave to you all my worldly possessions to try and ease this burden my absence has brought. I know it can't give you family, but maybe this is a way for you to keep me and your father in your heart. This includes my remaining monetary assets, my car, and my house in Salem once owned by your father and me.

I could never bring myself to sell the house. Salem, despite its now-painful memories, was my hometown. It's the place your father and I grew up together, fell in love, and where you were born. In my absence, a close friend has been tending to it. Don't let this affect your choice though, it is now yours to do with as you please. Whether you use it or sell it, all I want is to be able to support you, even though I'm not there anymore.

Be warned, my loving and kind daughter, that the world is not as good as you. Be forgiving, but be wary of those who come wearing disguises of knowledge and gentleness; sometimes they only wish to hurt you. The world has dark forces at play.

This world has some gems though, and finding out whom to trust will be one of the greatest challenges you will face in this life. Choose wisely and trust yourself first, my darling.

Love, Your Mother
Anne Elizabeth Harris

5: THE GOODBYE

"Come on, take the damn photo." Lucy laughed as she prepped her hands to jump in the background of their selfie. "3, 2, 1!"

She launched her body in the air while Mackenzie burst into laughter and held the shutter button.

The cavernous main concourse of Grand Central Station echoed with dissonant sounds from hundreds of people moving through the busy venue, the noises bouncing from every part of the massive chamber. The architecture was breathtaking, unlike anything Mackenzie or Lucy had ever seen. When they had first arrived, they had spent minutes just staring at the grand domed ceiling and observing how undeterred others were by the vastness they walked through. The detail stretched so far above their heads and surrounded them in every grand pillar that towered over them.

"Did you get it?" Lucy asked as Mackenzie slipped the phone into her bag, where it sat on top of her suitcase. Mackenzie glanced at the bag that housed all her belongings, a lump forming in the back of her throat as she fought to swallow.

"Yes, I got it." Mackenzie sighed with a smile as Lucy put her backpack on and glanced around at the busy space around them.

No one they knew, no one to look at Mackenzie in pity. A whole new world, so different from the small Oregon town the two girls had left behind.

"You know, I read that there's a place here where you can whisper on different sides of the hall and hear each other perfectly!" Lucy squealed excitedly as she looked for the place in question.

Mackenzie checked her watch.

"And we can find it when I come to visit you, but I do have to head off to the other station for my train, Luce…" The excitement in Lucy's eyes dimmed slightly at the reminder of their impending separation.

"I'm sorry!"

"Don't be, darling. It's a gorgeous place and I wish I could stay to be a total tourist with you, but I did book my second leg today." Mackenzie wrapped her arms around her friend tightly. The moisture in her throat disappeared, sapped by her anxiety. She'd be completely on her own, heading for something entirely unknown. "I'll be back before either of us know it. I need to explore this city with you. Please try not to see it all without me."

"That's not possible!" Lucy laughed softly, her voice thickening with unshed tears. She squeezed her friend so tightly, that Mackenzie was sure her own organs would make a popping noise and she'd die happy.

Silence fell between them as they held each other tightly, neither wanting to be the first to let go. Mackenzie had to bow out though, aware that the minutes until her train ticked closer.

"Okay. I have to start moving, Luce. I'm sorry," she said, taking a deep breath as she prepared herself for the goodbye they'd both been dreading.

Lucy had other ideas as she rolled her shoulders back and grabbed the handle of her bag.

"I don't have to be anywhere for a while. Let's go!" she said defiantly, changing Mackenzie's dreading sad frown to a surprised grin.

"Okay." She grabbed her bag, slinging it over her shoulder, and pulled the suitcase handle with a jerk.

Both girls took one last glance at the enormous magnificence of the station before they slipped out the door, and headed for the other train station Mackenzie needed.

As they hit the busy road outside, the sun reflecting off the high-rise buildings around them, it felt like they were being fried on the sidewalk. Sweat coated Mackenzie's skin nearly instantly and her movements turned slow and sluggish to conserve her energy as she pulled her phone out to check directions on her maps. Leading the way, Lucy by her side, she moved towards the train to her new life, anxiety and excitement warring in her stomach.

"So how did Josh take you dumping him? Or are we not calling it that because it was a one-sided situationship?" Lucy queried, but Mackenzie knew it was all a distraction tactic from the impending goodbye as they walked, clumsily dodging other pedestrians.

Mackenzie opened her mouth, closed it, and tried again to speak, unable to find the words. She knew she'd forgotten to do something the second Lucy had mentioned Josh. She cringed as Lucy watched her expression, Lucy's mouth popping open in shock.

"You *did* talk to him, didn't you?" she pushed, her face shocked and yet trying not to laugh.

"Well, I mean, we haven't really talked in the last month, so I figured he knew…" Mackenzie said slowly, watching Lucy's expression and hoping she'd confirm her theory. She pinched her nose for a moment with a sigh as they stopped at the traffic light.

"Did you not talk for a month or did he try and you were just too busy daydreaming about Kai to notice?" her best friend asked with a grin, as though she already knew the answer.

"I was not daydreaming about Kai!" Mackenzie breathed out, shocked, a smile creeping onto her lips at the memory of their time together.

"Hand me your phone!" Lucy commanded, holding her hand out flat.

"What are you going to do?" Dread temporarily squashed both her anxiety and excitement, wondering if Lucy wanted to text Kai.

"Do you trust me?" Lucy said slyly, a challenge in her eyes that said Mackenzie couldn't ask any further questions without implying she didn't. She knew Lucy though, and her best friend was the kind of person only ever to do things with Mackenzie's best interest at heart.

She reached out and dropped the unlocked phone into Lucy's hand, after checking how long they had on their current heading.

Lucy spoke aloud as she found her contact and started texting, Mackenzie not reaching to stop her.

"Dear Josh, over the past 18 months you have shown immense support and have been a great comfort in my life. I'm sorry I couldn't give you more. I've just moved to Salem MA, so I'm afraid our time has come to an end. I wish you all the best for the future and hope that you find someone worthy of your love. Happy Trails, Kenzie."

"Worthy of your love?" Mackenzie finally questioned with an incredulous laugh as Lucy handed the phone back to her, the message waiting to be sent.

"A guy doesn't exclusively sleep with one girl who barely notices him for eighteen months unless he's in love," she said, as though it were obvious. "Believe me, plenty of other girls knocked on that door and he turned them all down."

Mackenzie looked at Lucy, making sure this wasn't some weirdly cruel joke, but Lucy was entirely serious. Mackenzie had been so blind to Josh that she had never noticed his feelings. She knew she'd been using him as a physical comfort, but she figured he'd just done the same. He had always seemed like the kind of guy that would.

"I'm a horrible person!" Mackenzie gasped as she pressed send on Lucy's message and turned to her map again for the route. Her mouth flapped open as the full weight of her numb decisions hit her.

It was horrid. It was a bad taste in her mouth and nose, worse than the whiffs of urine she got as she passed the hot, grubby alleys. Her stomach began eating her from the inside out and not even the comfort of running away to Salem could make her feel less guilty.

"You were caught up in your grief, it's understandable so long as you turn over a new leaf and learn from it," Lucy said, holding an arm out and stopping Mackenzie in her tracks.

"Luce, I was caught up in my grief for *10 years!*" she said incredulously to her friend, feeling the guilt and terror chew through her.

"Hey, none of that! You're acting like this is new information and it's not. Yes, you were numb and distant for ten years, but you don't have to be for any more of them. So, learn from this is all I'm saying. Don't let yourself be numb in Salem, feel everything. There's going to be bad stuff that you're going to have to work through but you can't just retreat again, okay? I won't be there to pull you into participating in life so you need to do it yourself," Lucy said sternly.

Mackenzie softened as Lucy took her hand, wiser than she had ever known her friend to be. Mackenzie smiled sadly as she knew that her friend's new-found wisdom would be a new thing to miss.

"Promise me," Lucy said.

"I promise," Mackenzie said assuredly, no doubt in her mind about how right her friend was. The chewing continued in her gut as her anxiety and excitement drifted from their hiding places; so many feelings she wasn't used to acknowledging making themselves known. "When did you become wise?"

"One of us had to be. I nominated myself." She grinned, and Mackenzie could feel the heavy weight of her bad mood drift off like a storm cloud on the horizon. "Now, speaking of participating in life and feeling everything... Are you going to text Kai and tell him you're moving to Salem?"

"I don't know. I'm still not certain I wasn't just a nice fling on his adventure in Oregon," Mackenzie admitted, the doubt she'd struggled with since she met him resurging.

"I'm certain!" Lucy spat with a grin. "I saw the look you two gave each other in the diner, and when he dropped you home, I saw that goodbye!"

"Yeah..." Mackenzie whispered, as her brain brought back the moment they said goodbye. Parts of her curled again as though he were there telling her the words and touching her like that all over again.

The engine died in front of the house, sitting out on the street. Lucy glanced out through the gap in the curtains; Mackenzie smiled to herself as she pulled her eyes from the pineapple-yellow house.

Mackenzie and Kai looked at each other in silence, knowing this was their goodbye.

This would be the last time she ever saw him.

They'd spent so much of their day in the forest, making love and exploring. Not once did she look out for her mother, she was too caught up in watching him. They barely learned a thing about each other but they didn't need to... It had been easy. They could exist chasing each other through the trees like children, exploring each other's bodies against the trees, wandering through parts of the forest Mackenzie wasn't sure she'd ever seen before—they'd never been on her search route.

At the end of it all, as the light had started to dim through the woodland, they'd had to call it a night. He drove her back in silence, both feeling the weight of their goodbye getting heavier.

He looked at her, his gaze soft and sad.

"I'll give you my number. If you're ever in Boston,

give me a call," he said, handing her his phone to input her number into the contact card.

She reached out, her fingers glancing along his, electrifying heat jolting up her limb where they'd touched, and it took everything in her not to pull him close and ignore the phone and just connect with him again.

She typed her number in, leaving the surname blank, hoping for a little bit of mystery. When she handed it back to him, she saw him click the message button, and then his fingers were flying as he typed a text to send to her. So she would have his number too.

She pulled out her phone just in time to see the message flash up: "Hello to the most beautiful girl I've ever seen." She couldn't help the grin that pulled at her lips, biting down on her lower lip to try and reign in her excitement.

"Don't do that," he rasped quietly as he watched her expression.

Her eyes glanced back to his as he stared at her lip between her teeth. Her lip slipped out to its normal resting position, and she watched him take a deep breath in response as though he was calming himself.

"Don't send me texts that make me want to do that then," she said simply, the playful mood that had existed between them all day striking up again. "I should probably go…"

As they looked at each other, the feeling of mischievousness between them died as quickly as it had returned.

"Until next time," he whispered to her, making her heart bash her ribs unevenly as it fought to hand itself over to him.

With a country separating them, she wasn't sure there was ever going to be a next time. She doubted if he meant what he'd said about her being in Boston, but let herself feel it true just for that moment.

"Until next time," she whispered as she leaned into

him, their lips meeting softly. She knew if their kiss met with anything more, she would never leave the car. Finally, she pulled back—it was time to get out or she never would—and opened the car door.

She hated the bittersweet feeling that stung the kiss on her lips, hated the idea that they'd leave on such a sad note that would make her feel sick for the next several hours.

As she stood on the road about to close the door, she turned back to him, still watching her leave.

"If there is even a next time, maybe all those other girls back in Massachusetts are just too much temptation?" She said her voice thickening as their eyes met, trying to revive the playful mood between them despite the idea of other women squeezing at her heart painfully. She deliberately slipped her bottom lip between her teeth and watched the expression fall from his face.

She shut the car door, not waiting for any further reaction, convinced she'd finally pushed the joke too far, and dropped her gaze from him as she walked around the front of the car, eyes watching the road as she prepared to walk over to the house. She heard the thud of the other car door as he left the cabin of the car and met her in front of the hood abruptly. Her eyes lifted to his, seeing an animalistic desire in them as he stared at her lip that still lingered between her teeth.

He pulled her to him, smashing her body against his as one hand reached under her butt, hooking one leg to his hip, and the other fisted in her hair. His lips pressed against hers desperately, his tongue seeking hers intensely. He leaned her back on the hood of the car, his body pressed against hers, hearing the metal of the bonnet groan under their weight as the electricity and heat of the kiss between them made her heart skip beats.

It was at that point she knew, somehow after one day, he had stolen her heart.

"I'm going to say again, there's never any other girls.

Just you," he whispered against her lips as he pulled her body up from the car, slowly pulling away.

She walked back to the house lightheaded, seeing Lucy staring out from her bedroom, mouth hanging open …

"Yeah…" Mackenzie repeated, her body racing like he could step out of the next alley and claim her body and heart all over again. It felt all too real and like a dream, all at once. She knew it had happened but wasn't sure how much was an act from him or if it had been serious. She wished she'd been able to read his mind or have a lie detector on hand.

"Anyway…" Lucy trailed as they stopped outside the train station Mackenzie needed. They both looked up and realized they were now going to have to say goodbye.

The heaviness in Mackenzie, from too many goodbyes lately, pulled on her once again.

"I think I can beat Kai's goodbye!"

"Oh yeah?" Mackenzie said, ears pricking up as she glanced at her friend with a smile, the heaviness lightening slightly.

From her pocket, Lucy produced a silver necklace with an engraved heart that stopped Mackenzie's for a long moment. Her mother's necklace dangled from Lucy's fingers. Tears pricked in her eyes as she thought of Lucy, who hated the outdoors with a passion, going into the forest to collect the jewelry for her. Her mouth tried to form words, sitting open as the tears slipped out.

"Luce… Oh my god…" she breathed, her teary eyes lifting to her friend's hazel ones.

"I know." She smiled. "You're welcome. I win."

The laughing smile that took control of Mackenzie's face squeezed more water from her eyes as she took the necklace and wrapped her arms around her best friend.

"You always win, Luce. Always."

6: THE NEW WORLD

The rumble of the local train underneath Mackenzie was almost therapeutic as she fought her watering eyes again. Fiddling with the necklace around her throat, she ran her fingers over the engraving of her mother's name and repeatedly glanced at her backpack where the letter from her mother resided. It made her feel too many things at once to continue re-reading it in public: confused, happy, upset, and nostalgic. It was like picking off a scab on her heart, but then bandaging it correctly this time—it felt like a proper, tangible goodbye, and even though it squeezed her heart until she wanted to be sick, she felt at peace.

Mackenzie watched the people around her on the train—the few that had boarded it—as they went about their day, curious as to what their lives must be like on this side of the country. Were any of them locals who had known her mother when she lived here? Somewhere in the train, she could smell fresh bread and sea salt, the smell only growing as the vehicle came to a stop. Pushing up from her seat and, taking her suitcase, she climbed onto the platform.

The train station was quiet. Only a couple of people moved around the area as Mackenzie wandered her way down the platform and hefted her bag up each step. One or two people looked as though they might offer to help her, but she put her head down and pulled it up behind her, her muscles complaining at her effort. At the top of the stairs, she exited the station and looked around, her heart leaping.

This is where her parents had grown up. This is where they'd met and fallen in love and where her father died. This was the place her mother had run from because it was too hard to be without him, and this was Mackenzie's new home. Tears filled her eyes again, but she blinked them off, determined as she dragged her suitcase across the road, pulling out her phone to check the address of the house.

Mackenzie wandered down the street, following the directions her phone gave, soon forgetting about the inconvenience of lugging her bags around as the town began to bewitch her. She'd never traveled out of her hometown before—never left behind the plain-looking, white-painted concrete buildings that washed out their small town and gave no variety to its inhabitants.

Here, there was a character to all the architecture. Mackenzie's eyes darted around frantically as her steps slowed. It was hard to absorb it all. The red brick building on one side of her showed its history in its structure but housed new and renovated shops and cafes inside.

On the other side was a white-and-cream building that looked far from boring, with pillars and eaves, freshly painted with no cracks.

And on both sides were ornate signs showing types of shops she'd never dreamed a small town could hold. Museums, cafes, and shops all embraced a history she was sure the town would have wanted to forget. Instead, they welcomed it, showing off tolerance she'd never experienced.

She walked along the rainbow crosswalk to look at menus in the shop windows—far fancier and more diverse than the diner had back home. Mackenzie wasn't sure she would ever be able to see everything

Salem could give her.

Mackenzie moved between the shops quickly but lingered at each window, eager to see it all. She needed to tell someone—she pulled out her phone to take pictures of the city around her and sent them to Lucy, eager to hear her voice, mirroring her own amazement as she kept going.

Breaking off from the road, Mackenzie followed a walkway between buildings until she returned to the road and everything grew peacefully quiet. One side of her housed even more touristy shops, while the other had beautiful buildings with gorgeous gardens, vibrant with color.

The Salem Common came into view and Mackenzie dragged her bag in, feeling energy inside her—unlike anything she'd felt—pulling her into the park rather than the direction she had been heading. The gazebo sitting in the center caught her eye—others around her age already sat in and around it, much to her disappointment—and she considered going up to inspect it further. Something was singing to her blood, telling her to go to it, touch it, stand inside, and just close her eyes.

Her self-consciousness, especially while carrying her suitcase and backpack around, took over and she turned away to go find the house that now belonged to her.

It wasn't hard to find, and she stared up at its navy expanse with white trim, overwhelmed by its size. It was the opposite of everything she'd known and the first glance at anything to do with her father. There were no pictures growing up, no belongings besides the necklace he'd given her mother, and nothing to learn about who he was other than small snippets of knowledge she'd been given by her mother as a child. Even Lucy's mother, Mary, had said Anne had never really spoken about the man she'd lost and left behind in her hometown.

This is it, she thought, pulling the key from under a

well-weathered front mat where her mother's friend had left it while she was at work that day.

Her pocket vibrated with a text and she checked what Lucy had to say, knowing she needed to see it before she got too engrossed in the house and forgot to reply.

LUCY: IT LOOKS AH-MAZING! I DEFINITELY NEED TO COME SEE YOU THERE SOMETIME SO I CAN TRY ALL THE FOOD!

MACKENZIE: CLASSIC YOU, ONLY THINKING WITH YOUR STOMACH!

LUCY: ONE OF US HAS TO, YOU'RE TOO BUSY THINKING WITH SOMETHING LOWER ;). YOU SHOULD INVITE HIM TO SALEM FOR AN ADVENTURE AWAY FROM BOSTON.

MACKENZIE: I DOUBT HE'D WANT TO. HE WENT HOME AND HAD NO IDEA I WAS MOVING CLOSER. HE PROBABLY WANTS TO HAVE HIS ADVENTURE AS A SEXY MEMORY AND MOVE ON.

LUCY: SCAREDY CAT! YOU KNOW HE MEANT IT. HE SAID TO CONTACT HIM AGAIN IF YOU WERE IN BOSTON. WELL, YOU'RE NEAR BOSTON! JUST TELL HIM!

MACKENZIE: I THINK OUR MOMENT'S OVER.

LUCY: IT DOESN'T HAVE TO BE. LIVE YOUR LIFE! AND SEND ME HOUSE PHOTOS!!

Mackenzie grinned, considering Lucy's words for a moment before putting her phone away. She slipped the key in the door, feeling as the lock welcomed it easily, clicking in response. With a deep breath in, she turned the handle and walked inside. The air was somewhat stale but also filled with a hint of fresh grass which she assumed meant that Vicki—her mother's friend who had been the caretaker of the house—had left a window open somewhere to air the house out before Mackenzie arrived.

To her left lay a living area, dust coasting most surfaces but in generally good shape, with a kitchen to her right and stairs in front of her, photo frames lining the wall up the staircase to where she assumed the bedrooms were.

Leaving her bags by the front door, she walked up the stairs slowly, admiring the different frames and photos. Her mother smiled out of one, the same ivory skin and green eyes as hers, and lovingly embracing her from behind was Mackenzie's father, with features she recognized in herself but had never known were from him. He was lean but muscled, with auburn hair that had been shaved into a buzzcut. A dog tag sat around his neck and fell over her mother's shoulder into view of the camera, and his smile had no trace of worry or pain. Sheer glee.

Mackenzie moved to the next photo on her way up the stairs, tears in her eyes. Her dad was in the photo cradling her as a baby in a hospital, looking down on her face with tears of joy in his eyes, her tiny body swaddled up and asleep in his arms. That had probably been the last photo he'd ever taken with her, she realized: he had died in an accident mere months after her birth. The third photo on the staircase was taken in the same hospital, with clothing the same on her father, and her mother in a medical gown lying in a hospital bed, holding the small baby in her arms with an inexplicably happy smile—despite the tiredness that pulled on the features in her face.

Blinking more tears from her eyes, Mackenzie climbed the last steps to the staircase landing, moving into the first room she saw and finding an abandoned child's room with a crib and toys still strewn about the floor. The room was coated with dust and the sun streamed in through the blinds making the musty, stale smell stronger. She crossed the room, tears in her eyes at how quickly her mother had left this house in her grief, opening the window and letting in the fresh air.

She knew how her mother must have felt in this town, despite Mackenzie having grown up in a different place. She knew the feeling of being in a town that knew your trauma and pitied you for it.

Would anyone remember or recognize her name here? It had been long enough; she could go relatively under the radar here. She hoped.

She thought of her best friend's wish for her and her mother's letter and knew, despite the memories that lay in this room, she would have to be hard at work on parts of this house later that day. She was determined.

Participate in life and live it vigorously, she reminded herself.

Moving on to the next room for inspection, she walked into another bedroom and felt her breath catch in her throat. This room had belonged to her mother and father. One side was decorated with artful trinkets; the other was basic and reminded Mackenzie of the only true thing she knew of her father besides his love for her mother—that he was a soldier. The folded American flag sat on the bedside table on his side of the bed along with a digital watch, a compass, and his dog tags. Walking over curiously, she picked his dog tags up, rubbing the collecting dust off the text, and stared at them.

"Brian Harris," she whispered, rolling his name over her tongue. She smiled sadly, finally feeling the relief at having answers, at connecting to the family she hadn't had in years, knowing her place in the world. Carefully, she undid the clasp on her mother's necklace around her neck, sliding the named dog tag off its current chain and onto her mother's before doing it up again and securing the memories of both her parents around her neck. Her breathing felt lighter as she willed herself to honor them by living in a way that they'd be proud of.

"All right, first things first... Mom, Dad, I'm taking the biggest room. Sorry," she said to the silent room, opening the window of their bedroom before moving downstairs to check out how much space she had to leave items in the basement she had spotted on her way up.

Slipping in the other key that had been on the chain for her, Mackenzie unlocked the basement door and continued. *Why on earth did they keep the basement locked up?*

Dropping down the stairs quickly, she found the entrance to the basement level and descended into the darkness below, using her phone flashlight to search for the light switch. It was incredibly musty, and something smelled like it had died. *Probably a mouse,* she thought. She flicked the light switch on and followed the room around the corner away from the landing at the bottom of the stairs.

Her body began to tremble.

Opposite her were ornate weapons, varying kinds of guns, swords, knives, and staffs—among others she couldn't name or recognize—displayed on the wall. Below was a workbench with a large, old, and dusty book resting on top. An unrecognizable symbol adorned the front cover. She stepped back and made a mental note to investigate later when she'd had some food and rational thought as to why any of this was here.

Racing back up the stairs, Mackenzie shut the basement door behind her, securing it with her weight as she let out a deep breath.

"What crazy stuff were you guys into..." she groaned, speaking to the pendants on her necklace as she forced herself to leave her bags behind, take her wallet and keys, and go in search of food.

She ducked out the front door, locking it behind her. Mere streets away from her was a pub with a decent menu she was eager to try out. She didn't look at other options, knowing that if she did, she'd become too indecisive. Instead, she walked in the door and looked around to see if she needed to be seated or if she could choose for herself. The waitress stood at the back of the room talking to a customer but flicked her eyes to the new entry and waved to a free table in the center of the room with two chairs.

With a small smile and a nod, Mackenzie let the waitress return to her conversation and sat down. The pub was recently renovated inside but designed to mimic an old English-style pub, complete with a full bar, booths, and classic wood furniture that had been painted black. The smell of food greeted her nose, the smell of frying food reminding her of the diner back home—only much better. She could already tell the food quality was going to be far beyond that of her hometown. Her stomach rumbled loudly as she glanced at the menu and the specials board.

Mackenzie wasn't used to deciding on her food and the choice was almost overwhelming. Flicking her eyes over the contents of the menu, she chose quickly, knowing otherwise she'd take forever.

She put the menu down and regretted it, feeling the itch to find Kai on social media pull on her patience. She didn't want to be *that girl* who obsessed over a guy she'd met once. Lucy was wrong; he wasn't going to visit her in Salem if she messaged him, he had likely moved on to his next adventure. With his body and honey tongue, she was sure he had girls fawning over him all the time. So instead, she stared at the menu again intently, running over its items in more detail, inspecting it further to avoid creating a habit she might not be able to get out of her system.

Every time she paused though, the memory—of his tongue, of him, of her body being claimed by his in every way—overwhelmed her. She'd never experienced that kind of ecstasy before with a person. He'd brought a part of her alive that she didn't know existed.

Putting down the menu and resting her chin on her arm lightly, Mackenzie slowly traced the places on her neck where his mouth had been. Trying not to get too turned on in the middle of the restaurant, she poured herself a glass of water from the bottle on the table and busied her hands away from her body.

"You're new around here," a deep female voice said.

Mackenzie started, looking up to see a waitress standing over her. She took in the woman's kind, dark brown eyes, flawless dark brown skin, and curls that looked wild and tamed simultaneously. It wasn't a question she had asked, merely an observation but Mackenzie thought to answer anyway.

"Yes, I'm new to town. I moved here for college

actually," she said, glad to not have anyone recognize her because of her trauma. It felt... nice not to be consistently reminded by those who only pretended to care. There was no pity in this woman's eyes, and it was refreshing.

"I'm going to college this year too. I mean, I've lived here my whole life but I'll be joining you on campus," she said, excitedly, and Mackenzie couldn't help smiling in response.

"Great, I'll have someone to look out for. It's a bit daunting not knowing anyone."

"I get that. Well, I'm Amari, nice to meet you."

"Kenzie. You too."

"So what's your Major?"

"History."

"No way! Me too!"

"Oh wow! That's even better!"

"Well, if you want some good people to know in your Major, there's also Teo," she said, turning back to the man she had been talking to who now sat alone at the bar. "Hey Teo, come over here, I want to introduce you to someone."

He turned on his chair, eyeing both girls with a soft, surprised smile before sliding off and moving towards them. He had brown hair in a Caesar-style cut, olive skin, and brown eyes that watched her attentively as he came to stand beside Amari. He seemed kind, calm, and a little shy to Mackenzie as he broke their gaze to look at his friend, eyebrows raised in question.

"Teo, this is Kenzie. She's joining us in History this year!" Amari smiled at him, then looked at Mackenzie, transferring his focus.

He turned to size Mackenzie up, still surprised but kindly smiling through it all, not afraid to meet her eyes with his soft gaze.

"Oh, I completely forgot to take your order!"

"Just the burger special, thanks!" she said, chuckling with Amari.

"Teo, can you keep our friend company? I just have to run this order and a couple of others!" Amari asked hurriedly, reminded that she was at work.

Her relatable frazzled state made Mackenzie smile.

"Go! Do your work!" he said, laughing as she sped off to look after Mackenzie's order and the other patrons that had appeared in the pub. He turned back to the table, watching her with a hesitant smile on his face.

"May I sit and keep you company?" he asked, touching the back of the chair opposite her.

She could hear Lucy in the back of her mind telling her to participate in life, so she nodded quickly before she could decline, and hoped Kai would magically walk through the door. "So, you're new here?"

"Yeah, I moved here today. It's very different to my hometown." She smiled, feeling a wave of calm wash over her as she spoke to Teo. His face had an openness that said he was truly listening to and connecting with her words.

"And that is?" he pushed, leaning forward in his chair and settling into a comfortable position against the table.

"A little town up in Oregon you would never have heard of," she said, chuckling to herself, still barely believing her new home.

"Well, that's a fair distance to come for college. What made you choose Salem?" he asked, leaning on the table with his elbows, listening intently for everything she had to say.

She loved the feeling of being a blank slate to a person, able to be any version of herself she wanted to be.

"My family comes from here originally and they're not around anymore, so I wanted to feel closer to them and be somewhere new," she said, the honesty flowing. She wasn't sure why her words spilled out so candidly, but the ease with which she spoke to him surprised even her.

But Teo was unperturbed by her unloading of personal history, seeming to take it all in excitedly, the sense of relief and calm in her putting out any worry or concern in her mind. Like a fire blanket over a small flame, his presence choked all the negative feelings in her and smothered the desire to see Kai. She couldn't help returning his wide smile.

"Well, I hope you like it here, and if you need any help orientating the town or just want some company, I'm available," he said softly, glancing up right as Amari appeared at their table with Mackenzie's burger and one for Teo also. They laughed as though his mention had summoned her perfectly on queue.

"Thanks, I appreciate it," Mackenzie said before smiling her thanks at Amari, who hurried off again. "Look at me go, been here less than an hour and I've already made two friends!"

"Look at you!" He smiled along with her, as she picked up her burger to eat and he followed suit, still smiling up at each other as their eyes held.

Any nervousness Mackenzie had about this new town or the house or feeling alone had disappeared in Teo's presence.

7: THE NEW RULES

Mackenzie sat cross-legged in the entry of her new house, the strong wood of the front door pressing against her back. She sat for a moment with her eyes closed, head resting against the sturdy board, forcing herself to take deep breaths as the weight of her limbs pulled on her. After leaving the pub so calm and relaxed, she'd made it home and the job ahead of her made everything in her clench with dread. She wanted to climb up the stairs to the forgotten bed, maneuver under its dusty old covers, and never leave. No one could stop her.

She knew no one would appear to move her, but that was also the reason she sat on the floor at the bottom of the stairs, knowing she couldn't give in. Despite the flame in her that wanted a life her parents could be proud of, there was a weakness deep in her gut, pulling her to quit.

Her stomach cramped as though it might swallow itself whole, tears falling silently down her cheek. She slid her knees up to her chest, wrapping her arms around herself.

Mackenzie let everything fall only for a moment, giving herself two minutes to break apart before she imagined Lucy standing over her, telling her to get up and work for her happiness and her life. She needed to focus on something instead of wallowing; to be productive and keep going to avoid dealing with the crushing weight of panic, pain, and fear.

One last deep breath, inhaling the stale air of the house, and she pulled herself from the floor, heading down the basement stairs to investigate what she could work with in terms of storage space.

Piles of old boxes were flat-packed in a corner. She pulled them from their long-abandoned cobweb coverings and took them upstairs.

She stood in the doorway of the childhood bedroom she wished she could remember, taking a moment to admire the care that had been taken in setting up. She began with the toys that were strewn about the floor, preparing a box and loading the loose items in before ferrying them down the staircases, retrieving a toolbox from the basement on her return.

The crib was next. Ignoring the peeling paint and dust on it, she used the tools to disassemble it into its original pieces and took them from the room too.

Slowly and surely, the room emptied to the basement until all that was left was a dusty room with pale white-and-yellow diamond wallpaper. Finally, she could see her progress in the house, feel her presence, and not have it belong to ghosts of the past. This was necessary. She had to move on—leave some of the past but embrace how she needed things to be.

A knock sounded on the front door below and before she could move to answer it, the door opened. Had she remembered to lock it? She was sure she had.

"Mackenzie, it's Vicki," a voice called out from the bottom of the stairs. "Are you home?"

"Hi, Vicki, yes! I'm upstairs!" she called, turning around and listening as the steps made their way up to her.

A woman came into view with dark brown—almost black—hair cut short into a bob, pale white skin that looked like she'd barely seen the sun, and blue eyes. She stopped at the top of the stairs, putting her hand over her heart when she caught sight of Mackenzie as she let loose a heavy breath.

"You look so much like them!" she said.

Mackenzie smiled slightly, unsure how to thank the stranger who knew more of her parents' lives than she did.

"I'm so sorry for your loss, dear. I know you've spent such a long time on your own, but I want you to know that if you need anything, I'm right next door."

"Ahh… Thanks. I would offer you coffee, but I haven't been to the store yet," she replied with an apologetic shrug.

"That's okay, dear. I understand. I appreciate the thought." Vicki smiled, moving closer to Mackenzie's place in the doorway to see what she had been doing, seeing the now-empty room.

Mackenzie stayed quiet, waiting for Vicki's reaction, observing the woman who had been so close to her parents, wondering if she could find out clues about their lives just by looking at her face. It was weathered with stress, tiredness pulling at every feature, and Mackenzie wondered if that was the loss of her friends or something else.

"I could never really bring myself to touch this room. She left it in such a hurry and in such pain that I just… couldn't do it. This was your room and you'd barely gotten to use it when you both disappeared." Vicki's voice cracked as though she could see the ghosts moving around in the room.

"And yet you looked after the place all these years?" Mackenzie whispered, watching her carefully.

"Of course! When you both disappeared, we had no idea if you'd come back. I looked after it and your mother knew that, but I had no idea that she'd died until the office for her will called to say the ownership had been transferred to you. Then you sent me the email saying you were coming to live here for college and I was beyond happy. I knew you'd never really seen it and a girl needs a proper home," Vicki rambled in response, but Mackenzie just listened intently, absorbing every word eagerly, feeling how her heart raced like she was experiencing Vicki's turbulent story firsthand.

When their gazes finally met, Mackenzie couldn't move, entrapped by Vicki's words.

"They loved you very much and wanted everything for you. It's wonderful to have you here and if you have any questions about your parents, please don't hesitate to ask me. They were my best friends, and *you* are their legacy."

"Thank you," Mackenzie managed, her eyes tearing up again, trying to spill as she fought her own emotions. "That really means a lot. I haven't been able to have that kind of discussion before, so I would love to know more."

The saltwater finally escaped, spilling down her cheeks.

Vicki's face softened as she moved forward, arms wide, allowing Mackenzie to move away if she wasn't comfortable.

Mackenzie let Vicki pull her in, feeling the warmth of the arms around her help keep her calm enough not to break further. These tears were different though, a relief as she let loose the tightness in her chest. She'd found someone who knew *something*—who could tell her stories about her parents to make her smile and know them in a way that wasn't just a local news story of their disappearance and death. She'd never known her father and her mother was a ghost she had chased in the forest for ten years. Finally, she felt as though she had found something tangible and real.

"You're always welcome, dear," Vicki said as she held her softly. "I'm right across the street should you need me at any time."

Mackenzie pulled back, met Vicki's eyes, and dropped the hug, enjoying her newfound lightness.

"Now, do you need any assistance around the house with cleaning items out, or even groceries?" Vicki asked, glancing outside the bedroom to the rest of the dusty house.

Mackenzie followed her gaze and shook her head slowly.

"No, thank you... I find it therapeutic to pack away their things. I'm learning who they were in the process. I'll let you know if that changes. But I might need directions to the nearest grocery store for later," she admitted.

Vicki perked up happily. She pulled her phone out and brought up her maps, zooming and moving around slightly to show off where Mackenzie's nearest options were and what Vicki recommended.

"Where was my mother's favorite place in Salem?" Mackenzie's hunger for answers presented itself. Her stomach fluttered with butterflies and she looked up, hopeful.

"You know, if I ever wanted to find her during the day, all I had to do was go to the Common and she would be there, reading in the sun. She'd sit out there for hours on a picnic blanket and sometimes your father would join her, just napping beside her, keeping her company. I've never seen two people more perfect for each other." Vicki smiled sadly, her eyes losing focus from Mackenzie's face as though she was seeing it all in her mind's eye.

"How did my father die?" Mackenzie whispered, feeling the excitement turn rough and edgy in her stomach as anxiety overtook it.

Vicki's eyes lifted, wide with fear as her lips parted in silence, unsure of what to say.

She didn't break her gaze with Mackenzie but there was something about it that made Mackenzie want to look away, something that made dread take over anxiety and weigh her down as her hands began to shake.

"Ahh... It was an accident... Did Anne not tell you?"

she stammered, waiting expectantly as though Mackenzie's next words could save her from her fumbling.

"I was a young child. All I knew was that he'd died. No one ever told me how and I never knew his name so I couldn't exactly look it up. Not that it stopped me trying…" Mackenzie watched the worry and fear in Vicki's eyes. It told her there was something more to the story, and part of her wondered if she even wanted to know the answer.

"Don't you want to remember your parents positively? I mean, you barely knew your father, surely you'd prefer to learn happy things about who he was and how he loved your mother." Vicki tried to sway her from inquiring further.

But Mackenzie put on a brave face. Her heart began to thud against her ribs, each beat like a shock she wasn't expecting as her hands vibrated with nervous energy and her legs became weak. But she was stubborn, always had been, and always would be. She couldn't just learn the good things about her parents; she wanted to know everything. She wanted to know the truth of it, flaws, darkness, and all.

"No," she said firmly.

Vicki flinched.

Mackenzie softened her voice and tried again to be clear about what she wanted. "I want to know everything, no matter what. I'm not a child anymore and I deserve to know the truth about my parents. If you're comfortable telling me, please do, otherwise, I'll go and ask on my own. I have a name now and a place to start."

Vicki shook her head clear of the worry, her eyes breaking the gaze and glancing at the ground. She took a deep breath and Mackenzie could see her shaking also.

"Your parents got in with the wrong crowd well before you were born. Unfortunately, despite trying to leave that life behind, it wouldn't leave them. Your father's body was found one night, stabbed to death. The police put it down to a robbery gone wrong and the culprit was never found. Your mom feared for your life and her own, thinking it was a deliberate attack, so she ran."

Mackenzie's knees buckled as the world spun. She grabbed the door frame, stopping her head from colliding with it as the full weight of Vicki's words hit her. Her mind raced so fast that she couldn't focus her eyes. Her mouth opened, but no cry escaped. Heat burned in her organs, a sparking fury that she knew she couldn't ever let loose.

There was no horrible accident that had taken her father from her like she'd once believed.

Someone had robbed her of a parent.

Murdered.

Her mind reeled as she ran over the possible ramifications of this information. What if someone had found her mother in Oregon and had a part in her 'disappearance' too? Did her mother really disappear, or had she been killed?

Mackenzie could feel the sickness coming up her throat and pushed onto her feet, bolting across the landing to the bathroom.

She didn't make the toilet.

The taste of her burger and fries burned its way up her throat until it had completely emptied in the sink. It came in droves until her body was empty and weak, her abs complaining at the work they'd done in ridding her of the food.

Mackenzie turned the tap on and barely registered the water running brown for a moment before it carried the contents of the sink down the drain. Just the sight of it made her ill, but she braced her hands on the sides of the sink, unable to move as she watched the water and tried to hold in the remaining food.

The rancid smell threatened to make her heave again. She kept breathing deeply, slowly feeling the nausea disappear. She didn't move though, afraid to set herself off again.

Footsteps wandered up behind her, but she didn't dare look at Vicki.

"Are you okay, Mackenzie?" Vicki watched her carefully.

The tears she hadn't noticed surfacing in her eyes slipped into the rush of the sink as the water ran clear, having washed her filth from its porcelain.

Vicki reached over, shutting the tap off slowly.

"I'm not okay. I wanted to know but... I can't help thinking... What if those same people found her... What if they were the ones who..." Mackenzie couldn't form the words, couldn't make them real.

"I never asked, how did your mother die?"

The question snapped something profoundly deep in Mackenzie's chest as she turned to the woman in the doorway.

"I don't know! She disappeared ten years ago without a trace and... everyone told me it must have been a bear or something, but... what if it wasn't? What if she went camping like she wanted to and they got her? Who were the people they got involved with... Maybe I can do some research...and—"

"No!" Vicki cut off the thought before Mackenzie could speak it. "You are not investigating those people. I don't know who they are exactly, but if I did, I would tell you to stay the hell away from them. Nothing good can come from digging into that. Keep yourself safe, your parents would have wanted that. I know that for certain. They did everything they could do to keep you hidden."

Mackenzie refused to break eye contact with Vicki as the woman stared her down. She knew her mother's friend was right, but it didn't stop the niggling part inside her that wanted to know more, wanted to know the truth no matter what. And it didn't stop the restless raging fire that had sparked inside her.

"Okay," she said in surrender, taking her hands from

the sink and righting herself. "I won't. Thank you for telling me though, Vicki. I know that can't have been easy."

"Damn right, it wasn't!" Vicki agreed.

"I think I probably just need to go for a relaxing walk and get some food to right my brain, if you wouldn't mind. I'll come to find you when I'm all settled and in a better headspace, and you can tell me all the wonderful things about my parents." She wasn't going to be able to keep her conversation with Vicki going when she was so impatient to get to other things. She was thankful for Vicki, but her body started to rush with adrenaline to check areas without her around.

"It's okay, you can come to me whenever you're ready," Vicki said, softening with the belief that Mackenzie's interest in investigating had abated. She made a move towards Mackenzie before thinking the better of it and, with a smile, turned and left the house.

Mackenzie stood in the bathroom, waiting for the front door to click shut before she bolted down the stairs and into the basement, speeding her way around the corner to the wall of weapons. She could feel the fear and wariness of the space evaporating within her as she stuck her head down and opened the book on the workbench.

She flipped page after page with a shrill growl as she began to realize the entire book was blank and her attempt at finding answers here was futile. She tossed the book across the room with a final screech and turned to the weapons, hoping they would hold an answer for her.

They were old, decorated in ways that knives and swords and daggers weren't anymore.

She reached out to one at her eye level—a short sword with a black stone in its silver hilt that seemed to swallow her soul the longer she looked at it. Her hands touched the metal, cold lancing up her arm like she had touched the block of ice. Fighting the urge to let it go and inspect a new one, she wrapped her hands around the hilt of the sword and lifted it out of its holder.

Immediately, her limbs gained new strength, and a liquid-metal feeling solidified through her veins. Her breath turned to fog in front of her face. Yet, despite the temperature falling upon the room, Mackenzie felt more alike than ever as her nerves buzzed with excited adrenaline and cold strength. She admired the sword in her hand, power resonating from it, and her eyes caught on the stone again as a shiver crept up her spine.

It reminded her of the creature's eyes—black, bottomless, mesmerizing—pulling her in as she relived her last day searching in the forest. As her mind flitted to the object of her search, her mother, and the utter need she'd had to find her that day, pain spasmed up her arms. She cried out, her hands releasing the sword.

It clattered to the floor.

The moment it touched the concrete, a smash echoed as tiny pieces of black stone flew through the air.

Mackenzie blocked her face with her arms, closed her eyes, and dropped into a ball on the floor, facing away just in time to feel sharp tiny pricks across her entire exposed side. She cried out as stinging broke out over her skin, the pain growing as the room fell silent and still.

When she was sure it had all ended, she opened her eyes and took stock. Tiny cuts dotted one side of her body, warm blood staining her shirt in some places as black shards glittered on her shirt.

Mackenzie surveyed the room around her, taking in the damage from the black stone in the space, unable to help the gasp that escaped her lips.

Every wall of the room twinkled with black onyx stone stars.

8: THE FIRST DAY PAINS

Mackenzie sat in the lecture hall between Amari and Teo, losing focus over what the lecturing professor was talking about. He was on an unrelated tangent for the third time, removing his mind from the expected topics and classwork that all the students wanted to know about. Every time someone had raised their hand to direct his conversation back to the expected workload for the semester, he'd found a way off the rails yet again mere minutes later.

Mackenzie rolled her eyes as he droned on about a life no one had asked to hear about. Instead, she drew trees in the margins of her notebook.

Amari reached over to the notebook, pen in hand, and scrawled, in gloriously curly handwriting, a note for Mackenzie.

'He might not be on task but damn the professor is totally hot. Not going to mind staring at that all semester. Intelligent. Hot. Looks like the shy type who's seriously freaky. What more could a girl want?' Amari wrote with a puckish smile on her lips.

Mackenzie was met with a wink as she looked at her new friend, and had to stifle her laugh at Amari's brazen comments, hyper-aware of the other students around them.

'Not really my type, but good luck with that! Haha!'

she wrote back, a bit jealous of Amari's writing as she stared at her plain, neat script below it.

Amari's eyebrows raised in question as she stared at what Mackenzie had put down, dropping her pen eagerly to the page in response.

'*So what is your type then?*' Amari asked, watching the penned response carefully.

Teo, on Mackenzie's right, had begun to follow the girls' distracted notebook chat.

Mackenzie's pen hesitated above the page as her mind instantly jumped to the memory of Kai. Biting down on her lip, she tried to pinpoint what about him made her so attracted.

'*Knows what he wants. Confident. Bold. No shame. Playful.*' She grew hot at the memory as her cheeks flushed.

Teo and Amari shared a look Mackenzie barely caught sight of. She didn't have long enough to translate the look on either of their faces before it disappeared, and she wondered if she had even seen it at all.

"It appears we are out of time. I will update you all on this in the next lecture. The resources online also give you the assessment dates for the semester. Dismissed." The professor cut their conversation short.

Mackenzie shut her notebook with a smile as the three of them got up and moved towards the exit.

Before they could get out the door, Amari tapped Mackenzie on the shoulder.

"I'll catch up with you after, I've got a question for the professor," she said as she waggled her eyebrows suggestively.

"Okay…" Mackenzie laughed, unconvinced, but let her disappear, continuing with just Teo in tow. Mackenzie walked out of the building, the sunshine warm on her face, taking a deep breath of fresh air. And enjoying the freedom after the stuffiness of the lecture hall.

They walked for a little while in silence, before Teo

filled the conversation void, escaping the crowds to the front of campus.

"Well, we made it through the first day!" Teo held his fist out triumphantly.

Mackenzie chuckled and bumped hers with his.

"That we did, and we only lost Amari at the end there!" she said, continuing his jovial tone, bouncing her energy off his.

"She'll turn up eventually. Speaking of, one of our friends is hosting a party tonight. You should come," he said, slowing to a stop and turning to her, watching her reactions with a soft smile.

She mirrored him, stopping and catching his gaze, embracing the serene happiness that washed over her. She couldn't imagine staying home in the empty house all night on her own.

"Sure! I'll be there!" she said, watching his face light up at her acceptance. His smile grew brazen as he took a step closer to her, leaning in to whisper in her ear, his breath tickling her chin.

"It wouldn't be any fun without you."

She swallowed hard, feeling the way her stomach curled in delight at his words before guilt dragged at her. What about Kai?

And suddenly the look Amari and Teo had shared made sense.

"Oh?" she said quietly, attempting innocence as her heart leaped about in her chest and her stomach sunk until all she could feel was trapped fluttering inside her, begging to be freed.

"Of course! I'd be so lonely without your lively conversation and beauty keeping me company..." he continued.

Her chest grew tight as she held her breath. With his body so close to hers, she was sure he could feel the heat coming off her body. Her smile fell as he swallowed, feeling the anticipation hit her body as he moved in slowly, leaning close.

The brazen smile broke out on his face again.

She rushed, flustered.

"I don't want you to have the wrong idea," she said quickly, reminding herself that participating in life also meant not creating another 'Josh situation'. "I'm not looking for a relationship right now. I just moved here and don't have the mental capacity to care for someone else's needs," she spilled, worried her new-found *friend* was going to hate her already, but knowing she couldn't be blind again like she had been.

"I'm not asking for that." He surrendered, his hands held up in defense, grazing her body as they lifted. "All I'm saying is that we can have some fun at a party together. No strings, no feelings, no expectations. Just come and have some fun, meet new people, and enjoy your first week of college the right way."

She softened, feeling like moldable jelly at his words. Her guilt disappeared like it had never existed, and her insides warmed at the prospect. Just harmless fun. She'd specified her limitations and he'd listened, and now she was free to enjoy herself as much as she wanted.

"Okay. Sure!" She caved with an enthusiastic grin.

"I'll see you tonight then," he said, leaning back, turning, and walking away.

Her body, acting of its own accord, mourned the loss of his closeness.

"Amari can give you the details," he called without glancing back as she struggled to breathe normally again.

Amari appeared beside her as if summoned, a knowing smile on her face. She didn't seem surprised by what she had walked up to.

"You knew?" Mackenzie asked Amari.

"Why do you think I asked what your type was?" Amari responded, getting an incredulous and confused look from Mackenzie. "To help him approach you! He had to know the best angle for success!"

"What? You were giving him the answers?"

Mackenzie asked, still reeling.

"Absolutely! I'm the perfect wing woman! He was smitten with you after the day in the pub when you talked for hours! He just didn't know how to approach it best, so I made sure to give him more of a chance at success!" She winked at Mackenzie, letting it all dawn on her. "But don't worry, he can do non-committal too."

"Hang on, so do you actually find the professor hot?" Mackenzie asked, questioning how much of their conversation in the lecture hall was the truth.

"God, no! He is definitely not my type—if you know what I mean?" she said, chuckling.

Mackenzie stared wide-eyed, her mouth open like a gulping fish, wrapping her mind around exactly what Amari could mean.

"You might have to spell it out for me. I'm still figuring out that *I helped him get the answers thing…*" Mackenzie said slowly and sheepishly.

"My type is my *girlfriend,*" Amari said with a smile and Mackenzie nodded, finally realizing what she meant.

"Oh! Okay, now I get it. Sorry," she said with a tight grin, feeling foolish for not understanding her meaning earlier.

"No need to apologize!" Amari laughed. "You're too busy dealing with that very hot almost-kiss to focus properly. I don't take offense!"

Mackenzie joined in the laughter, breathily, still trying to figure out her feelings. Somehow whenever Teo was around, her yearning for Kai completely hid itself and her desires were a mystery to her, foreign and out of touch until she was free of him and clarified again.

"Speaking of," Amari continued, "maybe we should pick out an outfit for you tonight?"

"Sure! But fair warning, I did walk here today." Mackenzie watched the surprise on her friend's face.

"I'll drive." Amari pulled her keys from her bag and

led the way to her parked car.

Mackenzie followed with a smile, glad to have a friend for the afternoon rather than being on her own while she waited for the party to start.

They found the car with no hassle but had to shuffle a few items off the front passenger seat before Mackenzie could climb into Amari's hatchback.

"Sorry, my car's a mess."

"Don't worry, I guarantee my pick-up was worse." Mackenzie chuckled as Amari's worry smoothed off her face.

The tightness in Amari's face softened as she shot her a grateful look, turned the car on, and began the route toward Mackenzie's house. It wasn't a difficult drive and it made it much quicker than the journey to college had been that morning.

Pulling up in front of Mackenzie's house, they both got out of the car, Mackenzie feeling Amari's amazed gaze, trying to make a point by looking at her.

"What?" Mackenzie said.

"You live here by yourself?" Amari asked with eyes wide.

"Yeah, I do." Her eyes dropped and her mood fell as she was reminded of her loneliness.

"Oh. I'm sorry. I just meant it was a beautiful place that I was surprised you could afford, I didn't mean—"

"I know. It's just hard to bring up my damage in conversations with new people, otherwise, I would have warned you. This is the house my parents left me," Mackenzie explained. The weight of her necklace pushed against her breastbone, hidden under her shirt. She reached to pull it out, letting Amari closer to inspect it.

Amari carefully placed her fingers under the pendants, reading the names aloud, her eyes widening in recognition.

"Oh! I remember my parents talking about this. They said it was so sad what had happened to your father and your mom just…" she started, recalling the information before stopping herself and checking Mackenzie's face.

"You can say it, she left," Mackenzie said in acceptance rather than pain.

"Yeah…" Amari said quietly, letting the conversation drift off into an uncomfortable silence.

The silence chewed into Mackenzie's stomach as if it were telling her that it was all her fault for bringing up such a difficult topic with such a new friend, but she pushed on, determined to resurrect the mood.

"On a happier note, I get to see the place they lived in and it has made me feel closer to them," Mackenzie said, offering up her optimism, relieved to get a smile in response.

"That's great news!" Amari said, dropping the necklace pendants and letting them clink back onto Mackenzie's chest.

"Let's go inside." Mackenzie led the way to the front door with her new friend in tow. "I'm going to warn you now though, I don't know if I have a lot of party-worthy outfits!"

"Now you tell me!" Amari responded mockingly, pretending that it was an issue before dropping the pretense quickly and surrendering. "We'll find you something."

Once inside, Mackenzie led the way up the stairs into the bedroom that had once belonged to her parents. She'd done some work cleaning it to make it her own space but left remnants of her family behind. She hadn't yet brought herself to go through the closet. Walking over to her suitcase on the other side of the bed, where her clothes were still housed, she opened it up and began pulling a couple of outfits out to show.

Amari hadn't noticed her change of direction, exploring the wardrobe and peering inside.

Mackenzie glanced up at the creak of the cupboard, ready to explain her friend's honest mistake when she spotted a dress—nestled in amongst everyday clothing—

that took her breath away. She knew Amari had found it too by the gasp that escaped her lips as her fingers reached for the material.

Amari pulled it carefully, untangling the coat hanger as if the dress were precious, while Mackenzie got to her feet and moved beside her, drawn by the magnificent piece of clothing.

The only thought that came to Mackenzie's mind while looking at it was that it looked like living magic. The dress was a dark sky blue with winding gold and silver threaded through its depths. It was fine enough thread that it seemed to shimmer in and out of view with the movement, and a variety of symbols she didn't recognize were sewn into it and made it feel… ancient. Reaching out her hand, she stroked the velvety fabric that greeted her touch, a soft fuzzy kiss.

"This dress was meant to be worn by you," Amari said quietly, only partly breaking through the spell the dress had on Mackenzie.

Mackenzie could feel the urge to slip it on and see, but a voice niggled in the back of her mind, warning her not to.

"This is my mother's. I don't know if I should be wearing it to a college party." Mackenzie's eyes never left the dress as she tried to imagine what it would look like on her.

"It was your mother's," Amari clarified quietly. "And I didn't know her, but surely she'd want you to have this dress, no matter where you wore it. So long as you look after it, you can keep her close this way, right?"

Mackenzie looked up at Amari, catching her gaze and seeing the sincerity in her eyes. Amari didn't budge or look away and Mackenzie knew that her good intentions were probably correct. She would feel closer to her mother, and considering how much adventure she was adding to her life lately, the little bit of comfort a gorgeous dress of her mother's could bring would help balance her out.

"You're right, I can. Thanks," she said quietly but assuredly, taking the dress from Amari's hands and placing it on the bed. "I can already tell we're going to be great friends."

The level of sincerity she gave to Amari surprised even herself.

Amari put a hand over her heart, her lips pushing together, touched by Mackenzie's words.

"We are, aren't we?" Amari said, sitting on the edge of the bed. "Well, we picked your outfit quickly, so now we can just relax until the party!" She sank back on the bed, letting the mattress claim her.

Mackenzie lay down next to her, avoiding lying on the clothing she'd left on the opposite side as she shut her eyes and took a deep breath for a moment.

"So… your girlfriend, hey? What's she like?" Mackenzie asked, realizing how oblivious and self-centered she'd been earlier. She turned her head to look at Amari, catching the bashful smile that broke out at the question.

"Lily is wonderful. She's gorgeous and passionate about people and the planet. She's such a kind person, who has such a depth for caring about other people's lives and emotions, I sometimes wonder how she can handle all of it. But she's incredible! Truly," Amari gushed, making Mackenzie smile as she imagined whom this description might belong to.

"And…? What does she look like? So I know when I meet her!" Mackenzie pushed, watching Amari light up further.

"She has bright orange hair, green eyes, and all the right curves," she said excitedly, bumping her elbow into her friend's.

"And how long have you two been together?"

"Two years—but I'm still as in love with her now as when we met, maybe more."

"That's wonderful! I hope I can meet this amazing woman one day!"

"Oh, she'll be at the party tonight so you absolutely will—if you're not too distracted by a certain guy who will not be named." Amari giggled, both girls overwhelmed by their grins, warmed by the wonderful company and conversation.

9: THE FOOL

Mackenzie stood outside the house, music blaring from its depths and a mass of people spilling over onto the porch and front lawn. She fiddled with the velvety dress, running her hands—which were beginning to sweat—down the front of her thighs, wiping them on the dress, and then immediately thinking better of it.

It was a gorgeous piece of clothing and once she'd zipped it up the back, it had secured to her frame perfectly—wide enough for her breasts, slim enough for her waist, and enough of a slide out on her hips to fall loosely and flowingly. It was long-sleeved, secured at the wrists, low cut in a V that showed off her cleavage just enough and stopped just above the knee with a small pentagram on her hip. Amari had told her that the pentagram was a reoccurring symbol in Salem, but as she stood in front of the house, fidgeting with the dress, she became wary of any connotations that could be taken from it, worried what strangers might think of her.

"Ready?" Amari asked, and Mackenzie took a deep breath, not allowing herself to procrastinate any longer. She nodded. "You're going to have so much fun, I promise!"

"I know…" Mackenzie responded slowly as she took her first step. "It's just getting inside."

"Didn't go to many parties in your old town?" Amari asked, seeing Mackenzie's nervousness.

"No, but I'm participating in life now."

"Then this really will be so much fun for you! Come on!"

Amari linked her elbow through Mackenzie's, slowly edging their way towards the house. Mackenzie took a final deep breath as she walked up the porch steps and was claimed by the cloud of music, smoke, laser lights, and the throng of bodies.

Immediately, her heart began to race—excitement and claustrophobia taking over her body as she glanced around, trying to take it all in. She followed all the people, their faces, what they were wearing, absorbing it all as much as she could. The bass of the room vibrated through her, urging her to join the group of people that had gathered in the middle of the living room and swing her hips to the rhythm.

She let Amari lead her to the kitchen though, where the people broke away only enough to allow others to collect drinks, and a bubbly, orange-haired girl bounded up to meet them, wrapping her arms around Amari.

Letting go of Amari's arm, Mackenzie let the two women have their moment, taking a step back and giving them space as they shared a passionate kiss.

A touch on the small of her back had her turning quickly to see Teo moving up behind her, glancing at his friends with a smile before turning to her and letting it grow bold.

"You came!" he said, sounding surprised.

"I said I would!" she retorted.

"True." He met her gaze.

The moment their eyes connected, Mackenzie's tight lungs loosened and everything fell into a state of calm. She smiled, relieved to be in Teo's company as his eyes traced down her dress.

She could see the admiration in his eyes, even before he spoke. "You look beautiful tonight."

"It's an old dress of my mom's that Amari helped me pick out," she said, looking up through her eyelashes. Again, not sure where her candid babbling was coming from.

Amari appeared beside the two of them to join the conversation as though summoned.

"This girl needed something wonderful for her first party ever and I saw the opportunity." Amari nudged her orange-haired companion. "Kenzie, this is Lily. Lily, our new friend, Mackenzie."

"Nice to meet you." Lily's melodic voice greeted her, a wide smile pulling at her lips before turning to her girlfriend. "Did you want a drink?"

"I could definitely use one! You two?" Amari turned to Teo and Mackenzie, and both nodded. The couple disappeared momentarily, leaving Teo and Mackenzie to watch each other quietly before their friends returned to save them from the silence.

"We're going out the back to play beer pong, you in?" Amari said eagerly.

Teo looked at Mackenzie, clearly taking an answer from her reaction.

"Ahhh... I'll come to watch... But..." She started, with Teo nodding his agreeance, understanding her intention.

"No stress—come see how the champions do it!" Lily declared triumphantly, leading the way out a side door of the kitchen and heading around to the back of the house where a ping-pong table had already been set up on the grass.

Amari and Lily embraced the others already at the table, acquainted with the men who cheered their names excitedly. Mackenzie's face grew hot as Amari and Lily's opponents wolf-whistled at her presence with Teo, reading something in their situation that made her feel embarrassed to be there.

Teo waved for them to shut up, before turning back to Mackenzie with an apologetic smile.

"If you want to, we can go somewhere else," he said quietly.

Too many things ran through her mind at once, urging her to stay. The first was that she refused to look like the girl who couldn't handle a bit of teasing, and she knew she was better than that. Second was a reminder of all the college movies Lucy had made her watch where the couple 'disappeared' and ended up in a bedroom. She didn't want that either.

"It's okay. I don't mind… Plus I want to see how this turns out for Lily and Amari," she said, shaking her head quickly, saving herself from explaining any further.

"Sure," he agreed, wandering to a nearby set of foldable chairs that had been set out for any onlookers.

"So… Amari tells me she gave you the answers on how to ask me out…" Mackenzie started, making conversation, and instantly regretted it when he turned to her, wide-eyed.

"She is such a gossip!" he said with a soft chuckle. "But yes, I wanted to be sure you'd say yes and needed to know the best approach."

"Well, I am here." She grinned. "But I meant what I said about not having a capacity for anything serious."

"That's fine. You are here and I feel honored." Even though he wasn't asking, she could feel the question beneath the words. He wanted to know more about why she hadn't ever been to a party before; clearly, Amari hadn't told him her story yet.

Calm washed over, allowing her to take a deep breath, feeling at ease around him suddenly, like they weren't strangers anymore.

"I've been a bit of a social hermit my whole life. Back in Oregon, my best friend used to be the one to take me things like this, but I never really ended up at a party with her, much to her disappointment and not for lack of trying." She dropped her gaze carefully to the red plastic cup of beer in her hand, taking a large swig.

"If I'm allowed to ask, was there a reason you were a

social hermit or are you just naturally an introverted person?"

She hesitated to answer, remembering how her truth had previously brought down the mood with Amari, but glancing up at him, she could see his genuine interest in her life and decided to take the plunge.

"My mom disappeared when I was young and I never knew my dad, he died right after I was born. I just withdrew from life until I moved here. I made a promise to do better and try to actually live my life," she admitted, relieved when he wasn't deterred by her brazen honesty. It was like he wasn't truly a stranger to her, but she couldn't place why.

"That's pretty horrible, I'm sorry to hear," he said, his lips scrunching for a moment in sympathetic tension before he relaxed and offered up a sad smile. "But you seem to be living well if you've made it a party with a date in your first week…"

"You're my date?" she asked, her stomach fluttering at the notion. Out of excitement or anxiety, she wasn't yet sure. It was fleeting though, disappearing before she could inspect the sensation further.

"Aren't I?" he said, his smile growing as he raised his eyebrows in question, daring her to say it.

"I suppose you are." She gave him a hesitant smile.

His gaze left her eyes for a moment to glance at her lips before returning, his smile slightly wider.

"Well, to fit with the tradition of college party dates, and because I know you admire shameless confidence now, do you want to dance?" he asked, holding his hand out with a grin.

Mackenzie couldn't help but return it. Her heart banged into her ribs enthusiastically as she took his hand and tossed her beer down her throat, warmth spreading through her entire body. She felt like she was going to melt as he pulled her along gently, leading her back into the house, ignoring the wolf whistles from his friends at the beer pong table who had noticed their exit.

Teo dropped his empty cup on a table as they moved past and turned to welcome her close as they reached the throng of bodies on the 'dancefloor' of the living room. His arms slid around her waist as his hips began moving side to side to the music, her body following slowly.

She felt everything loosen and warm as the alcohol worked its way through her bloodstream and she let the music take over her body.

He pressed closer and, as he did, she could feel her breath shallow, aware of everywhere his body grazed hers.

Memories of Kai disappeared as fleetingly as they arrived, the music pounding into her consciousness and moving her body like a siren song. She laid her hands lightly on Teo's shoulders, happy to dance together and let the experience wash through her. Lost in the music with time blurring, they moved together in their beer-addled fog.

Teo's hands slid down, and his hand moved to her hips, pulling her in tighter until she could feel every hard line of his body pressed against hers, bringing his lips a breath away.

She didn't dare exhale too heavily as his cinnamon musk swarmed her nose with the inhale.

On and on they danced, pressing and pushing against each other, with each other, finding rhythms that Mackenzie didn't know her body could find. Her insides turned themselves inside out at how close his lips were to hers the whole time, yet they didn't connect. She could feel his breath against her face and neck, a constant reminder that he was merely an inch away.

Finally, he closed the distance, connecting their lips.

It was soft but passionate at first, as if he was afraid she might disappear in a puff of smoke if he pressed too hard or too fast. And yet, ecstasy filled every space in her mind.

Her body ached for more—ached to be touched,

caught in the moment, her body merely following sensations and forgetting rational thought.

His fingers lightly traced her hips through the fabric of the dress, before lowering around the back towards the top of her butt, snapping her from her stupor with a gasp.

She pulled back slightly, feeling her balance tested.

He lifted his hand defensively, a concerned look on his face.

"Too fast…" she whispered, her voice drowned out by the loud thumping music that controlled the room and its occupants.

He understood though, nodding slowly as he rested a hand on her shoulder carefully, his face free of hurt or annoyance.

The reactionary feelings eased as she read the 'It's okay, I'm sorry' on his lips that never carried to her ears.

He leaned closer.

"Do you want some air or would you like to keep dancing?" he said loudly over the noise.

She thought about it for a moment, considering the outside world and space it offered her, and was about to reply 'air' when a brand new sensation hit her. A desire to dance, to pull him close, hit her out of nowhere along with a severe dizziness. It was foreign and yet it was there within her unquestionably.

He seemed to understand her as she looked up, blinking at his interested expression, unsure of what had triggered her internal change.

It's probably the alcohol, she reasoned lightly.

He moved quickly, wrapping his arms around her waist as he lifted her feet from the ground, carrying her further into the mass of dancers.

When her feet returned, his arms remained wrapped around her, and his hands were careful not to return to their earlier position.

His lips claimed hers again as the music guided their bodies again.

His tongue touched her lips, and her mouth opened to him.

He never took more than before—keeping his touches light as they traced her body, avoiding more private areas. Shivers ran up her back as he traced his finger slowly up her spine over the dress, starting in the middle of her back and finishing at the back of her neck.

His arms tightened around her and then, like he couldn't hold the tension any longer, he pulled back carefully, meeting her eyes. A fiery desire burned in his irises.

"Let's get a drink," he said, his eyes flicking to the people around them that Mackenzie had forgotten were there.

She nodded, breathing heavily as she tried to calm her heart rate down.

The dizziness in her still made it hard to concentrate on her rational thoughts as she searched her mind for them. She welcomed the break from his body as he released her and took her hand instead.

Following him into the kitchen, Mackenzie waited on one side of the kitchen bench as he released her hand, moving to the other side to collect drinks for them. With his distance, she could finally feel clarity return to the fog of her brain. Blinking herself clear, she started to feel more herself.

That was when she felt the eyes watching her—the prickling on the back of her neck—that forced her to turn around quickly to meet gray-blue eyes. She would recognize those eyes anywhere.

Her jaw dropped and her eyes went wide as she spotted Kai standing against the wall, watching her with a tight frown. A girl was standing with him, pressing her breasts against his arm as his focus remained intent on Mackenzie. There was no hiding that he'd seen her and no secret she'd seen the other girl. His eyes traveled down her dress and she couldn't tell if he was admiring it or remembering the body he'd made love to underneath it. Mackenzie couldn't move, frozen under his gaze.

Despite her presence at the party with Teo, her mouth soured at the sight of another woman clutching Kai.

Mackenzie felt a touch on her lower back as Teo appeared beside her, handing her a cup of beer and turning his attention to where her gaze had been stuck.

"Do you know Kai?" he asked, his voice growing rough with suppressed anger. He glared at Kai with a ferocity that claimed history.

Mackenzie felt the lie forcing its way up her throat.

"I had a very brief run-in with him not too long ago, but we're not close." She cast a bitter last glance at the desperate woman and Kai, touching Teo's free hand lightly, catching his attention. "Let's get some air."

As if realizing his anger, Teo relaxed with a nod, leading the way back to the beer pong table outside.

Mackenzie dropped her gaze as Teo took her hand, pulling her along. She refused to meet Kai's eyes as the sick feeling overcame her. She wanted to vomit her heart out of her throat where it sat cold and silent. As they moved, she could feel eyes on the back of her neck, and Kai following behind as they stepped into the backyard.

She closed her eyes, taking a deep breath as, the cooler air welcomed her, trying to calm the nervous jittering that had taken over her senses.

This could turn ugly quickly. Hopefully, Kai is merely an inconvenient viewer.

"Should I know what your problem with him is?" Mackenzie asked Teo quietly as they returned to their viewing of the beer pong. Guilt chewed in her stomach at not telling him the truth, but his jaw clenched tightly as he noticed Kai watching them from a distant corner of the yard, and she thought better of remedying her dishonesty.

"Let's just say he's not a good sort. He thrives on

other people's pain and no one should be that eager to hurt others," he spat quietly, his eyes never leaving Kai's. There was obviously history, but Teo did not elaborate and she feared asking, the few words he'd spoken already haunting her.

The idea that Kai enjoyed the pain of others gave her ugly shivers. She tried to ignore the thoughts that had begun to intrude upon her mind, instead turning her attention to Lily and Amari, who were finishing their round at the table to the sound of cheers.

Mackenzie smiled at them as they glanced around to share their triumph.

"Congratulations!" Mackenzie said, Teo nodding his agreed praise beside her. She opened her mouth to ask about his silence but thought better of it and returned to her victory parade.

"Who's up next?" one of Amari's friends called from the beer pong table, clearly trying to initiate another beer pong round for his growing audience. By the way he preened around in the backyard, taking ownership of the table and its surroundings, Mackenzie guessed that this was either the host of the party or a very close friend.

"I will."

Mackenzie didn't have to look around to know exactly who had called into the quiet chatter of the area in a low, silky voice. Most people were silent, eager to see who was joining in the fun; others could see who it was and had a physical reaction of disgust or hatred, just as Teo had.

"And I'm issuing a one-on-one challenge to Kenzie."

Her mouth felt like sandpaper as she swallowed and tried not to look up or react to Kai's words. She wished she hadn't heard him as the rest of the group responded with a collective 'ooh' at his challenge. The ground did not feel stable enough as she glanced up at Amari, who was watching her with an eyebrow raised.

"Kenzie?" Amari whispered, pointing out the

nickname Kai had used for her, her tone full of disapproval at Mackenzie's association with such a character.

Finally bringing her eyes across the crowd, Mackenzie saw Kai, leaning casually over the table as others reset the cups and beer, while Teo looked like he was about to choke at Kai's words. She wasn't sure if it would be worse to say no and deny the challenge; would it make her look more guilty? Would it motivate conversation as to why?

She sighed and nodded in acceptance, onlookers jeering as she stepped forward to the other side of the table, keeping her face blank.

The host of the table looked at both parties carefully, pulling a coin from his pocket.

"She can call—heads or tails?"

"Heads," she called, initiating the coin flip before seeing the apologetic teeth of the host as he checked the top of his hand where he'd captured the coin. Kai would have his turn first. Her stomach crunched in on itself, and she internally kicked herself for not denying this challenge when she knew she was going to lose this game.

"I'm going for that cup," Kai called, pointing at the one directly in front of her before tossing the ping pong ball quickly and landing it perfectly, no bounce required.

Mackenzie's eyes widened and her jaw dropped as she realized how screwed she was, pulling the ball from the cup and downing the drink quickly. The bubbles messed with her stomach for a moment and she knew it was going to get harder to throw them back, but she straightened her shoulders, resumed her calm, expressionless demeanor that refused to give anything away, and pointed at the mirroring cup on his side.

"That one."

She tossed the ball. It bounced off the rim and continued, only saved from landing on the ground by

Kai catching it off the table.

Pointing to the next cup, he lined up and managed again, with no bounce.

Holding her frustration in, Mackenzie picked the ball out again, ignoring the sounds of the crowd, and calmly drank it down, feeling the warmth push through her body quicker. She shut her eyes for a second, taking a deep breath before looking at his cups and picking the one that she was sure she could get. Tossing the ball, she let loose a relieved sigh as it landed inside.

He nodded his approval and downed it.

She fought the urge to grin at her triumph. No celebration was allowed yet.

He slipped the drink down easily, downing it so smoothly it seemed like he barely needed to swallow. Taking the next target on her side, he threw without bounce or issue once again.

Fire in her flared in anger at how easily this was for him. Not to mention Mackenzie hated how Teo was watching so intently, glancing at her as though she'd done something wrong.

Amari looked thoroughly entertained, ignoring the way Teo and Kai looked at each other.

Everything about Mackenzie felt on edge and ready to lash out, but knew to do so would bring questions she didn't want to answer in front of her new friends.

Cup after cup she missed, and shot after shot he landed, and as each drink slid down her throat, it struggled more. Her stomach complained as the yard began to feel unstable. She stayed upright though, leaning against the table to brace herself now and then, trying to make it look natural and not show how the alcohol was affecting her.

Kai got smugger, and every time her eyes accidentally met his, she grew more and more frustrated as his amusement grew.

Chewing her lip in frustration, Mackenzie watched him point to one of the last two cups before glancing up and pausing. His eyes caught her lip between her teeth, an obvious shiver taking over his body; he shared a second of silence with her as the memory hit them both.

"Don't look so worried, Kenzie. It's all just a game," he drawled, his words emphasizing how much he was enjoying his success. He had another motive here that she couldn't quite place, and as she breathed in, her chest tight, panic seized as Teo retaliated.

"Don't act like you know anything about her, Kai," Teo spat, and Mackenzie prayed Kai wouldn't bite on those words.

She knew he could, and she'd felt the way the ammunition was loaded into the gun before Kai even pulled the trigger. She met Kai's eyes, trying to plead for him not to bite, not to let that bullet of truth loose.

His face hardened into a sadistic smile and his eyes turned to Teo.

She was in trouble.

"I do know her, Teo, much more intimately than you ever will…" Kai said, smiling, his words harsh under the surface, sending shivers up Mackenzie's spine as the color drained from her face.

Teo picked up on the standout words, his eyes widening as they turned to Mackenzie questioningly, probably hoping to see denial written all over her face.

All he found was the truth.

Teo fought back, despite seeing how her lips pulled tight and her eyes wouldn't meet his. "Nice try, but you're a slimy good-for-nothing dickhead that isn't worthy of an ounce of Mackenzie's time. Go fuck yourself!" he told Kai, his voice rising louder and louder with each word.

Once again, Mackenzie glanced at Kai, hoping to see some sort of change on his face that would say he didn't want to do this to her. She spotted it, keeping his gaze as he softened slightly, looking at her whole body the way he had when he'd claimed her in the forest.

She grew hot under his eyes, hoping no one would

notice as he spoke just to her, ignoring the room, as he glanced from her eyes to her thigh and back.

"Have you still got that bite mark on your thigh, love? Or has my brand faded?" he said, loud enough for the quiet of the yard to hear.

Mackenzie couldn't move, her body frozen as it flushed with heat. The ground swayed. The memory of it had her warm between her legs as she remembered their day in the forest. She knew everyone was watching her, but she couldn't make her body lie, couldn't hide the heat and surprise on her face at how much information he'd given up.

Her heart raced on while her body seemed to shut down; nothing but her heart and lungs seemed to function, though she didn't know how. She remembered him from that day in Oregon, and she could barely wrap her mind around how these were the same people. She felt like she'd been stabbed, and she hadn't seen it coming.

Reeling, her eyes tried to catch Teo's, but he was stalking Kai.

Amari raced over and grabbed his arm as it tensed into a fist and wound up.

"Teo, don't!" she said, meeting his eyes. As though they had a silent conversation, Teo held Amari's gaze and then dropped his arm, before giving a curt nod and walking off.

"Teo," Mackenzie said quietly, hoping he'd look at her and she could explain this was all before she knew him, but as he met her eyes with a coldness that was like a slap in the face, she knew it wouldn't matter. She had a history with his rival and it was unforgivable.

She dropped her gaze to the beer pong table where her two cups sat. The people around her had gone quiet, unsure what to say aloud but whispering amongst themselves.

The ping pong ball splashed into the cup and she looked up in disbelief, mouth wide as she met Kai's grinning face.

Her fire flared. She picked up the cup and, not breaking gazes, drank both cups remaining and tossed them on Kai's side of the table, ignoring the nausea that crept up as the bubbles hit her stomach. "I'm done," she spat as she turned and walked towards the side gate of the house.

She couldn't do this anymore, she couldn't be here facing any more judgmental stares when she'd been sure she'd left it all back in Oregon.

As she left the view of the party in the backyard, she lost her insides at the base of the tree. The vile taste of beer returning up her esophagus burned, but she knew she couldn't fight it back down.

She pulled her hair back off her face as the second wave hit her and more beer made its way between the blades of grass like a small chunky lake of regret.

10: THE DEVIL

Mackenzie heard steps behind her and tried to ignore them until she'd finished throwing up, but foreign hands took her hair off her, helping to hold it back.

It didn't make it easier as she braced her body against the tree and shut her eyes in frustration. With a final spit of bile, her stomach quietened and her whole body vibrated with weakness.

The scent of sandalwood wafted to her between the whisps of her own sick and she groaned. "Leave me alone! Haven't you done enough damage for tonight?" she said weakly as she wiped her mouth, making sure to avoid the sleeve of the dress and just use the back of her hand for the mess. She pushed herself up to standing and then turned to Kai, who stood over her, his face softer but still holding the air of amusement he couldn't hide.

"Oh, come on, you can't tell me you like Tantrum Teo!" he said, throwing his arms up with a slight smile.

She huffed a breath out and tried to watch his face to see how seriously he meant his words. It became clear to her that Kai had just as much disdain for Teo as the reverse. "I do like him, you dick. You just have to hurt people with the truth?"

His smile faltered. "You're mad that I told the truth? It's not my fault! He was being high and mighty and thought I wasn't worth your time. He doesn't get to decide who's worth your time." The smile disappeared from his face entirely as he took in her anger. He stood over her as though his height could intimidate her.

Despite her size, she stood tall and strong, meeting his confidence with her own. "I was the one who told him we barely knew each other. *That's* why he was sure of his words," she snapped back, making him straighten as though she'd zapped him. "He trusted *me*."

"You lied to him?" he said breathily, chewing on the words, like they had a bad taste before moving on. "Well, I guess that's on you then, isn't it?"

"Oh, fuck off!" she hissed, turning on her heel and giving up on the conversation. She didn't care if he followed her. She hoped he would give up when he realized she wasn't going to stop and indulge him anymore, walking in the direction of her home.

"I have to say, drunk Kenzie is very different from the girl I met in that tiny town on the other side of the country," Kai said from behind her, following in step as she struggled in her high heels in the grass.

"And you're very different from what you were like when you met me too. What's your point? I just, for once, wanted to be the girl who didn't have a whole town judging her! Now I'm going to be the girl that fucked you. Not that you care!" she called back, feeling him stop.

For a moment, she trudged forward, glad to finally be free of him, before a flash of curiosity made her turn and glance back. His eyes had dropped to the ground and he looked... defeated.

His shoulders sagged as he rubbed his temple with his fingers carefully. As though he could feel her stare, he looked up, his eyes meeting hers.

"Why do you think I did all this? I saw you with him and I *did* care. I hated it. If I'd known you'd be moving to Salem, I wouldn't have let him get his hands on you," he said, sighing as though the answer was obvious.

It took a moment in Mackenzie's drunk mind to piece together that all of this could have been done out of jealousy and not just for fun. He was petty, sure, but he'd wanted to hurt Teo because he was *jealous*. Her eyes widened at the realization as her mouth opened and closed uselessly, trying to figure out what to say. It was surprising, but she couldn't let him off the hook for what he'd done, regardless of motives.

"I'm not yours, Kai. You don't get to decide who touches me," she said, trying to sound confident. Her voice wavered at the memory of his hands on her.

If Kai had been an option when she'd arrived, she would never have indulged Teo in the first place, but she refused to tell Kai that.

As though he could sense her thoughts, his eyes lifted to hers and caught in her stare. Neither looked away, as they searched each other's faces.

The weak shaking limbs of her body felt like they were buzzing and she swayed.

"Are you saying you don't want me to touch you?" he whispered as he took a step towards her, his eyes never leaving hers.

She swallowed hard as he moved in closer. She didn't back up or back down, holding her ground despite how her body shook, coated in goosebumps. Every part of her skin felt hot and cold at the same time.

He slid his arm around the small of her back and pulled her a step closer, waiting for her to push him away and deny what she knew she wanted. He leaned down slowly, his hand sliding to hold her neck as he tilted her face up to keep his gaze.

She knew she could pull away at any moment, he moved so slowly, taunting her, daring her to stop it. But despite her anger, she still wanted him too, and he knew it.

He froze a breath away from her lips, waiting with a small smile, feeling her fidget closer. He held himself just far enough away to make her ache for him.

Their hips pressed together and with the height her heels offered, she could feel him hard against her hip as her upper body arched back over his arm wrapped around her waist.

Trembling, she bit her lip deliberately.

He seized upon it, his mouth claiming hers desperately.

Mackenzie opened her mouth to welcome his tongue and slid her arms around his shoulders, desperate to pull herself up onto his hips again, but he didn't lift her this time. She could tell how strongly he wanted her, feeling the way his body stiffened in delight when she rubbed herself against his jeans, but still, he held her carefully.

She was impatient, she wanted him so badly that she ached to feel him inside her again. The ghost of the bruise on her leg where his teeth had been pulsed with a fury, begging for return.

She released one of her arms around his shoulders, holding it back against her chest. Her eyes widened as he broke their kiss, and she could feel a ball of lead manifest in her stomach as she searched his face, confused.

"You don't want me like that anymore?" she asked breathily, trying to joke around and tease him with a soft smile despite the dread growing in her stomach, fueled by doubt that threatened to claim her entire existence. She could feel the hold he had on her soul and it terrified her. If he rejected her now, she was sure she'd become a melted puddle in the middle of this grassland.

"Of course I want you! Just not here like this. Not when you're drunk and throwing up in the bushes because I beat you at beer pong," he said, in an amused tone that shocked her.

She breathed out, mouth wide open as she watched him.

There was no disgust on his face, he had completely softened, showing the side she'd known when they met;

the playful, confident guy who could be rough with her but knew her soul. "Despite your thoughts of me, I can sometimes be a gentleman. But don't tell anyone, it'll ruin my reputation."

He winked and moved backward, sliding her out of his arms, instead taking her hand, his fingers intertwining with hers.

"I don't think anyone would believe me if I tried." She smiled, watching his face twinge slightly as he nodded his agreement.

"Probably not. How about I walk you home?" he said, looking back at her, his eyes tracing down her body, admiring her dress. His gaze was soft but she could still see the hunger on his face that he fought against and she nodded, her own need chewing at her too.

"Sure." Mackenzie led the way as she gripped his hand. Quickly she realized that her heels were going to be an issue to walk across the grass with and took them off, holding them in her free hand. "So you really just got jealous of me being with Teo, huh?"

"I was. Yes," he admitted sheepishly as she peered at him. "Trust me when I tell you that I would have torn his head off if it meant he'd stop touching you like that."

"Touching me like..." she started, trying to remember when he would have seen Teo touching her before realizing he must have spotted her earlier than she had seen him. "Oh..."

The insides of her curled, pulling in and out of guilt as she realized the amount of action she'd gotten tonight and the fact that it had not been just one guy.

"God, I feel like a slut!" Mackenzie choked, more to herself than to Kai.

Regardless, his eyes widened, pulling her to stop.

"No! Don't ever think like that. Please. Neither one of us could've known the other would be in Salem." He pulled her close, meeting her gaze confidently.

"Well, maybe we could have told each other back in Oregon?" she suggested with a sheepish smile as she glanced up at his gray-blue eyes.

His smile mirrored hers as the worry between them ceased and they began to move again, Mackenzie leading the way through the quiet, cool night.

The wind had begun to pick up, encouraging goosebumps under the sleeves of her dress. Mackenzie's stomach filled with a heavy feeling as they finally made it to the Salem Common, the air thick and heavy with a magnetic power she couldn't quite place.

"You okay?" Kai asked as her hand stiffened in his.

His speech brought her out of the sensation, breaking the spell that was forming like a haze in her mind.

"Yes, sorry. Thought I heard something," she lied, not wanting to explain and let him think her crazy. She glanced at his face, seeing that he didn't believe her—opening his mouth as though he were going to say something before he dropped it and nodded.

She pulled him towards the house, stopping for a moment and letting him absorb their destination, ready for the inevitable conversation.

"This is a nice place. Do I want to know how you scored this?" he asked with a smug smile. She could almost hear the unspoken murderer joke from their first day.

"I didn't murder anyone for it if that's what you're thinking." She smiled, only letting her smile falter slightly as she told the truth. "My parents left it to me."

"Your family came from here?" He watched her curiously.

"Yeah, it's why I came back. I wanted to know the place they'd met and grown up… and where I was born before my mom left." She paused, waiting for the inevitable questions. She breathed deeply, preparing to try to be as open and honest as she could with him—when he listened as interested as he did, it made it easy.

Between all the active curiosity, she could see his brain processing her words, his lips tightening as a question formed in his mind.

"It occurs to me, you didn't tell me your full name..." he said, not quite asking but piecing information together as he looked from the house to her.

"Mackenzie Anne Harris," she said, letting the information settle with him, watching his eyes widen in recognition. "Yes, my mother was the one who left Salem after my father's murder."

"I'm so sorry for your loss. My parents were friends of yours, and I know what happened pains them. They wished they could have done more to help," he said solemnly, his gray-blue eyes glistening in the moonlight as he stayed strong in his gaze, not breaking from hers.

"Really?" Hope squeezed Mackenzie's heart as yet another connection to her parents presented itself.

"Yes! I've seen the photos of them in the albums. It was terrible what happened to them and I'm sorry you've had to live with that." Pity shone in his eyes.

It made her feel sick; she didn't want to be pitied and treated as fragile—you couldn't trust people's true feelings or intentions when pity was involved. Working quickly, she told the truth, hoping to remove the pity while she could.

"It's fine. I guess." She kept his gaze firmly to show her sincerity. "It was hard, don't get me wrong, but I only learned about their story here and that was what I wanted. I came here for closure, answers and to feel closer to my parents. No matter the form it came in, I'm grateful to have what I wanted."

His face pulled back as he watched her, surprised. The pity departed and she gave a reassuring smile to cement her positivity, his face softening as he mirrored it.

"Well then, I'm glad you got what you were looking for." He turned to the house with a new-found admiration.

Mackenzie watched him, feeling closer to him than she thought possible.

"Did you want to come inside?" She grinned,

catching his eye again and squeezing his hand.

"I'd love to," he said, squeezing in response. "But I don't trust myself not to surrender to you in there."

Her stomach jumped and flittered around inside her at Kai's words, almost tempted to ask again. She watched though, her heart warming at his restraint. A playful part of her wanted to test it, to see what it would take to get him to surrender.

He moved closer, a hand pushing her hair behind her ear, cupping her cheek as he leaned in to kiss her forehead.

Her heart smashed forward in her ribs, trying to find its way to Kai as she shut her eyes to his touch, a sense of safety cocooning them both. She slipped her arms around his waist, feeling him welcome her touch, pulling her closer in the embrace. She turned her head to the side, ear pressing against his chest as his hand stroked her hair, the other holding her tight.

"What's so wrong about surrender?" she whispered, feeling his heart thump faster under her ear in response. She pulled her head back to watch his face.

"Nothing is wrong with it, love. I just want to do this right. We're both in the same place now, we can afford to slow it down and learn more about each other, if that's what you want too?"

Her breath caught as everything lurched excitedly in her.

"What do you mean, what are you asking?" she asked, hyper-aware of the quiet as she waited for him to come up with his words.

"Do you want to give us a try as more than just a fleeting adventure?" he asked, his hand fiddling with her hair as he held her gaze.

"Yes," she breathed, the word barely audible as she smiled in the moonlight up at him.

He leaned forward, breaking the distance between them and meeting her lips again. He was soft and passionate, with no urgency in his touch. Everything in her cried for more.

"You know…" Mackenzie whispered against his mouth after releasing his lip and feeling him tighten against her. "If you wanted to stay tonight, you'd be most welcome."

"Someone's keen…" He chuckled against her, his thumb caressing the back of her hand. "And trust me when I say there is nothing I'd want more, but not tonight, love."

"Are you sure?" Mackenzie pulled back, a teasing grin on her lips as she watched him fight his own urges.

"I'm sure I want all your faculties about when I have you. Plus, I have to take you on a real date first…"

Everything inside her tightened. Her lungs threatened to suffocate her.

He leaned back down to her mouth, claiming it feverishly, reminding her of the first day in the woods. It was insistent, passionate. His tongue claimed hers without resistance as he pressed against her, his other hand resting on her back clutching the dress in his fist.

Testing his resolve playfully, remembering his previous reactions, she bit his lower lip softly. The rumble of a growl sounded from deep within his chest, making everything in her flush with heat.

He pulled back slowly, every muscle in him straining and tightening as she plastered an innocent smile on her face, as though she had no idea why he might be struggling. He chuckled to himself as he caught sight of her expression.

"It might be time to call it a night before we push my self-control too far." He smiled. "God knows you don't have any."

Her mouth dropped open as she clapped a hand to her chest, pretending to be offended as a swarm of giggles escaped her.

He smiled as he pulled her in again, resting his lips on her forehead before stepping back.

"Have some water, get some sleep and I'll text you

tomorrow," he said, far enough away from her that she got the message.

She walked up the porch stairs carefully, turning back to Kai as she produced her house key from her bra, earning a raised eyebrow in response.

"Goodnight," she said with a smile as she opened the door.

"Night, Kenzie. Sleep well." He slid his hands into his pockets and waited for her to disappear into the house.

Mackenzie closed the door, still giddy with blissful butterflies as she walked into the living room and let her body fall back onto her couch, vaguely away that it caught her.

She heaved a loud sigh, finally feeling her breath return to her as she lay in content silence.

When the knock at the front door came a moment later and the excitement seized everything in her once again, she had to suppress her laugh. Bounding up, she hurried back to the front door, opening it up eagerly.

Amari and Teo stood on the other side.

Mackenzie's smile faltered.

"What? What were you two doi…"She started as she glimpsed them, but could barely make it to the end of her sentence before a wave of dizziness overcame her. Head spinning and vision blurring, she teetered forward, vaguely aware that Amari moved forward to catch her.

Unconsciousness claimed her before confusion could.

11: THE MAJOR ARCANA

The first thing Mackenzie became aware of was the biting pain in her wrists. The way it gnawed and lashed into her skin as she tried to move them anywhere except for the place they were pinned at her sides.

Blinking her eyes open, her pupils struggled to adjust to the dim light. Flaming torches on walls in the distance were the only sources she could see.

Silhouettes formed in her view. She couldn't see their faces.

The cave-like room and strangers surrounding her created a panic that seized her into alert consciousness.

Her head thrashed around as she tried desperately—and unsuccessfully—to ascertain where she was.

Her heart clutched in on itself, hiding from the outside world.

Her lungs tightened, threatening to rob her of oxygen just like the rope.

It pressed down on her chest, tied across the height of her breasts, her waist, and her ankles.

Unable to release herself despite her struggling against her bonds, her organs writhed in her body as though their discomfort could help her escape.

She looked at the silhouettes, tears forming in her eyes as she pleaded with the mysterious onlookers.

"Please let me go! There has been a mistake or

something, *please* let me go!"

None of the silhouettes moved to assist her. They watched as Mackenzie fought the light to see their faces to no avail.

No one was coming to save her. She thrashed against her bonds more savagely, desperately hoping someone would give. Her muscles began to hurt, feeling the wear from her futile fighting as her skin rubbed raw under the strong braided strands of manila hemp.

A pressure began to build in the air, pushing on her head like a sinus migraine, her ears popping and her breath feeling thin.

Mackenzie halted her attempts at freedom as she searched the room for the sudden source.

Nothing presented itself, no answer could be found in the cave-like room with her body tied to a stone altar.

Something inside Mackenzie shriveled up and the dread gut feeling told her she couldn't get out.

As the headache built, she shut her eyes tightly, trying to block out the pain that slaughtered her brain as the room began to heat. Tears streaked down her cheeks to her ears as sweat beaded her body and face. She breathed heavily, the air too thin and her body too hot to absorb the oxygen well enough.

Like lightning in the air around her, crackling and popping noises sounded near her head, zapping her extremities as she screamed out.

"Make it stop, make it stop!"

But no one came to assist and no reprieve came.

She opened her eyes, her skin so hot it felt like it was ablaze, to witness purple lightning flash through the air, striking her body.

Agony, unlike anything she'd felt, seared through her body, radiating from her stomach outwards. Every muscle and organ in her lower abdomen felt like it had shut off, robbing her of function and life. When it reared awake a moment later, it gripped so tightly in on itself that, Mackenzie was afraid her insides would disappear into oblivion.

"Let me go!" she shrieked.

It stopped.

Nobody moved.

The ropes disappeared, purple fire consuming them instantly, burning them away from her body with a cold sensation against her skin.

The pressure in the room dissipated, her head and ears returning to normal as though it had all been a dream.

Mackenzie lay on the table, despite being free, trying to catch her breath and figure out what had just happened.

Slowly the figures moved, coming in closer to her from their places around the room. The circle closed in on her, setting her heart afire with fear.

Jumping to the ground and ignoring how weak her legs felt, Mackenzie bolted for the dark corner she hoped was an exit.

The strangers—who Mackenzie could now see were wearing hooded robes—descended upon her. As Mackenzie tried to dart between them, the exit finally in sight, one hooded figure dashed into her path and grabbed her shoulders in each hand, securing her in place.

She pushed, tossing her shoulders to each side, trying to break the stranger's grip as she searched the darkness of the hood for a face.

"Mackenzie, stop! Please calm down!" a deep, raspy male voice said soothingly.

She stopped—in shock at hearing her name.

As her eyes caught those slowly coming into focus under the hood, her fight melted. A warmth filled her, soothed her, dizzied her—extinguishing any resistance in her like a calming tea.

The person noticed her changed state and slowly took one hand from her shoulder, pulling the hood back from his head. Teo's deep brown eyes stared at her, a comforting—if confusing—sight.

As her mouth opened to form the questions and the panic fought to rise in her at what had just happened, a slow 'sshh' escaped his lips, as if the terror she held deep within her could sift away with his words. "Listen to me, it's going to be okay. You're not trapped, we just need to explain some things to you. That's all. If you can just wait a moment, and let us talk, you'll understand everything soon."

She stood for a moment, feeling as though her body was fighting itself internally. Calm flowed in her like a drug trying to wind its way through her veins and tell her there was nothing to fear, but the pit deep inside her had questions and fight, things that told her to run from the room as fast as she could while his guard was down.

"Why am I here?" she asked defiantly, not running but not entirely comfortable staying. Her limbs were ready and alert, fighting the calming feeling inside her to make sure that she could run if the answers weren't satisfying.

"I'm sorry we had to get you here the way we did. It was essential for the timing to just explain later. I would've told you at the party but, well… Things developed in a way I didn't expect," he said, his gaze dropping from hers, ashamed.

Mackenzie could feel her cheeks flush as she too remembered what she'd put Teo through.

Kai. The memory of where she had been when she'd passed out was like electricity through her system. Did he miss all of the visitors and get away okay? Had Teo kidnapped him too? Was Kai in on the whole thing? Her mind reeled with too many questions and any involving Kai were ones she feared to ask Teo, considering his clear dislike of the man.

"So explain *now.*" She crossed her arms and hoped she looked more confident than she felt.

"Your parents were involved in an organization known as the Major Arcana—it has lasted hundreds of years and is passed down by bloodline," he started, barely meeting her eyes.

Her stomach twisted at the notion of her parent's involvement in anything—remembering Vicki's words about getting in with the wrong people.

"Every lunar eclipse, the power converges here in this place and those with the right bloodline can be awakened."

"Awakened?" Mackenzie whispered, feeling the shivers run up her spine as she thought over what had just happened and how he was talking. Her heart fluttered up her throat as though it were going to choke her, and her lungs shriveled until it felt as though no air was getting into her. The way he spoke seriously about something so ridiculous tightened her limbs to run, and she hoped the next words out of his mouth were not what she feared they were.

"Your family has magic, Mackenzie. Well… your father did," he said, and the words snapped something inside her.

She took a step away from Teo, the calm in her body run out by the utter dread at what he was saying. He had kidnapped and tortured her for…magic? She doubted the sanity of his logic, or that he would even let her go as he said he would.

"This can't be happening. Magic isn't real, Teo. That's nuts," she said quietly, backing up another step and watching his gaze finally lift to meet hers. She could see the belief, the absolute truth he was sure of, and cold iced her veins.

"I know it's hard to believe, Mackenzie, but I'm telling you it is. Each of the family bloodlines is imbued with the powers of one of the tarot. When you were old enough to carry the mantle, your parents would've told you all about this, if they had lived." He said it carefully, but her stomach still felt like a hole had been punched through it.

Her breath left her.

"This is a sick joke, Teo. I get that I hurt you with Kai, but this is low. Really fucking low of you!" she spat, sure that this was revenge for the beer-pong incident and that she was being punished for her intimacy with Kai. "This is a horrible thing to do!"

"I swear to you, Mackenzie, what I'm telling you is the truth." He took a step closer, trying to raise his hands to take hers.

She moved back, sliding her hands behind her back and watching him carefully.

"That my family is… that I'm *magic*? I think I'd know something like that," she scoffed, laughing at the stupidity of his fantasy.

"That's why we brought you here and what I'm trying to explain. We've awakened that power for you here and now," he said, his steps halting their advance.

She temporarily paused her retreat too. She could feel a wave of anger burning in her, bubbling as she watched the hood-robed figures wait on the edge of the room, seemingly ready in case she decided she did want to run. All hidden, all anonymous as Teo explained it all to her.

"And if I didn't want the power?" she challenged.

"The creed states that the lineage must continue. I'm sorry, Mackenzie, it doesn't take consent into it," he stated, sounding like a religious fanatic.

"Creed? You've got to be kidding me," she spat, feeling the anger inside her burst forth. She wanted to hit him. Her arms crossed across her chest, trying to hold her anger in as pieces of information she'd known about her family fell into place. Major Arcana must have been the 'wrong crowd' Vicki had spoken of that had gotten her father killed.

"I know this is really hard, but your father was a part of this organization and he would've wanted you to be too."

"I'm not going to be part of your *cult*." She swore, feeling the curling of disgust in her gut. How dare he speak of her father as if he knew what he would have wanted? "For all I know, you psychos got him killed."

She couldn't take any more lies or explanations of things that couldn't possibly exist. Instead, she pulled her shoulders up straight and confidently strode past him, hoping his words about letting her go were correct.

He didn't try to grab her, but she was ready in case he did. Instead, his words struck her frantic, raging heart with ice and halted her in her tracks.

"Your father was killed by a magic wielder, but they were not part of the Major Arcana."

Mackenzie stopped, afraid to turn around and face Teo. They *knew* who had killed her father. A world of answers seemed to be at her fingertips if only she'd indulge their fantasy and listen. She was at war with herself, needing to be free of the room but the answers begging her to stay.

He had obviously known they would, that was why he'd said it.

"What did you say?" she whispered to the air in front of her, but Teo heard it all the same.

"I shouldn't be telling you this, but the Arcana knows who killed your father."

His words were like a gunshot through her chest, confirming the answers she so desperately wanted. Whipping around, desperation in her leaked like poison as she faced Teo and walked back to him.

"You should be telling the police!"

"It's a matter for the organization, it's too dangerous for the police," he said, and she couldn't help gaping at him. He truly believed their magic was too dangerous for 'normal people'.

"Then tell *me*." Would he reveal the information without a commitment to Major Arcana? If it took joining them to know the answers... she would. "I deserve at least that."

"First, you have to understand the Major Arcana. Each family bloodline is imbued with the powers of each of the tarot—" he started, repeating items she had heard him say the first time and feeling the restless frustration of having to hear it again for answers.

"Yes, I got that much,"

Unperturbed by her interruption, he continued.

"Your family line is that of the Magician in the tarot. There were twenty-two bloodlines in the Major Arcana," he explained, and Mackenzie couldn't help noticing his choice of words.

"Were?"

"Two families sought power for themselves and instead of helping people as we do, used their powers for selfish gain, cutting down anybody in their path. Your father sought to help them, turn them back to the right path, and make them see reason. They killed him."

Mackenzie's heart fought against the ice that threatened to stop its beating and the rage inside her was ready to be directed at someone.

"Who were the two families?"

"They represent the Devil and Death in the Arcana. The Devil at the time murdered your father before passing his powers to his son, Kai, and disappearing."

Her knees buckled and collapsed, smashing into the ground as she struggled to draw breath, swallowing Teo's words. Her heart ripped itself into pieces as her mind fought the image of a Kai doppelganger stabbing her father. *There is no way Kai knows,* she tried to tell herself. Replaying their conversations, she was sure that he couldn't have, he'd described their parents as friends and if his father had disappeared—same as hers— maybe he had no idea.

"But… there's no way Kai could've known," she whispered raspingly to the air, not speaking directly to Teo, barely able to speak between her gasping breaths.

"Answer me this honestly… Where did you meet Kai?" he said, squatting down beside her broken body on the ground as she gulped air into her lungs, hoping to push away the feeling that she was dying.

The question stirred her memories, making her think about the daze of numbness and pain she'd been in when she'd met Kai, and how he'd met her right when she needed it to pull her from the depths.

"He was on a road trip around the country and..." she said slowly, trying to absorb how the question tied to her experiences.

"And met you in Oregon? In that small little town, no one would've heard of?" he asked, already knowing the answers but drawing her gaze to his, making her forget her inability to breathe.

"Yeah..." she whispered, wondering where he was going with this train of thought, not wanting to admit the truth.

"Don't you think it's a completely bizarre coincidence that your mother ran away to hide in a small town on the other side of the country and the son of the man that killed your family turns up and meets you? Are you still sure he didn't know who you were?" He seemed to know exactly what button to press to make her realize her stupidity.

How had she never questioned it? How had she run into Kai in Salem, found out his parents knew hers and never questioned if their meeting had been accidental?

Teo saw the shock in her eyes, saw the tears that welled and slipped without resistance. He rested a hand on her shoulder and suddenly her body cooled—the rage inside her was turned from a vicious simmer to low heat, and her heart overtaken with shame subsided. "You don't have to join us right away, but for your safety—while you digest this information and your magic starts to present itself—please stay away from Kai."

She nodded quickly, no thought needed as she processed the rest of everything she'd been given today. She didn't believe a word when it came to whatever magic they were sure existed in her or this world, but she knew his words were true about Kai and his family and for the moment, that was what had stuck with her.

"If you need us, Mackenzie, we are here to help and protect you," Teo said, placing an arm under her elbow and helping her to her feet carefully. "Let's help you get home. You need rest. I'm sorry for tonight, I realize this has been a lot but I hope in time you'll understand our reasonings."

12: THE EYES OF THE MAGICIAN

Mackenzie lay on the bed, focusing intently on the way the paint twisted across the ceiling. The cracks had formed in it over its time unoccupied—she supposed they would have even if someone had resided underneath.

Her eyes hadn't shut since Teo had left her at her front door and she'd climbed the stairs of her empty house and dropped back on the bed. She was vaguely aware the sun had risen, only because the cracks in the ceiling became more visible.

Her cell buzzed on her nightstand, snapping her out of her numb daze. She reached over and checked it, not quite sure what she was hoping for, but found herself disappointed to find an update notice for her phone software. With a groan, she dropped it back on the wooden bedside table and flopped back to the mattress. With her focus finally broken from the ceiling, all the thoughts she'd been pushing down were inescapable now.

Kai had known who she was when they'd met. He'd pretended not to, sought her out, seen all her pain as an orphan, had sex with her, and then gone back home victorious as she unknowingly followed him home to Salem. How dare he! Mackenzie's hands balled into fists, her nails biting into her palms as the memories of his body on hers turned sour in her mouth, the thought boiling all her insides.

And in amongst all this, Teo had kidnapped her for his cult and "awakened" her magic powers. What sort of chaos was this town festering?

She felt homesick, missing her best friend and her hometown. Even though they were judgmental, it seemed an easier burden than this. Religious cults, murders, and amongst it all, she'd found herself tangled. How had her parents done this?

Like she'd been zapped by the purple lightning again, her upper boy shot off the bed. Her back was straight and alert, her heart pounding heavily, struck by an idea.

As quick as she could manage, Mackenzie vaulted off the bed and down the two sets of stairs, heading for the wall of weapons, grabbing the book from its place strewn on the floor. This had been the only occult indicator she'd found in the house.

As she surveyed the weapons, she felt she was seeing them all anew. Everywhere she looked—blades, guns, swords, daggers—glinted with a purple light. She checked the room around her, expecting to find something to explain the purple, but came up empty. Her gaze flickered to the book in her hand that had been empty, watching the edges of the endpaper noticeably shimmer, robbing her of breath.

Putting it down on the tabletop, Mackenzie glanced it over carefully. She lightly traced her fingers over its cover, gold embossed symbols over it that she'd never seen before. They rippled dimly with purple light until she couldn't take the anticipation chewing through her gut and pulled the cover open. She hoped the pages would stay blank—hoped that the insanity of it all—was a trick or lie, or some ill-placed belief.

A family tree stretched out on the once-empty page— the Harris ancestry line unfolded in tiny writing and branches, stretching back further than Mackenzie had considered she could have a family.

But her focus lay on the bottom of the tree and the purple glint that wrote her name underneath her parents. She rubbed her eyes, sure it was a trick of light.

When it didn't disappear or change, she considered whether she could have been drugged. Despite the shock of the situation, she felt too in charge of her mental faculties to entertain that idea further as she stared at her name on the page.

Mackenzie wasn't sure how her body was functioning and upright when she felt like she was going to puke. She didn't want to believe Teo's words, but it was getting increasingly hard to ignore as she stared at the self-drawing tree.

She'd seen the creature in Oregon, unexplainable by normal standards, but she knew what she'd seen with her own eyes.

Teo's words hadn't resonated with her until this very moment. Now they gripped her, a stranglehold on her mind that would not release her until she faced it. She glanced at her hands, expecting to see purple lightning or something magic fizzling on her fingertips. She took three deep breaths, waiting and feeling disappointed by the lack of action, then finally turned the page and saw the title "The Magician" glitter back at her.

Her breath caught as she skimmed the page, tears prickling the corners of her eyes at the use of her family name. She couldn't help the sad smile that stretched her lips as she ran down the page eagerly.

The Magician
Current Family Name: Harris
Traits: Willpower, creativity, action
Power Description: One of the most elusive of the tarot, the Magician's power stems from the wielder's willpower and creativity. It relies on manifestation and manipulation and is only limited by the Magician's mind and imagination.

Mackenzie stared at the page, trying to process how her powers would manifest—how she could make them—if this was to be believed. So she could just will anything into existence?

Shivers passed over her body as she was reminded of her awakening. No one had touched the ropes to free her but she had screamed out for freedom after the lightning had struck her, telling them to let her go and the ropes had complied. Was that her doing or theirs? Was that the willpower manifestation that the book had spoken of?

She'd need to experiment some more on her own before she could be sure.

For now, her curiosity pulled her through the pages of the book to see what other powers existed in the Major Arcana.

She didn't recognize any of the family names, but she supposed she didn't know many to begin with. The powers across the families were so varied: influencing emotions, seeing the future, control of the elements, and so many more.

She came to the Devil's page and scanned her eyes down it, dreading her discoveries about Kai's family line. Her stomach lurched so violently at what she found that it felt like she'd been punched in the gut when she'd read the page.

The Devil

Current Family Name: Logan

Traits: Primal Instincts, Personal interest, Truth

Power Description: The Devil's power revolves around primal power and truth. The powers of the Devil are wide-ranging. The Devil can take several forms, depending upon the individual's inner state, but the most common amongst the wielders of the power is the beast form—a creature resembling that of a hellhound

Other aspects of the Devil's power revolve around the truth. They are the wielders of it and cannot lie to a direct question posed. Can also sense truth and lies in the mouths of others.

Mackenzie stared at the drawing at the bottom of the page, the back of her neck prickling as though the drawing were watching her through the page at that moment. She didn't realize she could be gutted anymore by Kai's behavior until her knees buckled to the floor.

The book stayed on the table as she fell out of sight of it, but she couldn't help the paranoia in her system, running through her body as though she needed to bolt at any second. Her breathing and heart rate came in so quickly that she feared she'd have a heart attack or feel her heart explode, and her mind froze for a moment in time, replaying the memory over and over.

The day she'd met Kai in Oregon, the feeling of it growing more bitter and rotten with every second as tears slipped down her cheeks. She hadn't even thought she was capable of crying, but her body had raced ahead of her mind.

How had she been given such a feeling of hope by this guy, only to have it dashed less than twenty-four hours after finding him again? How had she missed every sign that this was only going to hurt her? How had she cared so quickly? Why did this hurt so bad? How could she have been so stupid and naïve?

But she knew the answer and hated herself for it. He'd brought her to life at a time when she was determined to live again. She'd started falling for him hard when she knew—deep down—she shouldn't have, and she'd let herself do all this without really knowing him.

She hadn't even known his last name, for god's sake. If he had been the creature in the woods that day, as she supposed he was, how long had he been watching her search for her mother? How could he pretend he didn't know her when he'd been stalking her in beast form…

Beast form…

Shivers crept up Mackenzie's spine again as she took deep breaths and forced herself to calm down. She dropped her face into her hands, straining to breathe slowly through her fingers as she shut her eyes tightly and tried to ignore the image of the creature—Kai's beast form.

Focus on something else, she told herself, pushing her body up slowly and painstakingly to get back to the book.

Flicking past the family pages, she stopped short when she came to pages of handwritten notes. Kai slipped from her mind as she spun through pages and pages of handwritten notes by multiple different people—all ancestors of the Harris name—leaving behind ways they had used their power differently.

The full extent of power explained in the book was incredible and her heart swelled when she reached notes written by her father.

"The willpower of movement," he'd written. "Manifest a wall into existence—invisible, slim, paper-thin but strong as steel, and then like you are the wind and it is a piece of paper, push it to the desired location."

On and on his notes went, more descriptive than anything written before until she came to a dated entry—the last entry.

My daughter Mackenzie,

You are barely born and I already know my time with you is coming to an end.

I have made some very powerful people angry and they are coming for me.

I know that they won't break the Magician's line so for now, you are safe. I have no doubt you'll be awakened eventually and you will find your way to this book, and so I leave for you, everything I know in this book.

For the awakened eyes of the next Magician only.

Rely on yourself, and find your true power. If you're anything like your mother and me, you will have the willpower and creativity to be the strongest Magician our line has ever known. Use it to your advantage and be wary of others; no one in this world will give you the real truth, that is something you must discover for yourself.

Please be safe and strong. I'm sorry I couldn't be around to see the woman you will become.

From your loving father,

Brian Harris

Mackenzie ran her fingers over the words, trying to imagine him etching the markings into the page, the tears she couldn't seem to dry falling again. And yet, despite everything she'd experienced so far in Salem, these tears warmed her face. They were bittersweet, providing her with a small amount of solace in an otherwise overwhelming life.

Mackenzie picked the book up and hugged it to her chest, careful not to let her tears fall onto the page. While the book and the ink might be magical, she could no longer imagine allowing any kind of harm to befall what had almost instantly become one of her most prized possessions. It rested close to her breastbone, pressing the necklace pendants of her parents closer to her heart. The weight of them both was a calming agent on her mind and body.

Climbing the stairs, Mackenzie moved into the living area with the book, finding an armchair by the window showered in comforting sunlight.

She slouched into the chair, curling her feet up under her as she dropped the open book and flicked the page all the way back to the start. Calm took over as she stared at the book, no longer frightened or nervous about the information it had to offer. A slight smile danced across her lips as the sunlight warmed her skin and the sense of belonging to an actual family warmed her soul. She ignored the painful boiling sensation in her gut as she passed Kai's tarot page and instead focused on the positive.

Despite what she'd seen lately and knew she couldn't explain, her belief in the magic that Teo and this book spoke of was still a struggle. But slowly she could feel herself opening to the prospect and she knew her father's and ancestors words were the cause. She moved through the start of the book, dedicated to each in the tarot and the magical family that represented them. Mackenzie realized how blind she felt, staring at the surnames as though time staring could provide her with answers on the individual wielders of the powers.

She took note of the others in the Major Arcana, hating the idea of ever coming up against them, feeling the cold snake of dread ice through her fleetingly as she took stock of the magic around her. Control of blood, emotions, nature, and luck as well as prophecy, flight, and illusion all stuck out at her from different pages.

But what bothered her more was that Amari and Teo were involved with the Major Arcana—with powers of their own, she supposed—and she had no idea what they were. Her new "friends" had pulled her close and learned so much about her, but she didn't even know their surnames. She had no idea what her kidnapper's powers even were. All she knew was that they weren't the Devil or Death powers—which didn't eliminate much.

The jingle of her ringtone drifted down the stairs, but Mackenzie stared out with a tight frown as though she could see its caller, making no effort to move. Turning her attention back to the book, she focused her annoyance down on it, wondering how she was going to prepare herself against magic society cults, murderers, and people who probably had more control over powers she still wasn't entirely sure existed.

13: THE CONFRONTATION

Mackenzie had been ignoring the jingling of her damn phone for hours. She was mildly amused that it hadn't run out of battery with all the texts and calls it had been announcing. Unless Amari and Teo had decided to include her in some Arcana group chat or Lucy had taken to watching their favorite show on repeat again, Kai had become desperate to get her attention. It was starting to feel pathetic as the embers of the betrayal sizzled away in her stomach. She refused to even walk upstairs and save her phone from having to announce each contact note. *Let the full weight of his insecurity sing out through the house,* she scoffed, letting it all be ammunition to go with the lies he'd told.

She flipped through more pages of her ancestor's stories and ways they had found to use their powers for good. The book had not been wrong when it said the options for what could be done were only limited by what you could think up. The only common strain throughout the line seemed to be the ability to hold the manifestation in place. All the Magicians before her had documented their experience with the power from the moment they were awakened until their early demise.

That was the other thing sticking out to her from the pages of those who came before; all of them died well before old age. Whether it be mysterious circumstances, accidents while helping others, or murder, there was no denying that becoming part of the Major Arcana made you a target for death.

Mackenzie's stomach curled up inside her painfully as she realized she'd been consigned to an early death by Teo and others. Kai had probably known what she was destined for and said nothing. They were all content to sign her up for a life she never asked for or wanted, and no one had even pre-warned her.

Finally, she reached the start of her father's journey. The bubbling rage inside her quieted for a moment as she looked at her dad's voice penned into its pages. Her grandfather, his father, had awakened him when he had finished college at Salem. He'd already met and fallen in love with her mother by the time he found out about the world. There had been no going back, he'd written in his first entry in the journal, unsure if he could bring Anne into this magic underbelly but unable to lie and keep her from it. He knew the choice he faced the moment he was awakened; he could leave her or allow her into his ancestral world.

A tear sped down Mackenzie's face, falling onto the page below. She gasped, and her hands quickly reached up to clear her cheeks and eyes of any other tears. She hadn't even realized she'd begun to cry. Swallowing the tight lump in her throat, she returned to her dad's written thoughts, knowing the decision he'd made had caused the set of events that had her sitting in this living room alone and filled with every negative emotion on the spectrum.

Most of all she was angry. Angry at Kai for lying, at the Major Arcana for not giving her a choice, and now her dad for making the wrong choice. If he'd made a different one, both of them might still be alive, her birth be damned.

The knock that rattled her front door had Mackenzie starting in her seat, the falling tears holding on to her cheeks as she glanced out the window to see the person on the other side.

Kai dropped his hand from the hard wood, waiting in the dying sunlight for her, staring at the door in anticipation as though she were about to appear on the other side.

She left the tears on her cheeks, resigned to letting him believe they were just for him as she got up from her place in the chair, leaving the book open carefully on the coffee table. She let the sparks of her fury blaze brighter as she strode to the door, jerking it open, watching his hand drop from where it had been about to knock again.

The flame sputtered at the sight of Kai in front of her, feeling that small part of her that still wanted to go to him and melt in his arms. But she had to ignore her heart right now as it both yearned and broke for him.

Kai took in Mackenzie's appearance too, and she watched the smile fade from his lips. He caught sight of her damp cheeks, the heavy bags under her eyes that suggested no sleep, and the black smudges of the night-before makeup that said she'd been crying on and off for hours.

She was still wearing the living magic dress, and the burns on her wrists and ankles showed up bright red and raw.

"Hey, Kenzie. Are you okay? What's wrong?" he asked quickly, scanning her body and catching on her rope burns. His eyes widened as though he knew exactly what had occurred to create the wounds, and she felt a pain twist in her gut at his recognition, a poison leaking and burning in every cavity of her body.

"Surely you know," Mackenzie scoffed bitterly, more to herself than him. "You can't be that innocent in all of this..."

Kai strode forward, concern scrunching his face as he reached to take one of her hands in his.

"What do you mean 'innocent in all this'? Kenzie, what's going on?"

The thought of him making her feel better was a physical pain. Mackenzie flinched, watching him stop in his tracks as a cold power ran through her veins, turning her resolve to shut him out into strong, thick ice. Her cold anger flattened her face into a frozen glare.

"I've been awakened," she said simply, her tone as flat as her heart rate as he faltered in his step.

His hands dropped, no longer offering for her to take as he retreated.

"Oh." His eyes bulged, taking her in again as though he could now see the magic that coursed through her veins.

Silence fell between them, prompting the blaze deep within Mackenzie to burn brighter in the quiet. It melted the icy stare and resolve she had used like armor, and she felt the fiery rage within her take control too quickly.

"Oh? That's all you have to say?" She wanted him to fight it, to tell her that it wasn't the truth. Her show of anger knocked fight into him.

"What do you want me to say?" he asked her seriously, leaving the space between them for her to ask for answers.

It only angered her more that she had to ask for any of it specifically. She gaped at him for a moment as all her betrayed pain and anger became fuel for the mouth she was quickly losing control of.

"The truth! You knew exactly who I was when we met and knew what the Arcana would want of me and told me nothing! I spent so long searching for my family and answers, and you never thought to clue me in!" she yelled, not caring who might hear in the dying light of the street, letting him know every way that she'd been stabbed by his secrecy.

"Kenz, I can explain…" he began, his hand held up defensively.

The gesture did nothing to soothe, instead flaring her anger; she hated the thought that him finally telling her anything could fix this. Her hurt was too great—and if he tried, some part of her might give in.

She couldn't let that happen.

"No! I don't need explanations anymore!" Her emotions exploded upon him like a flood she wasn't going to be able to stop. "I trusted you… I let you in… in a way, I haven't done before… I slept with you… I was even starting to…"

The words flowed out of her as her eyes drifted to the porch, swarmed with tears that flooded but never spilled, messing with her vision and making her feel unbalanced. She reached out, holding the doorframe as he tried to suck in enough air and strengthen her limbs to stay standing.

"Kenz…" Kai whispered. She could hear the pity and care dripping into his voice.

The burning electric feeling of the purple lightning jolted through her, reinvigorating her anger and giving her a new bout of strength. She blinked her eyes clear as she took her weight off the door frame and raised her gaze to his with all the her strength and magic could muster.

"No! What I need now is straightforward answers to direct questions. Did you know who I was the day I came to talk to you in Oregon?"

"Yes." His face scrunched, falling in regret. His eyes dropped from her leveling stare as he fidgeted with his fingers and took deep, visible breaths.

"Was that the beast following me that day you?" Mackenzie continued, asking the next question before he could add, explain or talk his way out of it. She knew as the Devil he could only tell the truth to a direct question and didn't know if that extended to extra explanations. She planned on using her words wisely.

"Yes, but I—"

"How long had you been following me before the day we spoke?" she pushed, feeling the burning magic in her come alive with her rage, changing it a way that electrified her veins and made her feel like a charged battery.

"Eighteen days. But you have to understand, I—" he tried again, but she was too agape to let him tell his side, every answer enraging her further.

"You don't get explanations. Had you been to my hometown before?"

"Yes." His lips pressed into a tight line as he respected her wishes begrudgingly—or held back from telling her the next part of the truth.

"When?" Somehow, she knew what his answer would be, dreading it all the same.

"Ten years prior... The day your mother disappeared," he said quietly, and she could hear the reluctance in his voice as her world stopped.

The lightning intensified and her body went numb for a few moments. When she finally reconnected with her body and the full weight of her feelings, she knew she'd heard enough.

"Get away from me," she whispered as she met his gaze unflinchingly, the pain of her betrayal turning into venom in her mouth.

"Kenzie, please. Listen, I can explain it all," he hurried, trying to fumble through his words before she could cut him off again, his eyes filled with fear.

"There is nothing more you could say that I want to hear."

"Please," he tried in a whisper, watching as her pain finally exploded into being.

"Get away from me!" she screamed, the magic in her coming loose from inside her body and taking control of the situation. Purple lightning exploded as she outstretched her palms, hitting Kai in the chest and throwing him backward. Like a ragdoll, his body was tossed through the air, landing with a heavy thud against the gutter on the opposite side of the road.

Feeling robbed of breath by the gasp that overtook her. Mackenzie held her breath as she waited the whole long second for Kai to move. She wanted to rush over and check for herself, but was still frozen in surprise.

Kai rolled over to his front slowly with a groan, glancing at Mackenzie for a second as he raised himself to his feet. He retreated down the street, movement slow and pained, as she let the events dawn on her.

Glancing down at her hands breathlessly, she studied them, expecting to see something different. All she saw was the same scarred hands they'd always been— tortured by the nail-digging too many times not to show.

When no other magic showed itself, Mackenzie stepped back and shut the front door. In the fading light of day, all alone and confused, she fell apart. She had more answers than before, but had never felt so lost.

She ignored the book she'd left on the table, her eyes glancing over it in the room with a sense of disinterest. Climbing the stairs sluggishly, feeling every limb pull with a tiredness that suggested utter exhaustion, she retreated.

The bed welcomed her like an old friend she hadn't seen in months, surrounding her as she fell into the depths of the mattress, saturating its sheets with the tears that escaped unrestrained.

She blamed herself. The first person she'd trusted in her vigor for living life and participating had betrayed her and until now, she'd never questioned it. She could have gone in with caution but she'd thrown herself in without a second thought. And yet she was surprised by how it had turned out?

Her mind spiraled with self-destructive thoughts, convincing her that leaving this bed was all too much risk, too much work. She had been so on board with the plan to live a life worthy of her parent's pride, but she feared what they'd think of her association with Kai.

On and on she fell, until she knew there was only one way she'd ever escape. Reaching over slowly, she picked up her phone and send a text before sleep claimed her overwhelmed mind. *SOS.*

14: THE EMERGENCY BRAKE

Mackenzie had expected a phone call in response, not a knock on the door hours after.

The first knock echoed through the house, and Mackenzie's stomach tightened up savagely, making her fear it would bring up what remnants of food remained in her. She wasn't sure who it was knocking, but none of the limited options were appealing to her. In fact, most—if not all—she wanted to avoid.

When the knock came a second time, she still made no effort to move, determined to stay nestled in the depths of the mattress forever, staring at the pieces her parents had left behind.

The metallic clunk of a key clicked the lock free and then the creak of the heavy front door opening sounded up the stairs. Mackenzie jolted upright in the bed, her skin cold without the comforter, prickling with alert nerves as she listened intently for the sound of the intruder.

"You know hiding a key under a pot plant is a real crappy hiding spot, KZ," a melodic voice called from the base of the stairs.

At the sound of her childhood nickname and the tone of the one person alive in the world she wanted to see, Mackenzie bolted out of bed. She skidded to a halt at the top of the stairs, everything that had been weighing her down disappearing at the sight of the girl with the perfect golden blonde curls waiting by the front door with her suitcase in tow.

"Luce!" Mackenzie cried, bounding down the stairs and launching herself onto her best friend without a second thought.

Lucy caught her in the hug, barely staying upright as the full weight of the two of them went backward with the momentum.

"Oh my god, what are you doing here?"

"You're kidding, right?" Lucy replied, pulling back out of the hug to check Mackenzie's face. "I got your SOS."

The two of them assessed each other slowly, having a moment of silence to study the state of the other.

"I expected a phone call, not a visit..." Mackenzie whispered as she looked at Lucy's frazzled, haphazard state. Her clothing didn't match, her hair while falling properly was not as perfectly kept as usual, and she was without the smaller touches of makeup Mackenzie had always known her to wear. It was very unlike her. She looked tired and as though she'd left New York the second her friend had messaged.

"Do you want me to go home then?" Lucy challenged with raised eyebrows.

"No!" Mackenzie said quickly. "Just surprised, that's all."

"Well, maybe next time you send for help, remember to leave your phone on charge when I call you, so you can brief me," she responded with a grin.

Mackenzie's face flushed.

"I'm so sorry. I completely forgot. I fell asleep and didn't realize."

"Fell asleep? Already? And did you plan on getting out of bed?" her friend questioned, losing all jokes and humor as she took in the living magic dress and the accompanying smells.

"Not until then," Mackenzie admitted honestly as she

met Lucy's gaze. She hoped the tight frown told her that this was due to new events, not just an inability to move.

"What happened?"

Mackenzie opened her mouth, intending to let the story spill out naturally—as naturally as a story of magic and chaos could—but came up blank about where or how to start. How was she even supposed to tell her friend that magic existed, let alone bring her in on a world of information that could put her in danger?

"It's a pretty long story," she found herself saying as she contemplated what she could tell her.

"Well, I'm going to assume you haven't eaten and I can smell you haven't showered or changed since whenever this was," Lucy observed, wavering her hand over the dress that still clung to her like it was made to be there. "So why don't I grab us some good old-fashioned comfort food while you shower and get all clean and snug, and then you can tell me everything."

Mackenzie nodded, suddenly noticing how unclean she was and feeling the itch to rectify that. She wasn't offended by Lucy's words, just very aware that if her friend was pointing it out, she had lost sight of her own state.

Lucy slid her suitcase against the wall and jingled the spare house key in view before disappearing back out the door.

In the quiet, Mackenzie focused on the task at hand rather than the silent loneliness of the house. She trudged back up the stairs to the shower, needing to be out of the emotionally charged dress.

* * *

Mackenzie came down the stairs, following the smell of fried food to the living room where Lucy had placed a variety of goods out on the coffee table on separate plates. Too much food for the two of them, but enough choices that it didn't matter what Mackenzie was in the mood for. That was the way it had always been with them. Her eyes glanced over the tater tots, mac 'n' cheese, chicken wings, Greek salad, waffles, Boston cream pie, New England clam chowder, and pizza.

"I've missed having you in the same house every day!" she found herself saying as she watched her friend set up the plates, cutlery, and drinking glasses, pulling more and more out of the takeaway and grocery bags she'd returned with.

"Oh, we're starting with the compliments already. Who are you and what have you done with my best friend?" Lucy joked, her words driving an edge of truth into Mackenzie.

"You have no idea how much I've changed already," Mackenzie responded, feeling the recent memories surface like a remembered nightmare.

"Well that sounds ominous…" Lucy waved for Mackenzie to take a seat on one of the cushions she'd set up on the floor around the coffee table.

Mackenzie waited for a moment, choosing to stand.

"I'm so done with life participation already and I haven't even been here that long! Being social hurts."

"Unfortunately, honey, that is the curse that comes with experiencing the world," Lucy said softly, a hopeful smile on her face as she watched her best friend's scrunch in disagreement. "You get the good as well as the bad."

"Not like this…" She sighed, feeling the weight of her time in Salem pull on her limbs again. "Why don't I show you around and give myself some time to think about how to explain all of it."

Lucy's smile lit up her kind hazel eyes as she nodded.

"Come on." Lucy gestured for her tour to begin, the warm food wafting its scents of goodness through the room and house. "Then you can tell me everything."

"Be careful what you wish for…" Mackenzie warned before she could stop herself.

Waving her hand around the living room, she showed it off. It still required some care but she knew she'd get there eventually—or at least that's what she told herself—as she ushered Lucy through the room.

The kitchen at least had been cleaned and stocked enough that she let her friend admire the cabinetry and old devices that she hadn't been able to bring herself to remove yet. Lucy looked the same way Mackenzie had felt the first day she'd been able to explore the house; Mackenzie couldn't help watching her bittersweetly, jealous that her illusion of the house had not yet been shattered.

Next, they wound back through the front entrance, ignoring the laundry, and up the stairs. Same as Mackenzie had, Lucy moved slowly past the photographs on the wall, smiling at them as she observed and absorbed their memories.

"They were so in love," Lucy said quietly to herself, looking at the photo of Mackenzie's mother and father, as though talking too loud would shatter the moment caught on film. She continued, a sad smile on her lips as she walked up ahead of Mackenzie and reached the landing.

Mackenzie hadn't put anything in her old room yet—with plans to eventually make it a study for her college assignments and work—but for the moment, as Lucy passed by it, she saw only an empty room.

When Lucy came into the room Mackenzie had claimed from her parents, she gasped at the mementos still left on the walls and cabinets. The folded American flag, the watch, more photographs, and their clothing were still visible in the open closet. She hurried in, glancing at Mackenzie's open, still-in-use suitcase. A raised eyebrow from Lucy said she understood what Mackenzie had been unable to bring herself to do yet.

Mackenzie led the way back down the stairs, finally prepared to show Lucy the craziness she'd been dealing with since coming to her parent's hometown. Down they descended into the dark, Mackenzie waiting at the bottom of the stairs before flicking the light on for dramatic effect.

Lucy gasped as she caught sight of the weapons. "Okay… Is this a collection of your dad's, or have you found a disturbing new hobby since we last saw each other?" She breathed out slowly and quietly as her eyes took the time to work their way over every weapon in more detail.

"This belonged to my father and has been added to and kept by my family for generations, apparently," Mackenzie replied. The weapons glinted at her, and she remembered a time before her magic when she couldn't see the power flowing through them.

"And you know this because…?" Lucy pushed, turning to her friend.

"My father left a whole notebook about my family for me."

"That's amazing!" Lucy replied, bubbling excitedly before nodding that Mackenzie's expression was still concerned. "It's not amazing?"

"It's honestly been really interesting getting to know my parents through their home. I've learned heaps, and the people from the town have helped too," Mackenzie said, hopeful but feeling the weighty reminder deep in her gut.

"Look at you go! Finding all the answers!" Lucy exclaimed, still reigning her excitement at Mackenzie's sad face. "What?"

"I'm not sure I wanted some of the answers I got," she admitted, some of her tension leaving as the words fell into the air, raking their power over her body with it.

"What do you mean? Were your parents good people?"

"As far as I can tell."

"Then there's nothing that can't be weathered," Lucy said with a reassuring smile. "Now come with me, I had a feeling that the SOS was going to spell a need for a heavy conversation so I brought vodka as well as fried food."

"Brilliant," Mackenzie replied, her lips lifting slightly at the edges. It didn't reach her eyes but it was a start.

Seeing her change, Lucy led the way back to the living room, pulling the bottle out of her bag while Mackenzie grabbed glasses off the table. Both girls sat on their pillows on the ground, Lucy pouring shots in their glasses and Mackenzie loading their plates with food.

"All right, lay it on me," Lucy said, holding her glass up in cheers to Mackenzie's. The glasses clinked and both friends threw the shot down their throats, trying not to wince as it burned its way to their stomachs.

"Well," Mackenzie said, "I got here and met my mom's friend and neighbor who has been looking after the house, only for her to tell me that my mom fled Salem after my dad was *murdered*."

"Oh, shit," Lucy muffled through a mouthful of mac 'n' cheese.

"Turns out he had gotten involved with the 'wrong kind of people' and pissed them off. When my father died, my mother fled across the country and went into hiding with me. And then ten years later, when she went mysteriously missing, the same people seem to have been involved."

"Oh my god."

"And I'll warn you now, it keeps getting worse. So I tried to live, knowing I now had answers, trying to focus on my studies and do as you and my mom wanted to and live my life. I made new friends and even got invited on a date to a college party with a guy named Teo."

Lucy's eyebrows shot up at the mention of a date, clearly impressed by her friend's new lease on life.

"And you went to a party?" Lucy urged, her face impressed so far but cautious as to where this story would go.

"I went, and for the most part, I was enjoying myself.

We were getting a little hot and heavy on the dancefloor…”

“And…?” Lucy smiled, clearly hoping at least this part of the story had a happy ending.

“And we went to take a breather outside and ran into Kai.”

“As in the Kai that you met back home and had sex with in the forest?” she verified, putting the pieces of coincidence together much quicker than Mackenzie had.

“The same one. He’s from here apparently and got incredibly jealous when he found out I was here and getting it on with another guy.”

“And we’re back to oh shit,” Lucy said as she crossed her legs and leaned in, chewing her tater tots like they were popcorn. Pouring another shot of vodka for both of them, she wasted no time tossing hers back.

Mackenzie followed suit, feeling the burn down her throat, warming her insides, and calming the stress that chewed through her stomach. Taking a deep breath, she continued.

“Yeah, Kai also told said date—who hates him by the way—that we’d slept together, so he left the party. I tried to as well, but Kai followed me out…”

“I’ll bet he did.” Lucy winked and a sick feeling twisted Mackenzie’s stomach.

“He told me that he wanted to have a relationship with me now that he knew I was here in town, and that he would’ve asked for that earlier if I’d told him I was coming to Salem,” Mackenzie continued, watching Lucy’s jaw drop excitedly. “And then he walked me home and I invited him in.”

“Yes…?”

“He politely declined and left me for the night. I got a knock on the door not long after and was knocked out by Teo and Amari.”

“Teo, the guy you went to the party with?”

“The very same. And Amari is one of my new *friends*

from college."

"And he knocked you out because of Kai?"

"No. I woke up tied to an altar, was struck by purple lightning, and then told that they had awakened my magic. That my family has had magic for generations and we are symbols of the Magician tarot card, sharing powers that emulate that." Mackenzie let the words sit in the air, awaiting Lucy's move.

Multiple things contorted Lucy's face as she listened and Mackenzie wasn't sure if it was confusion, anger, or worry.

Lucy poured herself another shot, tossing it back, then poured one for Mackenzie.

"Do you believe it?"

"I didn't at first. I accused them of being a cult, of kidnapping me, but in all this, they gave me an answer to a question I'd been searching for but wasn't sure I wanted."

"What did they tell you?" Lucy asked as Mackenzie tossed her shot back too.

"That Kai's father was the one who killed mine."

"No!" Lucy gasped, her hand coming up to her mouth as Mackenzie relived the same shock she'd felt the night before.

"And I didn't want to believe in magic this morning. I tried not to, but then Kai came over."

"I hope you punched him!"

"No, I... I asked him if he knew who I was before that day back home. If he'd been there before..."

"He said yes, didn't he?" Lucy asked, and Mackenzie looked up to see her eyes tearing up.

At the sight of her friend in tears because of her, she got watery also and the two watched each other with sad smiles and welling eye floods.

"He last visited the town the day my mother disappeared," Mackenzie said. "I was so mad that I tossed him across the street."

"What?!"

"With my magic. I used it on Kai."

"So this isn't a trick. Do you actually have magic? Real magic?"

"I do." Both girls were stuck somewhere between shock at the events and elation at the idea of magic existing and Mackenzie having access to it. "It's why my family has all those weapons and the book just over there. It's true, everything they told me when they awakened me, it's all true."

"You're going to need to tell me more about this Magician's tarot power. But first, a magic show?" Lucy proposed.

Mackenzie couldn't help the girlish giggle that escaped her throat. She thought for a moment over the notes she'd read, trying to figure out what she might be able to achieve. Figuring that the purple lightning was an uncontrollable, emotionally-driven magic, she held back from using that indoors. "Be warned though, I have not practiced this at all," Mackenzie cautioned.

"Then this could be very entertaining," Lucy responded with a grin.

Mackenzie put her fork in the center of the table away from everything else as Lucy settled forward eagerly to watch and Mackenzie forced her tipsy mind to focus. Outstretching her hand, palm facing towards the cutlery piece, she thought about how her father had described it. In her mind's eye, she could see an invisible card the size of a credit card sliding under the fork and then she willed it into existence. A shimmer of purple caught her eye on the table, and disappeared almost immediately, letting her know it was in place. Using her focus, she lifted it slowly, drawing the card up with her mind as flat as she could manage, watching with wide eyes as the fork lifted in the air, levitating.

She could feel the moment her surprise and excitement muddled with her focus, and the fork clattered to the tabletop.

It was harder than her father's note had made it seem

- just willing it into existence and moving them—and
required a great amount of focus that was mentally draining.

"You're amazing, KZ," Lucy whispered in the silence of the room as her hazel eyes widened larger than she'd ever seen before.

Mackenzie stared back similarly wide-eyed, wordless for a moment, a silent conversation between their pupils that said how much they needed each other.

"You really think the power is a blessing and not a curse?" Mackenzie questioned just as quietly, finally glad to be with someone who knew her so wholly and not just the power she now possessed.

"I think you'll make it one," Lucy responded without hesitation.

"Well, I guess I'll need to study its capabilities some more then." She smiled, her voice wavering as she felt the reassurance of Lucy's words warm her the way she needed to hear. "Luckily, my father left notes on the powers too."

"He really left you all this to learn on your own? Why not enlist someone else in that society to help tutor you or something?" Lucy questioned.

Mackenzie sat in silence for a moment, mulling it over as though there should be some complicated answer known to her, but came up short.

"I really don't know…" Mackenzie admitted, slowly working through the thought, feeling the way it sat uneasily in her gut.

"That's a red flag for me!" Lucy said, not hiding her unease.

Like the tension had been let out of her, Mackenzie let loose a heavy sigh. "A red flag of my dad's or the Arcana?" she checked, hoping her friend's unease was held in the same place as hers.

"The Arcana, of course! I think you need to be careful around them. If your father didn't trust them to teach you, there's probably a reason and it's probably because he didn't trust them."

Mackenzie's chest tightened as more questions were raised in her mind at the statements. "What if they're the only ones who can give me more answers on the things the book doesn't cover?" she said, her gaze focused on the food between them, barely seeing any of it. Her brain spiraled with questions she couldn't answer. It was working too hard, sorting through too many of them to be able to register anything other than her thoughts and anxieties.

"Then I'd say let them think you trust them but keep your secrets close to your chest. Don't let them see your full potential and get better at lying," Lucy said defiantly.

Mackenzie glanced back up at her best friend, feeling her heart squeeze happily at the idea of having her back for the moment.

Lucy's eyes lit up with mischief at the idea of tricking a secret magic society, but Mackenzie could feel a twist in her gut at the notion. Lucy was correct though. It would be the only way.

Until she was sure who she could trust, she'd play them all to get her answers.

15: THE ORIGINS

Mackenzie stood outside the lecture hall door, bouncing on her toes and flicking the extra nervous energy out of her fingers, mentally preparing herself. Deep breaths in and out as she rolled her shoulders back and mustered the courage to face what she knew was coming.

She'd have to face Amari and Teo eventually, and avoiding college was just going to end up ruining her future as well. It didn't matter if her world had shifted, college had always been the goal, and passing it even more so.

She needed to act normal. She wished she could go back to when she felt that way - when her biggest problem was whether she could get herself out of bed to face being an orphan.

Now it was whether she could enter a room as a magical orphan to face the people who had kidnapped her to awaken her powers without her consent for a secret society that she wasn't sure could be trusted.

But Lucy was right, she had to play along.

Taking one step at a time, letting her tension release with her breath, Mackenzie opened the door. Disappointed to see that the professor hadn't arrived yet and that she'd beat him, she scanned the room, finding her 'friends' easily.

They acted as though nothing had changed between

them, beckoning her over to the empty seat they'd left between them. She plastered a smile on her face and climbed the stairs to meet them before dropping into the chair and focusing her attention forward, thankful that was the moment the professor had decided to arrive. A hush fell over the lecture hall as the students realized he was about to begin and those who had not yet found their seats hurried to do so.

Remembering the plan she'd concocted for herself, Mackenzie turned to Teo quickly before the class. "Can we talk… after class?" she asked, battling her eyelashes innocently, and he nodded carefully, his face a mask of concern. She reached her hand over slowly to touch his and let her lips fall into her best reassuring smile, his body and face relaxing slightly, emboldened by her comfort.

Amari's eyebrows heightened and she gave a 'what are up to' look as the professor finally addressed his audience.

Once class began, Mackenzie used it as the perfect excuse to rescue her hand from Teo's touch, cringing internally at the contact.

"Your first assignment and our focus for the next two weeks will be on a bit of local history. The infamous Salem Witch Trials are everywhere here, and we will be looking at the political, religious, and financial atmosphere, and how that contributed to the turn of events that occurred. So let's begin with what came to pass in February 1692."

Teo reached over and sought Mackenzie's hand confidently, lacing his fingers through hers with a squeeze.

Mackenzie fought her instant reaction to pull away in disgust, stiffening only for a moment as she kept her eyes focused forward.

Teo barely noticed.

She fought off the scoff that wanted to push its way up her throat at his naivety. How did he believe that after kidnapping her, tying her to an altar, awakening her magic against her will, and telling her it was all because he had to, she'd just want to fall to her knees before him? Or did he imagine that because the Arcana had ordered him to do it, he was blameless in all of it?

Mackenzie's stomach chewed over her mind's flurry of questions. She was thankful for the lecture—it hid how much she was stuck in her head, unfocused. She roused on herself stewing on her anger at him, knowing it would make her act harder to keep up. Lucy and her had agreed that making him believe he still had a chance would be the key to getting all the information out of him about Major Arcana and magic. If only Lucy could be here to back her up and make her feel invincible. But instead, Lucy was doing her college work remotely from Mackenzie's house. For her safety, she needed to stay hidden. Mackenzie's secret counsel.

Mackenzie took deep breaths, trying to tune back into the lecture as the professor discussed people who had become involved in the initial accusations.

Sarah Good. The name stood out to her from Amari's notes as she remembered her family tree from the book. The first entry had been a Good... the coincidence made her heart leap in excitement. A place to investigate without the Arcana. She tried to listen, but the list of questions she wanted to ask Teo overtook her focus.

"Dismissed," the professor called out, snapping Mackenzie out of her inner ramblings to realize she'd missed most of the lecture.

Amari hurriedly packed up her things, about to leave alone when Mackenzie halted her.

"Amari, do you mind if I borrow your notes from this class? I had a lot of my mind and I'm not sure I took it all in very well," she admitted, knowing the best way to play this act of hers was to stick as close to the truth as possible so there was less acting involved. Lucy had always said she wasn't good at lying.

"Absolutely! I'll send pics of them later, okay? I have

to run!" Amari replied, waiting for confirmation.

"Sounds great!" Mackenzie agreed, thankful to at least have saved herself from missing college work, especially for an upcoming assignment.

Now she just needed to get through this conversation with Teo and find some more answers, then she was sure she'd be able to focus on the mundane things again. She hoped.

Amari waved goodbye and raced off, leaving Mackenzie and Teo to disentangle their hands and get up from their seats.

Walking down and out of the lecture hall, Mackenzie watched the people around them carefully. Weaving between the many students and teachers ducking in and out of earshot, she felt the chewing in her return as she waited impatiently for the chance to talk.

Teo watched her in quick glances, no doubt seeing her face tighten and scrunch as she tried to plan what to ask first.

They exited the building into the fresh air and the comforting smell of mown grass, and Mackenzie began to feel like she could breathe a little easier. She stepped off the path, Teo following and stopping as he waited for her to speak.

She stood in silence, lips pursued as her brain blanked. "Ahhh... I..." she started, hoping the words would find her as she opened her mouth.

Teo stiffened as his eyes caught over her shoulder at something.

Turning quickly, her gaze caught the gray-blue of Kai's eyes as he flickered between her and Teo. She could see his jaw tighten from his place ten feet away, sitting on the grass where he'd been reading his book.

She closed her fists tightly at her side, nails digging dangerously into her palm as warmth flooded the area. Purple sparked at the end of the arms as her stare drove him down, her anger—she was incredibly in touch with—taking over her body.

The purple lightning sparked over the outside of her fists, willing her to open her hand and direct it at him again.

Teo's hand gripped her shoulder, cold washing through her veins like ice, pulling her from her anger.

The purple lightning fizzled out as it finally drew Kai's attention.

Mackenzie gasped like she'd been dowsed by ice water as Teo slipped his arm around her shoulders carefully, turning Mackenzie and leading her further and further away.

Her mind reeled as she went with him, horrified that she'd been so close to losing control.

"It's okay. Emotional magic can be hard sometimes when you're hurting," he said quietly, squeezing her closer for a second. "Let's focus on something else. What did you want to talk about before?"

"Oh, I just wanted to talk more about the Major Arcana and my family's bloodline. I wasn't receptive the last time we spoke and I'm sorry. I believe you now and I'm ready to listen, I just hoped there was more you could tell me..." she said, stumbling through the words as she tried to stay focused on Teo.

Her neck prickled with Kai's gaze as she fidgeted, even with her back turned. It fueled her anger as she remembered him watching her in Oregon.

"Absolutely! Glad you're open to it now. How much time do you have before your next class? Did you want to sit down and talk about it further?" Teo asked with a growing smile as he turned and gestured to the other side of the grassy area, even further from Kai.

Mackenzie couldn't help glancing back at where Kai still watched them, paying no attention to the book in his lap.

Teo followed her attention, before offering his solution. "Hey, don't worry about him. Do you want to go somewhere else to talk?"

Meeting Teo's gaze again, she nodded, feeling Kai's

eyes constantly on her turned back.

With a reassuring smile, Teo laced his fingers with hers and led her away again, headed off out of sight of Kai.

The moment they were out of view, her whole body relaxed. As the sensation on her neck subsided, her breathing eased, her muscle tightness melted, and she fell into a calm pace beside Teo.

"Better?" Teo asked, glancing at her.

"Much," she replied with a breathy sigh, feeling the magic that had been exploding to her skin completely fade from reach, calming her further. She flexed her hands and removed the tension, shaking her free hand in the air.

"You know, if you want better control of your magic, Major Arcana can help," he said as they moved through a less populated area of the campus.

"Yeah? And what would I have to do in return?" she quipped, cursing herself as she felt the venom bite in her tone. She tried to change her expression, softening the grimace she'd created into an amused smile.

He looked at her quickly, hearing the sharpness, but slowed at her attempt to seem like she was joking. His eyes narrowed but he continued. "Help people?" he countered.

Shock opened her face, her eyes struggling to hide the double take at his words.

He smiled wider. "You join them, they give you jobs to use your magic to help people, and in return, they'll help train you and your magic. Sometimes you get paid for the jobs and tasks too."

"Oh?"

"Yeah… It's that easy if that's what you want to do, but no pressure," he said casually like he wasn't trying to sell her on membership.

Mackenzie's step slowed as she stared at the pavement, trying to wrap her head around it. That had not been the answer she'd been expecting. Teo was pulled to a stop beside her, watching and waiting for her quietly as she mulled it over in her head.

"I'll… think about it. Let's just improve my understanding of my family line and the organization first, then I can make an informed decision," she said, looking back and continuing their journey to a small, secluded grass area, currently empty of students.

"Very mature of you." He chuckled.

She glanced up, her stomach tightening at the idea of being alone with him and joining a magical society she knew nothing about. She was relieved if it came off as rational thinking.

"Thank you!" She smiled, glancing down and checking her prospective seat, knowing the expression didn't reach her eyes. Sitting down, she released his hand as he took a seat beside her, both absorbing the sunshine that beamed down on them. She wasn't sure what question to begin with.

Teo's features tightened. "I just want to apologize for everything that happened the other day. My behavior at the party was abysmal and I shouldn't have taken my frustration out by leaving you there like that, you couldn't have known Kai's true nature. He's good at manipulating people and I shouldn't have held that against you. I also want to apologize for how we got you to the sanctuary—that was not how I'd envisioned the night going and it must have been so terrifying for you. I can't fix it now but I want you to know that was not how it was supposed to go and I'm so sorry." He met her gaze unwaveringly.

The flood of dizziness that always seemed to accompany her warmth toward him struck again and she heard herself say the words before she realized she was asking, "How was it supposed to go?" A small, surprised smirk lit up her face, even as a sour taste overtook her mouth.

"Well, I would've taken you to the party and we would have had an amazing date without Kai to ruin it. I would've taken you for a walk afterward and told you about your family and magic, and showed you proof, then taken you to be awakened of your own volition and belief," he explained, watching her carefully.

Mackenzie searched his expression for any possibility of lies, but he honestly believed that was how the night should've gone. She could feel her stomach turn to goo in her as he took her hand, brushing his thumb over the back of her hand.

"What proof would you have shown me? Your power? What is your tarot?" she asked, leaning in curiously, considering placing her head on his shoulder to see if the lightheadedness would fade.

"I'm the Fool bloodline, we can read and influence emotions."

Mackenzie's back straightened as she leaned away, feeling everything in her go cold.

"Yes, I know you've been anxious today and kind of disgusted. I also supposed that's because of my horrific behavior the other night, but I only sense emotions, not reasons."

She couldn't move as he explained it casually, her entire plan of secrecy to infiltrate the Arcana disappearing out the window. "And influencing emotions?" she asked, her voice breaking mid-question.

"I barely ever use those powers and I can't make anyone feel anything they don't already have, I just… enhance it. Like the other night, you were already tired. I pushed and you fell asleep," he said.

Her eyes widened at the realization.

"That was how that happened?" she squeaked, her mouth flapping open as everything in her told her to run. Then calm dizziness washed over her as it all eased like it was disappearing in a cloud of smoke, the alarm quieted and quickly forgotten.

"I can promise things like the other night won't happen again," he said to her, his hand squeezing reassuringly.

She smiled, letting it slip onto her face without conscious thought.

"Now, what were the other questions you had?"

"Uh… I was wondering how the Major Arcana started. Surely every society has an origin story, and I was really curious," she said, feeling excited at the notion of answers that she could link to her family tree.

"It all links back to a witch in the trials in 1692. Well-timed with the topic in class at the moment. Sarah Good was a magic wielder of the time and for generations, her family held all the tarot powers. When she was accused, rather than running, she passed the powers out to families she deemed worthy, accepting her fate."

Mackenzie listened intently, still aware of Teo's hand holding hers, a comforting anchor for her as she wrapped her mind around the information. Her ancestors had been related to Sarah Good, she was sure of it. The family that had once held all the powers was her ancestor. She wasn't sure if Teo knew of her family tree and worked to keep her lips from spilling it to him despite the warm fuzziness inside her chest that said she could.

"Any other questions you had that I can answer?" he pushed, his smile returning after the brief reprieve from the serious tragic story.

His calm openness had her fumbling, expecting some sort of secrecy or resistance in giving answers, making a tingle of pain in her gut resonate at hiding things from him.

"I… I just wanted to know more about them. You mentioned using powers for good but for what exactly? What sort of things does the Arcana do?" she asked, feeling the niggling inner stomach that told her she'd pushed too far or asked for too much.

But as quickly as it appeared, it disappeared again as Teo nodded, approving of her question. "So the Major Arcana is an organization that has connections with many parts of society, working for the betterment of humanity," he said, puffing his chest as he squeezed her hand excitedly. "Hiding from society, we use our powers for the betterment of everyone. I've helped trauma victims by easing their anxiety so that they can talk about their experiences on witness stands, or sensed emotions for hostage situations so others can negotiate to save as many lives as possible. Whenever we can help, the Arcana do."

The warmth that spread through Mackenzie's body was unbelievable. The amazing work Teo had outlined was hard to believe and she couldn't help how she froze, her lips pursued as she watched again for any sign that he was lying or dramatizing it, finding none. He met her eyes excitedly, eager to share his triumph and she let her lips fall into a bright, excited smile, feeding off his energy.

"That's amazing!" she said. "You weren't kidding about doing good!"

"Just tell me you'll at least consider joining," he said, tracing his thumb over the back of her hand again, his entire tone altering as he leaned in close. "We could use a talent like yours in the organization to do wonderful things for the world."

"I don't know if my poor attempts at magic can be called talent." She chuckled, her eyes dropping, her face heating. The prospect of helping people warmed her up, but she wasn't sure she could do anything with her abysmal attempts yet.

"Then let the Arcana help you learn your power and you can help them change the world," he said to her pleadingly. Her eyes glanced back up, only to be caught in his gaze, unable to look away.

She nodded slowly, dizziness ebbing.

"Wonderful. I'll let them know you can start tomorrow."

Mackenzie grinned so widely her cheeks hurt. The idea of being able to make a difference in others' lives was so overwhelming. Everything else faded away except for that and the notion that she would be able to use her magic. "Thank you," she said.

Her phone buzzed in her pocket. Lucy. Waiting at her house for an update.

Mackenzie hurriedly removed herself from the ground, letting go of Teo's hand. "Text me the details and I'll be there. I just remembered I do have somewhere I need to be, so I should probably be going."

"No problem, but just remember, I'm here if you have any more questions," Teo said calmly, unfazed by her sudden departure.

She nodded quickly and took off for the bus stop, the chewing anxiety and weight of dread growing in her stomach the further she got from Teo.

Mackenzie got on the bus as it pulled up, climbing abroad as a sick feeling ate at her stomach. When the vehicle finally peeled out onto the road, her dizziness dissipated, giving her clarity that had her covering the audible gasp that drove up her throat.

The calm relaxation had disappeared from her mind and body.

Teo had used his powers on her.

Shit, she cursed as she yanked her phone out of her bag.

We have a very real problem, she texted to Lucy.

16: THE DECISION

Mackenzie wandered down the streets from the house, feeling the eyes of her best friend on her back, peeking through the front window curtains. She clenched her hand tight, wishing she could have Lucy holding it as she strode down the street to the Salem Common through the darkened street.

Her nerves danced along her skin, leaving goosebumps in their wake as the cooling night air brushed along her limbs. Her stomach churned in on itself as she finally reached the edge of the grass.

Despite the cold, her hands were clammy.

She wiped them on her jeans for the fourth time, aware that they were already sweating again. The street around was eerily quiet for so early in the night, the gazebo lit up, the only light in the middle of the park like a beacon.

"Hey," the rough low voice said quietly from behind her shoulder, making her jump.

Teo chuckled.

Holding her hand over her chest to calm it, she faced him with wide eyes, waiting.

"Thanks for meeting me."

"You said you'd take me to the headquarters and give me an intro to my magic," she said, taking note of the distance between them as he moved up to stand beside her, facing the Common. She followed his gaze, turning back to the place that had entranced her so much before arriving and yet had not been enjoyed because of all her life chaos.

"I am," he said with a mischievous grin. "Follow me."

Her heart sped as she watched him stride out onto the grass, pausing for a moment to offer his hand to her. She thought about not taking it, remembering how he'd used his powers on her the last time and at the party, and lied about it. He couldn't be trusted, but she needed the Arcana's intel and he was the key.

Let him think you are being manipulated. Let him think he could have you. Don't fight and see the information you can get, just don't give up your own information.

Lucy hadn't been a fan of her going off with a guy who could knock her out with a thought—and to be honest, neither was she—but she wanted answers more than anything else. This organization was the only tie to her family's lives before their deaths.

Mackenzie took his hand, aware that he could feel the warm dampness that coated her palm.

He said nothing but offered her a reassuring smile as he walked by her side toward the stone gazebo.

When they finally reached it, she looked around curiously, searching for some secret entrance as Teo grinned at her, eyebrows waggling, walking away from the stairs, leading her to the back of the structure. A blue mosaic sat behind bars at its base, probably to avoid damage.

Mackenzie looked at it, expecting something to happen as the silent motionlessness continued. "Okay, what am I supposed to be seeing here?" she asked, looking at Teo.

He grinned wider as if he'd been waiting for her to ask that question.

She glanced between him and the gazebo as he reached his free hand forward and touched the soft stone above it. The caged tile shimmered with black fog. She lost sight of it in the cloud and when it all disappeared, a small trap door sat in its place. Her stomach curled nervously at the prospect of crawling into it with Teo, and she sincerely hoped this wasn't going to lead her into trouble.

"Let's go," he said, releasing her hand as he opened the little door and went first into the dark tunnel.

Taking a deep breath, she watched him disappear into the dark, the urge to run readying her muscles with tightness. Another deep breath and she crouched down, crawling on her hands and knees into the black.

The air was musty, the smell of damp earth readying her nose as her fingers met cold dirt, packed tightly in a tunnel. Her eyes adjusted and the tunnel formed into view around her. It felt tight and claustrophobic but not tight enough that her body touched anything other than the floor.

Ahead, light slipped past Teo's body as he crawled in front of her easily.

Finally, the tunnel broke away and she found herself slipping down into a cavernous room that looked all too familiar. "What?" she squeaked, twisting to survey the room she'd been awakened in with wide, confused eyes. "There was no tunnel the other night. We left through the door that came out…"

"In the back of Amari's pub?" Teo offered as the words faded out of her open, flapping mouth.

"Yeah!" she said hurriedly, the grin growing on his face as he watched her flounder with confusion. She turned. The tunnel she'd just come through had disappeared, more of the cavernous room in its place. She raised her eyebrows at Teo, a silent question on her face.

"Magic!" he exclaimed, laughing.

She scowled as his amusement grew. "Okay, let's get

on with this intro magic then..." she said, her cheeks flushing red and hot at her own stupid question.

His laughing quieted as he took in her state, nodding in agreement. "Okay, come on..." He led the way again to a doorway that had appeared in midair.

She looked around, amazed at the extra room they'd found themselves in that looked like a living area in a cave.

"So, the Arcana leaders have left instructions for me to help you," Teo explained.

"They don't have a teacher for these kinds of things?" She smiled with a challenge in her eye, confused as to why she was leaving herself vulnerable with him when she could have been taught by someone else. She'd hoped it would have been.

"No, they the information on powers which they pass on and it's up to us to help each other using that. Do you have a problem with me teaching you?" he asked, clearly sensing the anxiety that ate at her.

She bit her lip, unsure if she should tell him the truth as her stomach churned. If she could give it a try it might minimize future issues. "To be completely candid, I know you used your powers on me yesterday when you said you wouldn't," she said bluntly, crossing her arms as she waited for a denial.

Instead, his eyes widened and he grew flustered.

"I... I... I could feel how anxious you were and I wanted you to feel at ease, and get your powers under control. I want you to feel comfortable with me," he explained.

It didn't soften her resolve. "You don't get to decide that for me. Don't ever do that again. I want to be able to trust my own emotions always," she said, sticking to her frustration stubbornly as she watched his face flush red with shame and his eyes drop. She felt powerful, feeling the anxiety disappear as she became sure she was safe.

"I understand. I'm sorry."

She let the silence of his apology stretch out until

finally, she caved. "Then yes, you can teach me for now. But the second something feels off to me, I'm out of here."

"Very well," he acknowledged, his face lighting again as he focused on her training and moved on. "Now, the first task of the training is learning how to hold the focus of your magic while other things are happening."

"That's impossible," Mackenzie scoffed. "I could only do it while I was wholly focused on the thing. The second I smiled or thought of anything else, no matter how small, the connection snapped."

"That's because you were thinking of your focus and will as all or none. You can build this skill of one central part of your focus always being tethered to your magic, even while chaos happens around you."

"A central tether…" she replied, chewing over the idea slowly. "Okay. I could try that."

"So your first task is to manifest and hold something in this plane of existence. As long as your tether to the magic holds, the object will stay."

"Okay, what did you have in my mind?" She dropped her smile as she set her muscles into position, coiled and tight like they represented her focus. She didn't care if she trusted the Arcana or him, she had a hunch their magic teachings would be true and helpful. And for now, she was sure she wanted to succeed at her magic.

"Okay, come take a seat and focus on the table. Bring a small rock into existence, will it into being, and hold it here. Just make sure that even if part of your focus fails, something is still holding it," Teo said, waiting to see if she understood or if he needed to give more explanation.

She didn't need anything more—she knew it was all going to come down to practice for her.

Taking a seat on the couch, she slid her shoes off and crossed her legs on its cushions, settling her body into a comfortable and readied position she wasn't going to need to move from. The sofa was perfectly welcoming, with just the right amount of softness for her muscles to embrace it but not too comfortable that she wanted to curl up and fall asleep.

"Do I use my hands?" she asked, her hands outstretched in front of her as though that was where her magic came from.

He looked at her demonstration and shrugged. "It depends on you. Some people with more physical magic, like you, prefer to, but others like me don't. Test it out and see what works best for you to keep that connection." He moved to a nearby armchair and took a seat. He was close enough to comment and assist if needed, but also far enough away to allow her to work on this individually—a comfort, her brain remaining free of the effect of his powers on her that usually made her dizzy and lightheaded.

Teo pulled out his phone and dropped his attention to the endless scroll of social media. Mackenzie was on her own.

With a sigh of mixed relief and anxiety, she watched the table intently, raising her hand and imagining the power passing through her.

Staring at the surface of the table, Mackenzie willed a small grey rock to rest there, relatively smooth with a couple of indents. She focused on the size and saw it in her mind's eye as clearly as possible before pushing with her magic, channeling it down her arm and through her hand to the table.

The rock faded into view as Mackenzie's face scrunched and tightened until it appeared exactly as she'd imagined.

It took every ounce of her to hold the rock in view, to not celebrate it and break focus, but she could feel the drain of it on her energies. She tried to focus on what Teo had told her, keeping a section of her tied to that rock in the center of the table, but she wasn't sure if it held.

"Good. Now keep it there but listen to my voice," Teo

said, glancing up from his device.

She felt the falter of the rock in this realm, watching it sputter in and out of reality as she fought to keep the tie in place.

"You're doing a great job, just keep the line open but be able to shift other parts of your focus. Come on, you can do it…"

The object completely sputtered out of existence and the table sat empty.

With a long loud groan, Mackenzie flopped against the back of the couch, feeling personally offended by the disappearance of the rock.

"Hey, it's only the first try," Teo said, seeing her frustration—and no doubt feeling her emotions oozing their way over to him.

He was right, but she was impatient and she had to work to swallow the foul-tasting thoughts that said she wasn't good enough.

She stuck her hand out again, sitting forward, eyebrows creased together.

This time it was easier to manifest, like slipping on a well-worn shoe, more comfortable with each use. Her mind remembered the shape and image she pushed for and barely a moment of full focus passed before the rock returned to the table.

Teo—despite having his phone ready for viewing—watched her adamantly.

Mackenzie's focus wavered at his attention. Should she even be practicing like this in front of him—giving away all her potential to someone she wasn't sure she could trust?

Still, he watched, the hairs on her body raising as she forced herself to ignore it—trying to keep her focus on the tie to her magic, making sure that it stayed as her mind tried to wander off, thinking about Teo and his actions until this point.

Her mind begged to run off on a tangent, to go back over his actions and try to find answers about whether he could be trusted. Was she overreacting?

The image flickered again, and the muscles in her hand flexed harder as though that could help push her outward.

The rock solidified in response. But the moment it was back in focus, Mackenzie found her mind wanting to wander again, wondering if she was paranoid and overthinking, or if she had every right to believe that she should be wary.

The image flickered and frustration heated her face. *Stay, damn it.* She swore at the rock silently, her anger holding it there for a moment as she glanced at Teo. Even when her direct eye contact with the rock broke, she could feel the drain on her energy that said it had stayed there, tied to her anger.

And as she smiled triumphantly, the anger fading, the rock disappeared.

"Fuuuuuuck," she droned, lying out on the couch and staring up at the stone ceiling, eyes shutting as her hands covered her face.

She heard Teo move before she saw him, sitting on the edge of the couch beside her, perched close enough for her to feel his warmth but not enough to be overwhelming. The closeness of his body was still tempting to her despite everything that had happened; her body was not listening to her brain on these matters. The forbidden nature of it ignited a spark in her.

"It's a good improvement, Mackenzie," Teo said quietly, taking her hand as she dropped it to watch him attentively.

She stiffened for a moment but kept his gaze, realizing that was as far as he was going to go. *He is respecting my other boundaries,* she noted to herself in shock.

No dizziness, no advances, just waiting for her. The idea of it made her soften, feeling warmer and safer with him than she had since their first date.

"Even just for the first day, it is good. Not many

people can even work that fast. Especially the Magician line, which is so complex."

Mackenzie smiled, glad for the encouragement as she sat up slightly, finding herself and her face closer to his. She waited for him to try to lean in or push further than holding her hand, but he stayed in place—not moving closer but not pulling away. "Thanks," she said. "I'm just impatient sometimes."

"You want to be better and there's nothing wrong with pushing yourself. Just don't be hard on yourself if it doesn't happen as quickly as you want it to." He smiled, his voice soft as her gaze met his.

She could feel the urge to lean in, to give in to that forbidden desire to just ignore his untrustworthiness and enjoy their bodies connecting. But if she gave in now, she'd regret it later and possibly open herself up to issues she hadn't considered yet.

Logic and rationality won out over her desire and she pulled back, clearing her throat, swallowing the extra saliva that had formed from her dark imaginings.

"Um…I know it hasn't been much, but I'm done with magic for the night," she said slowly, dropping her gaze from his to her lap.

He nodded in her peripheral, standing up slowly. Tension lined his jaw muscle with the frown before he pushed a soft smile on his face when he saw her looking.

Cold shivers crept up her spine.

"I'll walk you out?" he suggested, holding out his hand.

She glanced at it, thinking better of taking it, the desire in her freezing solid to a heavy weight in her gut.

She stood, plastering on a smile also.

"Sure."

17: THE TRAINING BEGINS

Mackenzie had barely finished the breakfast burrito Lucy had made her when she caught her best friend staring at her, an excited expectant grin pulling her lips.

"Come on, you *have* to show me," she whined, the grin never leaving her lips as she tried to sound commanding.

Mackenzie rolled her eyes, remembering her friend's disappointment when she'd come home and had been too exhausted to show off her new abilities. "I don't have to do anything," Mackenzie quipped, knowing it was driving Lucy's impatience wild not to know.

"Nice try. I'm the best friend, it's a requirement to show me new tricks," Lucy said, watching the laugh as it exploded out of Mackenzie's throat along with the food she'd been midway through chewing. Lucy dissolved into giggles at the sight.

Both girls grew red-faced with amusement as they caught each other's gaze.

It took a few moments before the amusement subsided enough for either of them to breathe, gaining composure slowly but surely.

"Let me finish my breakfast and then I'll show you before I disappear to college again." Mackenzie smiled, looking at the unappetizing chunk of chewed breakfast burrito that sat on her plate and the tiny piece of it uneaten in her hand.

"Aww, you have to go already?" Lucy said, pouting even as her eyes glimmered with amusement.

"Actually…" Mackenzie smiled, thinking over her schedule in her head. "It's a Tuesday, yes? My mistake, I have a few hours left."

"Brilliant! Magic show, let's go!" Lucy cheered, grabbing their plates and dropping them in the sink, hurrying off to the living area, clearly expecting Mackenzie to follow.

Mackenzie grinned to herself, popping the last bite of her burrito in her mouth, and jumped up from her chair to follow her best friend. Walking into the living area, she sat opposite her friend who had already reclined out on one of the couches. Smiling, she sat down, crossing her legs the same way she had done the night before.

"Okay, so as per last night's instruction, the point of the exercise is to manifest something into existence and hold it there and make sure that I can keep a tie of focus to my magic even when I'm doing other things," Mackenzie explained slowly as she reached in front of her, palms out towards the coffee table between them.

"So… it's magic multitasking…" Lucy verified with a grin she was trying to hide, unsuccessfully.

"Yes." Mackenzie gave a tight grin. "Except it's mentally draining."

"So it's magic multitasking," Lucy repeated with a giggle.

"Stop!" Mackenzie said, unable to control her own laughter. "Do you want me to do this or not?"

"Okay…" she said. "I'm sorry. Off you go."

Taking a slow deep breath, Mackenzie tried to pull her focus inwards and ignore Lucy's expectant stare.

Mackenzie imagined the rock in her mind's eye, the same one from the night before, seeing its smooth surface with the indents on the base and top. Pushing her power out, she manifested it into existence, feeling her power comply easier this time. And then she held, feeling the tether between her and the object, breathing deeply and focusing on a way to keep the tie.

Without looking up at Lucy, she explained, the rock already beginning to flicker. "Now I'm supposed to move my main focus to something else but keep the rock here regardless. But it's hard."

"Well, did you do it last night?"

"Yeah… When I got angry," she said, remembering the mental rage that had driven her.

"Well then, get mad," Lucy reasoned. "Keep that rock here and think about how badly you just want to hit Kai with it."

Mackenzie flushed with heat as her hands twitched tighter, her eyes blazing with a direct, intense focus into the rock's surface as though her eyes were lasers blazing a hole through it. Her magic flowed strongly through her hands, holding the rock there, tied to the anger she focused on.

"Okay, now hold it there, look at me, but vent about your anger?" Lucy suggested. Mackenzie's eyes lifted to her friend's and the rock flickered for a moment but held in place. She let herself feel all her anger at Teo's manipulation, at the life her parents had left her to, and at Kai's lies. Her blood ran hot, boiling in her veins as she let her mind spiral into her hatred ignoring the fact that she was staring at the one person who could dispel it all. She fought to hold on to the negative feeling, letting it flare in her gut and burn brighter.

For a moment, she worried about what would happen if she let it consume her.

"I'm pissed that he lied, that he made me feel things I hadn't before, and that he doesn't even seem to care that he hurt me. He just wants to stay blameless in this and make excuses or explanations, but there's nothing he could say that would change anything his family did, and what he didn't tell me when I gave him the chance," Mackenzie said, letting the anger flow through her limbs to the rock in a constant stream, the connection unbreaking as her anger fueled it. "I'm annoyed that Teo had posed as a friend but he's clearly trying to manipulate me and thinks I won't notice. Whether it's for the Arcana or because he wants me as more than I'm giving. I don't know and I don't care. He used his magic on me to get a make-out at a party, for god's sake. I mean, who the fuck does that? And he thinks now he's not using it that he's the good guy and I'll just climb on his lap? Fat chance."

Lucy nodded, frowning. A flash of pity crossed her face.

Angry tears welled in Mackenzie's eyes as she glimpsed the fleeting expression, the pity making the heat burst outwards like it had been doused in ethanol.

"And I'm angry that my dad decided to pull my mother in on this life when he had the opportunity to save her life. He had a chance to save me from *this...*" The tears slipped down her cheeks. Her fingers burst with energy and the rock disappeared in a flash of purple lightning from her hands.

Both girls flinched with a gasp as they looked down at the place on the table where the rock had been and the scorch marks burned into the table. They watched it for a moment with wide eyes and silence, neither daring to let their breath loose as the tension grew.

"Maybe anger isn't the answer," Lucy said quietly, breaking the silence and the tension along with it.

With a sigh, Mackenzie's shoulders sagged forward, finally feeling the drain her angry power had taken from her as she continued to stare at the singe mark on the table, feeling numb and exhausted. She supposed it was a very good thing Lucy was here, or she'd be crawling back up to her bed and never climbing out.

"Does it have to be angry? Do your father's notes have anything that could help keep the tie?"

"When I looked at it, he always said his focus lay in his determination, which he knew would never fade... It was a part of who he was." Mackenzie replied, thinking about exactly how her father had described it in his notes, or how the others had described their manifestation focus.

"Determination…" Lucy echoed, mulling the word on her tongue, struggling with the thought, like a honeycomb stuck in her teeth.

"They all had an emotion. Something in them that was consistent. The way they all described the Magician was that the manifestation and willpower were all tied to an attribute that was set in who you are. Lucy, I don't think I have something like that! I mean…Besides what, being an orphan… Numb…Naïve? Those are pretty stupid things to have as a magical powerhouse. Isn't it?" she rambled as nerves clutched at her heart. What if she couldn't do magic the way that her family had? What if she was destined to fail at this because she had nothing left in her life that was consistent besides misery?"

"Now you're being ridiculous!" Lucy snapped halting her hyperventilation before it had a chance to take hold.

Mackenzie's heart stopped as she glanced up at her friend, deadly serious and staring at her like she was an idiot. With raised eyebrows, she waited.

" *Willpower*, you dummy."

"Willpower?"

"Yes! You have the trait of your tarot, of your *family*, in you," Lucy said. "Don't you see that? I don't care if you've had days you wanted to give up and even some days you did, you always ended up leaving that behind. Mackenzie, you spent ten years looking for your mother *almost every day*. Even when people tried to tell you differently, you got up, searched for her, went to school, searched more, went to work, and just thrived even if you didn't feel like you were. You stood through everyone's opinions, and of your own sheer will you made it here to your family home on a scholarship. That was *you*! You never gave up hope and fought every day to either find your family or like now, find somewhere to belong. None of us would have made it this far if we'd been through what you had. You had your family with you even before you knew it. *You are willpower, KZ.*"

Mackenzie's face went limp, her mouth sliding open, but her mind found no words. She stared at her friend, feeling the tears slide down past her lashes and cheeks as a smile found its way onto her lips. Pressing them together tightly, she cleared the table with a jump, Lucy standing to meet her as she swung her body around her friend.

"You're welcome," Lucy whispered with a breathy laugh as she squeezed Mackenzie close. "It's true though, you have so much more willpower than you give yourself credit for."

Mackenzie and Lucy pulled each other closer, a comfortable silence falling between them as they held on and absorbed each other's comfort. Moments slid by as they enjoyed the safety of the embrace.

As usual, Lucy was the first to break it with her comments.

"But until you get control, we may have to move the magic show to the yard. Regardless of what's in control of it…" Lucy said, and Mackenzie could hear the grin in her voice.

Rolling her eyes as she stood back, Mackenzie took her best friend's hand and led her into the yard.

"Are we doing it now?" Lucy said with raised eyebrows.

"Yes. My willpower and I have to figure these powers out."

* * *

Figuring out how to pin down willpower as her magical powerhouse was harder than Mackenzie had expected, even now that she knew what her trait was. Happiness, anger, and love were all emotions she could recognize, but willpower...

As Mackenzie brought things to life again and again, Lucy watching on curiously, but she lost them the moment she drew her main focus away.

"Well, maybe we just need to figure out the source of your willpower?" Lucy suggested after a couple of hours of practicing in the high-fenced backyard.

Despite the calming scents that wafted through the area, Mackenzie's frustration was rising, and making everything in her zap with electrified impatience. She was beginning to regret her decision to skip college to practice her magic. "Do you have a magic-friendly shrink and a couple of years to figure it out? Cause I don't," Mackenzie replied, the venom of her annoyance dripping like poison through her tone.

"You don't need it. It's not *that* hard," Lucy quipped, ignoring the edge that wasn't meant for her. "You just need to think about *why* you're so determined with everything you do."

"I don't know..."

"Quickfire answer," Lucy commanded. "Go!"

"Because I want to make them proud!" Mackenzie let the words fall from her lips and hang in the air.

Lucy's eyes narrowed as she thought over her friend's words. "That's why you looked for your mom for so long?"

"Well... I had this image in my head of her being cold, alone, and lost in those forests and it was all for her. I couldn't deal with the idea that she might be out there, wishing for a rescue." It wasn't something she'd ever kept from Lucy deliberately, but at the time it had been too personal to share. It was a fear that had consumed her in ways she could never explain.

"And everything else was because you wanted them to be proud of who you were? As if they were watching you?" Lucy finished for her, swallowing the shaking that wavered in her voice.

She nodded in reply as her friend finally smiled.

"We found it! See? Wasn't hard at all!" Lucy sat on the neglected grass. "Now, try it but imagine your parents are watching too."

Mackenzie smiled slowly, letting her hands ready into position as she took a deep breath and watched the dead flat area where the grass didn't grow. She reached deep within herself to find the part of her that always longed for her parents to see what had become of her, imagining them watching from some secret place as she pushed, willing the rock to appear.

It complied easily and before she even had to focus on a consistent tie to her magic, she could feel it holding strong. Her eyes lifted to Lucy's, a triumphant smile on her lips as the rock stayed in place, not a single flicker on its surface.

"I think we cracked the code!" she squealed.

Lucy met her eyes with raised eyebrows and a mirroring smile. "Hold it and keep it there, I have a great idea!" Lucy replied, getting up and bolting into the house.

Mackenzie waited, the rock staying with her, the tie to her magic connecting to a part of her soul that made it much easier to manage. The drain on her energy had lessened dramatically and the excitement of figuring her magic out after hours of trial and error invigorated her with a new-found vitality.

Lucy finally reappeared, carrying an armful of balled-up pairs of socks.

"What's the deal with the socks?" Mackenzie prompted, but Lucy merely grinned back.

"You'll find out a little later when it's necessary," she said cryptically. "Can you summon something else? Can you manipulate that or even, like… make it fly?"

"I think manipulating the manifested object might be the next task."

"All right, KZ, make it fly." Lucy cheered.

Mackenzie's attention returned to the rock, her hand rotating at the wrist as though she were going to reach down and pick it up. Then, ever so slowly, her hand lifted, pulling the rock up with it. It required more focus than before, but she could feel it lightly. She smiled, glad her powers no longer required her to keep holding on to negative feelings. Triumph warmed her chest as she imagined whether her father would praise her power now, if he would think she'd learned his ancestor's power quickly and well. She was so busy smiling at the rock, imagining what her parents would say, that she didn't notice Lucy's movements.

Lucy took one of the balls of socks and tossed it at Mackenzie, thumping her straight in the face.

Mackenzie jolted.

Lucy gave a devilish grin as she lifted a new sock ball from the pile in her lap. At Mackenzie's absolute shock, Lucy keeled over in laughter.

Mackenzie's face softened, still wide with confusion but enjoyed the way Lucy's shrill giggle of a laugh echoed through the yard. Despite the chaos and corruption in the world around them, having Lucy in her corner made everything about this stressful journey happier—made her feel less apprehensive about the future.

"I don't know what I would do without you," Mackenzie said, drawing Lucy's attention out of her laughter.

The connection of smiles never broke between them as Lucy wound her arm back.

"Well, you won't even have to find out. Now, bring the rock back so I can try and break your focus again."

18: THE SEDUCTION

"I hope you know what you're doing," Lucy warned Mackenzie as she gave her a quick hug at the train station. "And if you get to the training and change your mind, it's okay. You don't have to go through with it."

"I appreciate your concern, Lucy, I do," Mackenzie said with a sigh and a sad smile. "But my mind is made up and I fully plan on following through with this, if only to see if I can get more information. I need to know more and I feel like he's not trusting me enough to tell me anymore. I need to do something drastic to ensure he thinks he's got me."

"Okay…" Lucy said, backing down despite the way that her lip creased in a disappointed frown. Lucy knew the impasse Mackenzie was at; after weeks of training with Teo every few days and with Lucy in her spare time, or catching up with her Arcana friends at college, Mackenzie still hadn't gotten any more real information out of Teo about the organization or her family.

"Well," Lucy said, "I'll be back in a couple of days after I sort this stuff out with my college roommate and bring a couple more of my things over. You promise you're okay with me doing my college work digitally and living at your house?"

"I welcome it," Mackenzie said with a smile. "It's

amazing."

"Okay then, KZ. Try not to have a crisis while I'm gone then."

"See you in a few, Luce." Mackenzie backed up away to the street, leaving her friend to sort out her train as she headed off to work out her own lack of information issue.

She walked back down the main street, amazed at how her life had changed in such a relatively short time since she'd first walked from this station. She took different turns, headed for a different entrance to the Major Arcana's tunnels, having learned quickly that there were many places where magic doors appeared.

Teo waited by the door to the witch museum, leaning against the outside wall, smiling to himself as he checked his phone. His eyes lifted as she approached, sliding his phone into his pocket as he grinned at her.

Mackenzie took a deep breath of the warm fall air and returned his grin. Now was the time to calm her mind and emotions, and she couldn't pretend this time: she had to find a way to make herself feel different while keeping her willpower in control of the show. She had to make him think she was falling for him, with no ounce of resentment, fear, or disgust in her body for anything. *Fake it till you make it and let yourself feel the dark thoughts for him,* she thought. *Embrace the forbidden.*

Teo pushed off from his place leaning to lead the way—as usual.

Mackenzie followed him up the stairs and into the foyer of the museum, watching as he brought tickets for both of them to see the introductory show. With raised eyebrows, she caught his glance as they filed in behind others waiting to see it, arriving just in time for the doors to the mini auditorium to open and invite them all in.

Searching for their seats, Teo took her hand and pulled her to ones he'd spotted that seemed perfect.

They both sat and she looked at the amount of people

around them in confusion, wondering how they were supposed to enter the Major Arcana's tunnel with so many around.

But he met her questioning expression with a wink as the final people filed in and the lights dimmed.

Red eyes lit up in the darkness, reminding her of Kai's red glowing beast-form eyes staring at her.

Calm down.

Teo squeezed her hand in the dark, indicating for her to stand from their place in the back row and guiding her around her chair to the wall.

She couldn't see where they were going but she felt a cold veil pass over her as she walked into where she could have sworn the wall had been.

Teo continued to lead, walking in the darkness where she didn't think it was possible, and then like the lights had been switched on, she walked into the Arcana's main cavern.

She'd gotten used to the feeling that she was Alice through the looking glass.

She'd also resigned herself to the fact that she wasn't going to be given great detail as to how they made it to the desired location every time besides "magic". It had become clear from Teo's ever-growing cagey answers of late that he didn't think she could be trusted yet—or that she wasn't ready to know.

Ignoring the twisting that was starting in her gut, Mackenzie forced herself to focus on the task at hand. She wished she had some alcohol to take the edge off, but unfortunately, she'd be left to her own abilities and controlling emotions. Looking at Teo, there was no denying he was insanely attractive; if she hadn't been so wrapped up in Kai when they'd first met, she might have even considered him an option and fallen for everything he'd laid on to her.

She had to focus on that. *He is hot. Majorly hot.*

He caught her staring him up and down. "What?"

"Uh… Nothing." Her cheeks flushed with heat. He'd

probably felt her checking him out too, that rush of primal attraction that had raced through her as she pushed all other thoughts and feelings of him aside. "Let's get on with training, shall we?"

This time, Mackenzie led, aware that he was grinning knowingly at her as she headed for the living area, letting herself feel the embarrassment. She embraced her confidence as she walked, grateful for her decision to wear high heels that showed off her butt this afternoon.

Just like every other time she'd met him here, no one else was around. It had been disconcerting the first few times she'd attended for training, but now she knew it worked in her favor.

She swung her hips as she walked, showing off the assets she knew she'd shaped from many hikes in the forest, feeling his eyes prowl her back as she moved. She dropped to the couch, unsurprised when he sat beside her, instead of in his usual armchair. She focused on the heat of their bodies close to each other in the cool room, just enjoying the physical sensation, ignoring anything that would have turned her off as though it didn't exist.

"So, what do you want to look at first?" she asked, keeping her voice low and sultry, leaving the double entendre in her words, implying with her tone as he watched her with interested eyes.

"Why don't we practice object summoning? I'll call something out and you summon it on the table," he suggested, to which she nodded. "Knife. Candy. Marble. Key."

As he called, she summoned, focusing on the first image that came to her mind each time, until he remained silent at the key, studying it carefully as he picked it up off the table. He handed her the key, which she took confused as he produced a lock from his bag. She knew the key wouldn't fit; why would her key fit a lock she'd never seen? But he showed it to her, a smile tugging his lips as he looked between her and the key she held open-palmed in her hand.

"Keep your focus on the key and manipulate it to fit the lock," he said.

Mackenzie stared at the padlock in his hand, a shiver creeping up her spine at the possible repercussions if she could pull this off. It both excited and terrified her. She nodded all the same, keen just to see if she could do it.

She and Lucy had worked on shrinking or growing objects or squishing them, but manipulating them to fit something else was a new concept she was itching to try. Taking the lock from Teo, she pushed the tip of the key into the lock, feeling the resistance of incorrect notches.

She closed her eyes, feeling her awareness creep to the key and the notches, focusing on making them malleable, letting them slide in as they met the correct answers inside the lock. It took several moments of concentration until finally, she heard the pop of the lock click apart.

With a triumphant smile, Mackenzie opened her eyes to look down at the lock and the key that sat perfectly inside it.

Teo's grin mirrored hers. "That's amazing, you're improving so quickly!" He reached over, squeezing her shoulder.

She didn't recoil from his touch, letting his warmth electrify her skin and leaning into it. Batting her eyelashes and looking up through them, she did her best to seem innocent, like she wasn't coming on too strong. She let her emotions do the talking as she admired him again.

"Enough to meet the rest of the Arcana now?"

"You really think you're ready to meet them?" he asked watching her and looking her up and down as though the answers to her readiness could be made based on her physical attributes.

"I think so," she said confidently, holding on to the powerful energy running through as his eyes scraped over her. She wanted him to feel it too. She wanted him to believe it was all because of his attention to her.

"Well, I'll tell them you're ready for your task to join and then you'll get all the information. How does that sound?" he said slowly, pulling his hand off her shoulder and letting it trail down her arm lightly, watching her skin goosebump in response. "I can't guarantee anything…"

"Perfect." She grinned, enjoying the fact she'd finally gotten the invitation to all the information she needed. Wrapping her arms around his shoulders, she hugged him quickly, sliding her whole body weight on him, letting her excitement at finally having answers flourish as she pretended to be excited by him. "Thank you!"

"No problem," he said, chuckling at her sudden excitement as his body weight slipped back to the arm of the couch, hers falling over the top of him.

Mackenzie lifted her face from his shoulder, drawing attention to the closeness of their faces with a glance at his lips. Sliding her leg to the other side of his body, she leaned forward, pressing her lips to his, sealing the promise of information with a kiss.

He wasn't insistent or rough like he had been the first time they'd kissed on the dancefloor, but more hesitant and soft as he waited for her to move to her limits. He only took what she was willing to give and she knew she'd have to make it clear she wanted him that way.

She needed him to believe it.

His mouth was warm on hers. Enjoying this was something so forbidden, but she knew to secure her information she needed to play the full act.

That was the plan, at least.

For now, enjoy the forbidden nature of it, embrace something dirty, and then pull yourself to reason afterward.

For a moment Mackenzie let herself enjoy the feeling of being wanted and needed by someone, feeling loved. She shouldn't be doing this, Lucy had hated the plan, but she also knew how heartbroken Kai had made her feel and for a single moment, this was a temporary filler.

So she just let herself enjoy the way Teo's hands began to expertly explore her body, her hair, her back, and the sides of her stomach. The way her body shivered under his touch with his rough fingertips tracing places of her she never knew were erogenous.

She opened her lips, letting Teo's tongue in where it lingered against her bottom lip, feeling the way they connected as they opened up to each other and letting the kiss deepen.

He relaxed into her, sliding one arm around her waist as the other came up to her face, pushing the hair back behind her ear before clenching his fingers in it.

She warmed, wrapping her legs tighter around his hips as she pressed their bodies closer.

The hand around her waist slipped to her butt to squeeze the cheek.

She enjoyed it, finding herself rocking, ignoring the deep pit that tried to get her attention from her stomach. Dizziness pulled at her, tugging like a weight on all her emotions for a moment, trying to pull away any negative ones that wanted to stop her in her tracks.

She wondered if she was getting enough oxygen for a second before any curiosity disappeared and the dizziness became like a drunk feeling that just let her feel her pleasure more thoroughly.

Mackenzie leaned forward to him again, enjoying the way he wrapped both arms around her and lightly traced his way with his fingers up the skin of her back under her shirt. Her body shivered and warmed under his touch as an ecstasy spread through her like strong alcohol, rushing to all her nerves, along with the dizziness she knew well. She couldn't help the gasp that escaped her throat and felt him smile in the kiss.

Like being taken over, body and soul, she slid her hips on his, feeling his soft touch grow insistent as he claimed her tongue. He lifted her, flipping over so that she lay on the couch with him over her as he moved down her throat, pulling at the ends of her shirt.

She felt his presence in her emotions, his control of ecstasy press into her mind. But just like any questions in her had been silenced, she couldn't hear any alarm bells that told her she wanted to stop. Everything was drowned by the dizzying ecstasy she couldn't help craving. She helped him, taking the ends of her shirt from him and whipping it over her head, and reaching for his.

His came off just as speedily, revealing the most defined set of abs she'd seen on a man in reality, and her eyes bugged out for a moment in surprise.

Teo embraced her surprise with an eagerness as his lips claimed her breast; she felt the ecstasy wash back over her as though she were going to burst with rapture. He moved to her jeans, looking up at her and meeting her gaze as he slowly and deliberately undid the button and fly, painstakingly slow, teasing.

She could feel the impatience coming in, needing it, not quelled by the pleasure that flooded her and she wondered if Teo pushed on her impatience, making it stronger to drive the need.

As quick as the feeling spiked, it disappeared as he pulled off her pants and kissed his way back up her body as the cool temperature of the room tickled her underneath his hot body.

His lips returned to hers as her fingers sought his pants, undoing them as he helped kick them off so that there was nothing between them.

She wrapped her legs around his waist; his help had already made her wet beyond what she thought she was capable of. He taunted entering her, making her mouth dry at the thought as she was flooded with a full-on release. She was almost ready to explode.

He entered her hard and she was done for. Stars danced in her eyes as a foreign noise, somewhere between a cry and a moan, escaped her lips.

"Oh god..." She breathed so quietly as his teeth kneaded her muscle and his length felt out every inch of her.

He chuckled against her skin as he continued to flood her body with pleasure, unlike anything she could compare. The only evidence she could breathe was the noises she made involuntarily as he pounded the way to their release, a sick feeling in the depths of her stomach that the dizziness fought to make her ignore.

19: THE FIRST TASK

The envelope for Mackenzie's first task had arrived that morning on her doorstep and ever since, her nervous system and organs had gone haywire. Her heart had been thrashing about in her ribs, and she was sure it would break out at any point now. The tightness in her chest made it seem as though no oxygen had entered her lungs for several hours now. And buzzing just under her ribs was the nervous energy of her stomach chewing in on itself.

None of this was helped by the lack of sleep.

This task is your key to answers and your way into Major Arcana. Get it together.

She shouldn't be this nervous. She'd been practicing with Teo and Lucy for weeks, making sure she could act on all aspects of her power: manifestation, manipulation, control, and magical focus.

If only Lucy could be by her side—but she wouldn't be back for a couple of days. Which made Mackenzie worry she wouldn't be able to keep her promise not to have a crisis while her friend was gone.

Not to mention her uncertainty about how much she should tell Lucy about her encounter the night before. The worst part of it all was that she hated to admit how much her body had enjoyed it. Teo was an escape she shouldn't have welcomed as much as she did.

It was addictive. It was the best feeling to lose herself in her pleasure completely and not be held back by any negative thoughts, fears, or emotions. She didn't love or care for Teo, and she knew they were using each other last night, but it was intoxicating.

Mackenzie shook her head quickly, as though she could shake herself free from the overthinking she was doing again.

She should be proud of herself instead of focusing on her anxiety. She'd managed to train and hone her magic while still taking her college classes and staying on top of the workload. And now she was ready to join a secret society—that may or may not help people. Either way, they'd thought her powers impressive enough to leave the handwritten envelope on her doorstep that morning.

The knock on the door had alerted her and when she'd arrived to open the door, only the envelope remained, the sender long since disappeared.

The first thing Mackenzie had noticed when she'd opened the letter was the feeling of old, rough parchment under her fingers as she pulled it from the envelope. Before she'd even begun reading, she could spot a long cursive script that looked as though a calligrapher had penned it.

The contents of the letter itself froze the blood in her veins and set her body into the frenzy she was now in, sure that this task was out of her skill and ability level.

The actual task itself had her questioning not only whether the Arcana was an organization that was good, but whether they might not be actually criminal.

Mackenzie Anne Harris,

We are delighted to hear of your desire to join the ranks of the Major Arcana. Teo has spoken at length about your training and provided details of your continued improvement and dedication. This is very befitting of your family's tarot and we are delighted to have your worth ethic as an asset to our organization.

The words had raced through her mind for hours and hours, electrifying her with their praise and confidence in her abilities but terrifying her at the same time. Was she sure that Major Arcana was 'the right hands' for what could be a magical weapon?

Despite the wording of the letter, something inside the twisting of her gut said that there was no option to decline this task.

What would happen if she tried? Nothing good, obviously. So, she worried, trying to ignore the way her body collapsed in on itself anxiously while she formulated a plan.

Surely the best idea was to go to the party undercover

and break into the basement and steal it then?

With a sigh, Mackenzie climbed the stairs to her bedroom and sat on the edge of the bed, staring at the open closet. She'd finally brought herself to house her clothing in it and stop living out of a suitcase. Some of her mother's clothing had stayed in there, and the rest—including her father's clothing—had ended up in a box in the basement.

Everything had to go smoothly tonight. She didn't want to know what it would be like if it didn't.

Mackenzie had stolen one of Lucy's dresses for the occasion. Her mother's dress—for reasons Mackenzie struggled to describe—seemed almost magical with its unfamiliar symbols.

Let's not draw attention to magic tonight.

There was an hour left before she could head to the party and throw herself in the deep end by putting her powers into action. But she couldn't stand being in the house any longer.

Slipping the red dress on, it hugged her body tightly as she zipped it up. She became aware of every crevice, curve, and roll on her body as she admired it in the mirror, aware now of certain shapes her body could make that she hadn't known before.

She took a deep breath in, swallowing down on her dry mouth to quiet the inner voice waking up in her head that said she couldn't pull this off.

Mackenzie ducked to the bathroom. Her makeup was an easy job—sliding on only enough eyeliner and mascara to make her eyes pop—before she turned her attention to her hair. It curled quicker and easier than she expected, for once behaving and giving her a small boost of confidence that something was going her way.

When she couldn't look at her reflection anymore, she grabbed her strappy heels from the night before slipping them on, and headed for the English pub Amari worked at around the corner.

Mackenzie barely saw Amari outside of class

anymore and knew she'd be currently working. Despite working for the Arcana—under a family tarot she hadn't been told yet—Amari seemed softer. She didn't strike Mackenzie as someone who'd go along with a corrupt organization, she seemed like the one to call it out. It was the only reason Mackenzie had given the organization the benefit of the doubt. Hopefully she'd get into the Arcana and find out she was being suspicious without reason.

Her steps to the pub sped along the sidewalk, along the edge of the Common to the corner. When she caught sight of it, the breath whooshed out of her and the tightness in her eased slowly.

As Mackenzie entered the pub, she headed straight up to the bar where Amari was working her way down the line of customers who waited on the other side.

At the sight of Mackenzie, the customer service smile Amari had been wearing lit up, the emotion reaching her eyes. "Oooh, you're all dolled up!" Amari cooed as her eyes ran the length of the tight-fit dress. "Lookin' hot!"

"Thanks, Amari. I have my first task, which seems to involve a frat party." Mackenzie glanced around as though people might listen in and understand what she was about to do. Her nerves jumped around again like electricity ran through her and her stomach chewed itself like it was insatiably hungry.

"Well, I'm sure you'll do great," Amari said, her eyes filling with recognition as if she knew exactly what Mackenzie had been tasked with.

"You really think so?"

"I do. I've heard Teo rave about your training as well as a *special session* last night, I heard." She shimmied her shoulder as he waggled her eyebrows.

Mackenzie did her best to grin and look embarrassed as Amari's eyes assessed her, not letting on how complex her feelings were about the night before. "Yeah…" She trailed off as she lost further words.

"You okay?" Amari said, her amusement flattening to concern.

Mackenzie couldn't tell Amari her true feelings about Teo, but she had to make sure Amari didn't think she was keeping things from her? "Yeah, I'm just stressing about the task is all..." she said quickly. Not entirely a lie, even if it wasn't the reason she'd made her faces.

Amari grabbed a glass behind the bar, filling it with cola, and then slipped some bourbon in it when other patrons weren't looking. She gave Mackenzie a reassuring smile as she handed the drink over, before disappearing up the bar to look after other people that seemed to be getting impatient as they flagged her down.

Mackenzie held the drink, slipping it between her lips and feeling the smokiness explode in her mouth between the bubbles of sweet soda. Her nerves suddenly simmered down—and a wave of lightheadedness hit her.

Her hold on the glass loosened too quickly and nearly dropped from her fingers. She tightened her hold again, jolting as she just managed to save it from slipping. Bourbon wasn't that fast-acting.

Mackenzie turned to the door, just in time to see Teo walk in with the breeze. The smell of his aftershave reached her before he did, sending reminders to her body of the night previous.

Teo's gaze trailed down her dress hungrily. The intensity made her feel naked under his eyes. It was as though he only saw her body and not the person it belonged to, and for a split second, there was disgust deep in her—squashed quickly by Teo's magic.

His eyes lifted and his expression softened as he joined her standing at the bar. "Excited for your first task?" he asked, his eyes lighting up eagerly.

"I'm terrified," she managed.

"Hey..." he hushed, taking her hand lightly where it rested on the bar as his face smoothed over with worry. "The Arcana wouldn't give you this task if they didn't think you could handle it. You told me you were ready."

"Thanks, but it's still a lot. It also doesn't seem like something you give a *novice* as their first task," she said. Surely they had someone more qualified than her. But even as she said it, she knew why; the targets had the same kind of magic as her, so she would be able to bypass their defenses.

Still, this seemed like a harder task for further down her training path.

"You can do this, Mackenzie, stop doubting yourself," Teo said sternly, putting an end to disagreement on the subject.

Her stomach twisted for a moment before Teo's power quelled it again, and she knew then she needed to be free of him for the moment. She needed to feel the warnings and messages her body was trying to tell her without interference.

"You know what? You're right. I just need to relax. I might go for a walk before the party, and get myself into the right headspace," she said. Knowing herself could be the difference between success and failure for this mission.

Mackenzie waved to Amari, who was glancing over at them—her bar slowly being swamped by a crowd of people wanting a drink—and headed out the door, Teo's influence slowly fading and her anxiety finding her again, making the buzz of adrenaline return to control her limbs.

On shaky feet, Mackenzie crossed the road and headed into the Common, her high heels sinking into the grass and threatening to roll her ankle. The further she moved into the park, the more she could feel her own emotions surging through her, and the brunt of it almost made her turn back to the bar.

When had she let Teo take such control of all her emotions? She wondered. But she knew the answer. She'd given him an inch last night when she'd allowed him in and he'd taken a mile. He'd taken full control of her last night and she couldn't help shivering at the memory.

And then she remembered his look in the bar and the shiver grew to a shudder. He was watching with that hunger like she could be his with just one small push of magic… and she'd barely had an inkling of discomfort. He'd squashed it before she could feel it properly.

If she had been aware of her own feelings, she would have realized how revolted that made her. To be looked at like an object, with no awareness of the person within, wasn't something that excited her. And now that she could remember it and feel it, it terrified her.

And yet Teo had withheld her own emotions from her, so she couldn't.

She couldn't do this anymore. She wasn't sure how to be rid of him, but she knew she had to be.

Walking through the Common, further and further from the pub, Mackenzie soothed herself. The grass stuck too tightly to her heels though and soon she had unstrapped her shoes to continue barefoot in the cool grass. The blades between her toes calmed her, her breath and nerves slowly stabilizing as she wandered through the dark park—and Teo had nothing to do with it.

The cool grass welcomed her, inviting her to lie on it, to become one with the earth and just escape.

She sighed, knowing the unlikeliness of the earth kidnapping her from reality. Though, to be fair, weirder things had happened in this town.

Noting the lack of people around, Mackenzie began focusing her mind and magic, manifesting a ball in her hand. It was rubber, firm, and real, and she watched it carefully as she tossed it, staying in shape and dimension until she caught it again. She could feel the tie to her magic, as though it were a real string flowing from her soul that she could snap at any time. But she kept it in place for the moment.

A smile spread across her lips as she noted the actual

progress she had made since she'd first discovered magic, remembering her failed attempts to keep a rock in mid-air without utter attention to it.

Dropping to the grass, Mackenzie lay back, letting her hair splay out amongst the blades as the green softness welcomed her. She let herself breathe the smell in deeply, enjoying the bittersweet earthy scent of the oak around her, and the dampness of the earth. She could smell rain in the air to come soon. For a moment, she held the ball tightly in her hand, feeling the way her own magic hummed from it, focusing on the sounds of the wind in the trees rustling its way through or the distant thrum of people chatter and just let herself feel… herself.

She tried desperately to push the task from her mind, not sure she even wanted to follow through with it anymore. But how could she refuse? What would become of her if she did?

20: THE HEIST OF WANDS

Mackenzie watched the throng of people move in and around the frat house, the party already kicking off before her arrival. She took a deep breath in, nodding to herself, glad that the many people could serve as a distraction for her to get in and collect the artifact with little attention from the house's occupants.

And still, she could feel her heart rate rising.

How many of the people in that house had magic like hers? Who might be watching her at the wrong time? The anxiety threatened to overtake her and drive her from the task.

Deep breath in… and out, she told herself sternly, following her own instruction.

She took the first step. Then another.

Feigning confidence, Mackenzie strode up to the house, following others as they entered past the frat-boy greeting guests at the door.

His eyes trailed up and down her body as she walked up to him. "You're new," he observed with a grin.

The buzzing of nerves in her quieted slightly as she realized he didn't have an Arcana photobook in his mind and clearly couldn't sense her magic; he honestly didn't know her real intentions as to why she was here. She needed to get her act together.

"I am!" she said, making her best impression of Lucy around boys after a few too many shots of vodka. "You noticed! I'm new to town actually, and was looking to make some new friends. When I was told of your party, I just *had* to come!"

He glowed, his chest buffing out as he moved from his position in the doorway to tower over her.

"Well, if you need anyone to show you around, come grab me," he said slyly, leaning in towards her, letting his face stop mere inches away from hers.

She made the effort not to pull back or show on her face how much she didn't want that. Instead, she took a deep breath and whispered her response, so her voice couldn't betray her. "How about I grab a drink and you can help me get acquainted with the area?" She let the innuendo seep into her voice as she glanced down at his chest and waist as though she could see through his clothes. She let the curious smile sit on her lips and then slowly moved past him towards the kitchen, glancing over her shoulder as he watched her retreat into the house. He didn't follow her, but she could tell she had him on the hook.

She reached the doorway to the kitchen and his eyes returned to the front of the house as more people walked up to the porch. Working quickly, she returned to the main entry hall and climbed into the crowd of people at the base of the stairs, hoping the tall people around her would shield her from the view of the frat-boy in the entry doorway.

Mackenzie glanced at the door under the stairs that she assumed led to the basement, and tried to see if anyone noticed her attention to it.

All the others around her stood chatting with their drinks, not paying her any mind, barely glancing at her in the red dress before moving on to someone else.

She shuffled through the people and pressed her back against the door as though she didn't notice it was there, glancing around at the room. There were too many people close by, too many possibilities of one of them being a frat-boy from the household who would notice if she opened the door. Feeling behind her with one hand, she clasped the doorknob, checking if it was locked.

There had been some hopeful place in her chest that had wished this would be easy and all she'd have to do was disappear through the door when no one was looking.

Things were not going to be that easy.

Her hand barely twisted before the lock stopped her from turning further. Her heart sank.

Cursing under her breath, Mackenzie looked out at the room. She'd need a distraction to get in the room once she'd unlocked it.

The first objective still remained; unlock the basement door.

Breathing deeply, she remembered her training exercise from the night before. She drew from the soul of her magic, forming a key in her mind before pushing her awareness out and manifesting it in the hand she had hidden behind her back.

Slipping the key slowly into the lock below the doorknob, she felt the resistance. Shutting her eyes the same as the night before, she let herself reach out, molding the key to the lock, feeling it click its way into the keyhole. Knowing it was in place, expanded to all the intricacies of the inside of the lock, Mackenzie changed her focus and the key shifted to be solid brass metal.

She waited a moment, her heart quickening as she slowly turned it in the lock, hoping.

It clicked, turning easily and setting her heart rapidly beating with excitement. Fighting the smile that wanted to break out on her face, Mackenzie kept her poker face and the string of magic in place until she was sure it was fully unlocked.

Her eyes snapped open. Now all she needed was a distraction.

Mackenzie's hand didn't leave the doorknob as she stared around at what she could see of the house. She could glimpse parts of the living room—which had turned into the dance floor –the main entry hall, and the stairs above her somewhat. She didn't have many options without moving from the door. She held on, knowing she couldn't leave the basement door unattended but knowing that the longer she lingered, the more danger she was in.

A plan formed in her mind. It was risky, but she was short on time.

And it would definitely be a distraction.

Taking a deep breath, Mackenzie pushed her magic out, leaving one string tied to the key in the door as she formed a large invisible mallet at the windows in the front of the house. She knew this would alert the frat boys that there was a magic user in their house, possibly even making it clear who she was. So the moment this was released she needed to run.

She let it fly through the glass, losing connection with the mallet as it broke through the largest window with an almighty smash.

The glass exploded outwards.

People around the room ducked in terrified gasps and screams.

The room quieted.

Everyone around her ran to the windows, those standing at the base of the stairs disappeared, and Mackenzie knew her timer had started. The frat boys would realize their problem soon enough.

Twisting the knob and slipping inside the door, Mackenzie removed the key and made sure to shut it behind her. The lock clicked across, trapping her in and she turned and raced down the stairs as quickly as her heels would allow.

Her hand opened, she let go of the magic tie, and the manifested key faded out of being before it even touched the floor.

Trying to get her eyes to adjust to the dark, she rounded the corner of the basement level and the need suddenly fell away. The basement was a near replica of hers. There was a stone floor with walls adorned with artifacts, although their artifact collection stretched around all their walls, rather than just covering one. Downlights illuminated items that Mackenzie reasoned were probably of major importance, and it was mesmerizing.

Reminding herself of the mission at hand, she scoured the items in an attempt to find the cuffs she'd been commissioned to find.

Item after item she glanced over, realizing none of these matched what she searched for. The clack of her heels on the stone floor made her flinch as her impatience drove her quicker. The progress was too slow for her liking. She was acutely aware of the muted sounds above as she tried to stay focused on the items in front of her but the longer it drove on the more her ears pricked up at every noise.

Knives, swords, maces, and even a few chain whips glinted back at her from the wall, and a couple of pieces of silver jewelry hung amongst them. She fought off the growl that wanted to escape her throat. *None of these are even close to what I'm looking for.*

Mackenzie swore as she glanced over the items again, unable to find the cuffs. She checked in the darkness, trying to keep her breathing under control as she looked again and again.

"Come on, Kenzie," she whispered as she tried to figure out her next move. "You didn't think it was going to be *this* easy, did you? Your magic could find it surely."

As the words slipped from her mouth into the quiet dark, she spotted a sword that stuck out to her. It was remarkably familiar. It was a short sword with a black stone orb in its silver hilt that called to her, the same as the last.

But the call this time was subtly different; the black stone orb seemed to glow with purple lightning from inside.

Mackenzie reached out and felt the hum of power glow like a vibration through her ears.

A deafening bang sounded as the power exploded from the orb.

She flinched, cowering down and sheltering her face as she held the sword.

She opened her eyes, the silence making her feel sick as she realized the noise could easily have been heard from above. Her skin and organs buzzed with a violent nervous energy that made her sick.

The damage done by the stone was different this time. It had completely missed her, embedding instead in the walls. This time, her wrists, which had felt ice cold after the explosion, were the home of two gold chunky cuffs. She'd bet anything they were etched with symbols on the insides.

"Found you!" she whispered, excitement flipping in her stomach.

The noise of the lock clicking above her sounded. Excitement turned to nerves. She let the sword clatter to the ground.

Mackenzie ran into the darkness of the room, finding a couple of boxes in the corner. She ducked behind them as multiple sets of feet clonked down the stairs. Covering her mouth with her hand as a precaution, Mackenzie lay back on the ground between the boxes and the wall, keeping as low as possible. The ground was cold, and she fought her body's instinct to sit back up as the frat-boys moved to where she'd been standing.

She waited, listening as they swore under their breaths at the damage and the sword on the ground. She heard movement as they surveyed the rest of the weapons, likely trying to figure out if anything else was missing.

"You know what this means, don't you?" the first guy

– the one that had manned the front door – said.

"Yeah…" the second one agreed quietly.

"It means the Magician is awakened and the Arcana's got their claws in them," the first one responded anyway, obviously uncaring that his friend already understood the implications.

"Well, we need to find them. They can't have gotten far!" the second said, heading back up the stairs, his friend lingering for a moment before following behind.

Mackenzie waited as still as possible until she heard the last step and then finally the door shutting above her. She puffed out a relieved breath, acutely aware of the cold metal of the cuffs against her wrists.

She waited a moment for the shakiness to pass, feeling the relief at not being found yet. But she still had a long way to go.

The new objective was getting out of the house undetected. Mackenzie sat up slowly, cautiously listening for any further sign that the door above her was going to open again. Surveying the basement area, she finally spotted her answer hiding in the darkness; stairs.

Opposite where she'd entered were stairs leading up to a tornado cellar door on the side of their house. Hoisting herself up off the ground, she ran on the toes of her shoes, wary that a single clicking noise might bring the boys back to the basement.

She climbed the second set of stairs and, using the same trick as before, she willed the key into existence, molding it as she found the perfect shape. Slipping it into the lock quickly, working the same magic as before, Mackenzie felt it turn solid under her fingertips. She wanted to smile at her fortune, excited by the feeling of power in her, the thrill of the situation making her heart skip a beat as she turned the key in the lock quickly and pushed the door open.

Peeking out, she checked to see if anyone was outside.

Glass littered the otherwise empty grass and she bit her lip anxiously.

She slipped out the door and tiptoed across the grass in her heels, not willing to take the shoes off yet and risk cutting her feet. She held her wrists in front of her, out of view of the house as she started to walk away calmly. If she ran, she'd be chased down easily. They were on the lookout for a thief after all.

She cleared the front yard carefully, with no shouts to announce her departure, and could feel her breathing start to return to a relieved, slower speed.

Mackenzie moved to the edge of the yard, lined by pristine white pickets, and placed her hands on the fence, vaulting over easily. Both her legs cleared the wood despite the dress holding her legs together tightly. Thank god for high school gym class.

She landed on the other side of the fence, however, her ankle rolled over uncomfortably.

Hissing in air, she dropped to the grass in front of the paved path and sank to her butt. She fumbled quickly with the straps of her heels, sliding them off and pulling herself to her feet again. Her ankle twinged and she couldn't help bending her knee and pulling her weight off that foot, grimacing at her own stupidity.

I have to keep moving, she told herself sternly.

Mackenzie stared across the street through the Common to see the opening of her own street on the other side. Should she even be headed directly home, considering she'd just stolen?

Stop delaying. Just start moving somewhere else, anywhere else. If you stay too long here, you'll get caught.

Holding her hands close to her chest, keeping her wrists out of view of the house, Mackenzie walked towards the Common, crossing the road. She walked past a willow tree, sliding her body behind the trunk and away from sight, the throbbing in her ankle threatening her entire task. She leaned against the tree, pulling the weight off her foot entirely. Home was so close, but she wasn't sure if she could make it.

Her feet left the ground entirely as she was suddenly tossed into the air.

For a moment she was weightless, her whole body flying headfirst away from the house she'd left—

And then she fell, hitting the ground hard, her head ricocheting against the grass, her spine jolting at the impact.

Black and white dots danced in her vision. Her brain throbbed painfully, everything in her skull rattling as the earth embraced it.

Her focus went fuzzy; *what happened?*

The frat-boys raced over to where she lay in the open area of the Common, away from the lights and the tree.

"Quick, Matt! Grab her!" One of them yelled, and the entrance doorman seized her upper arm before she could register what had happened.

She was pulled to her feet, her ankle twinging again, a pained cry escaping her lips.

Matt didn't care. He held her up, letting the weight fall to one leg and supporting her enough to keep a good grip on her. He looked almost pleased with her injury – until his eyes rested on the gold bands that hugged her wrists. His lips pressed tightly and his hand gripped her harder as his friends made it over to her too.

As her awareness of her surroundings returned to her slowly, Mackenzie counted four frat boys in total.

She had no idea what these guys would do to her and didn't want to find out. Something told her that magical artifacts didn't fall under police jurisdiction.

Taking one deep, centering breath, Mackenzie manifested invisible walls between Matt and herself, and the other frat boys, ramming them out and throwing the others away.

She dropped the magical tie and brought a knife into her free hand, slicing quickly at the fingers that held her arm.

She ran quickly, leaving her shoes and holding on to the knife.

But the frat-boy recovered quickly, launching after her and manifesting what looked like handcuffs.

Flailing, she swung the knife as he came closer to her, unable to outrun him. The knife missed him entirely.

He dodged and ran at her again, then fell back, giving her more space to run in the general direction of her house.

She knew she couldn't give away her home location but she needed to be closer to the public. *Surely they are limited around normal people,* she reasoned.

Maybe she could get them close enough to the pub and the people there so that she could get away.

As she bolted past a tree on the outskirts of the park near her street, she was off the ground again. Her head hit the tree, but this time she didn't fall.

A tightness wrapped around her throat and she struggled to suck in air.

Panic set in as her legs dangled, but the more she struggled, the worse she felt.

Her windpipe crushed in and dizziness threatened to rob her. She couldn't make her magic strong enough to manifest anything; the tie to her knife snapped and the weapon dematerialized.

No way out.

They raced over to her, and she was vaguely aware that Matt's hand was outstretched.

He reached her, holding something to her throat, keeping her in place.

Her vision blurred.

A large black mass grew in the darkness behind the frat-boy...and red glowing eyes emerged. Mackenzie's awareness finally started to fade to black, and she could feel herself slipping as the red-eyed beast pounced on Matt.

21: THE TRUTH

Mackenzie's body clattered to the ground as the magic holding her to the tree disappeared. Her knees buckled as she tried to catch herself, falling forward onto her stomach and hands.

She pushed up slowly, worried that the frat-boys would be upon her again in an instant, but they were not concerned with her, they were too busy with the animal that had claimed their friend in its teeth.

The black furry mass shook his head vigorously, throwing Matt's body around until finally, it released its teeth, flinging him across the park. Some of the boys screamed, one running in an attempt to escape, and the others to check on their friend. The beast growled at them, prowling toward them. Matt – miraculously alive but injured – struggled to his feet as his friends reached them. They all backed away from the creature, hauling their friend alongside them, moving off. The beast only followed them for a short time, ensuring they disappeared.

When the men had gone far enough to be sure they were leaving, the creature padded back towards Mackenzie. He looked proud of himself as he moved over towards her, but even the sight of him had her retreating in a crawl until she was backed against the tree, her heart hammering in her ribs as she held her breath.

He slowed, moving tentatively, keeping contact with her eyes as he drew close.

A rush of wind blew her hair as a flash of light blinded her, and when her sight returned, Kai was crouched down in front of her.

The fear and hesitancy in her that had been brought on by his beast form was replaced quickly with fiery hot rage, her heart hammering for a different reason now as she let her breath loose in an almighty command.

"Leave me the fuck alone!"

He moved to check her injured ankle.

"I don't need your help!"

He looked up at her, his eyebrows raising so much she thought they'd leave his forehead. Abruptly, they settled into a scowl as his eyes iced over with a hardness she'd never seen in him before.

"*Clearly* you fucking do! What the hell were you thinking going up against them, you were probably going to end up dead!" His hands moving away from her ankle as all care for her injuries disappeared.

"That's none of your business!" she said, pushing her wrists underneath her butt as she tried to pull herself up onto her feet. Her ankle complained but as she worked her way slowly, he stood up beside her, watching curiously.

She crossed her arms, determined to be free of him as soon as possible and prove she was fine. She stood tall on her ankle, holding her face as still as possible through the twinges of pain—

And Kai caught sight of the gold bracelets around her wrists. "Tell me you did not steal those for the Arcana." He said it so quietly, his voice breaking as his anger dropped and his eyes widened with fear.

"What does it matter if I did?" Mackenzie said, not denying it but not confirming his theory either as she crossed her arms tighter, hiding the cuffs from view.

"Because that would be the stupidest thing you'll ever do," he said, his eyes meeting hers, pleading silently for her to heed his words.

"And why would I trust a word you say?" she countered. She could barely stand to look at him, but she was even more stubborn about not wanting to back down. "Your family murdered mine."

"What?

"You heard me," she spat, holding her ground as confusion twisted his face.

His eyes didn't leave hers.

"Why would you think that?" he questioned.

She blinked a couple of times, reeling. Her frown turned up in disgust as she prepared to watch him try to fake his way out of it. "Because you told me that."

"Hate to break it to you, Kenzie," Kai said, his face slowly falling into an amused smile, making her body radiate with raging heat. "I didn't tell you *that.*"

"I was in hiding from your father after he killed mine and you just *happen* to find me? Not to mention the fact that you were in my hometown the day my mother disappeared too!" she said, her voice growing in volume as the venom of her anger dripped into her voice, aimed at him. She kept her arms crossed, worried she'd fry him with purple lightning again.

"I was there to protect *you*," he yelled back as though it were the most obvious fact in the world.

She froze, her heart stopping as her breath caught in her throat. "What?" she breathed, barely a whisper.

"Ask me what you want direct," he told her. "Be specific. I can't lie and you know it."

"Did anyone in your family murder my father?" she asked, her chest tightening as though everything rode on this one answer.

"Absolutely not," he said confidently, releasing all the tension in her, and with it, her anger. "I thought you were pissed at me for lying to you about knowing who you were, but fuck… Kenz… My family would never have murdered yours!" he said, running a hand through his hair.

"I don't understand..." she said, unable to make sense of all the information being thrown at her.

"My family and I were there, yes. We were supposed to protect and we failed. My dad failed. I didn't tell you that I knew who you were, but I'd never hurt you or your family, and neither would my parents!"

Mackenzie stood still, watching him, meeting his eyes, seeing his truth.

A wave of relief washed over her.

Unable to keep up her stubborn pose anymore, adrenaline wearing from her body, she sunk to the ground.

He moved to her quickly, and she couldn't help curling into the warmth of his chest.

She hadn't realized how tight her body had been wound by the hatred she had tried to feel for him or by the rage of betrayal she had felt. Now it was gone she sucked in air, finally escaping from the depths of the ocean of negativity she had kept herself in the past several weeks. Tears escaped her as she breathed deeply, his arms around her, the tightness in her body gone.

"Hey, it's okay..." he whispered, his hand stroking her hair. "We need to get you out of the open though, in case they come back."

She didn't move, couldn't move. All efforts to leave his arms had evaporated the second the truth had slipped from his lips.

He didn't try to ask her again. Instead, he pulled her closer into his chest, hooked one arm under her knees and the other behind her back, scooping her up and walking in the direction of her home. As they walked, he glanced back and forth, side to side, checking to make sure no one was following.

At the house, Kai paused at the front door, looking at her expectantly.

She pulled away from his chest just enough to reach

into her bra and pull out a key.

His eyes followed the plunging neckline of her dress, eyebrows raised before his gaze followed her hand to the front door, a smirk pulling his mouth up.

She chuckled as she slotted the key in the door, turning it easily and opening it for them.

Kai maneuvered them through the threshold before placing her on the couch in the living room, leaving her for a moment so he could close the door, then returning to sit by her feet.

They kept each other gazes in the silence, drinking the other in, nothing but the sound of their breathing filling the dark room.

She wanted him on her.

I'm being selfish, right? After everything I've been through tonight, a bit of emotion running this show is allowed, right?

Only the need for answers held her back.

The silence filled the space between them, her heart beating rapidly as her cheek heated. As the quiet continued, she had to fill it, sure if it strung on too long he would hear how her heart raced.

"What's the truth?" she asked, seeing his questioning eyebrows and tight lips in response.

"About which part?" he asked quietly, keeping her gaze.

"All of it. What's your involvement with me, the Arcana, my family… All of it," she responded. She wouldn't make her decisions with only half the answers ever again.

"Okay… My parents were close to yours. They got in trouble and my parents were in it too. Your father was the one who got the worst of it, and when he died, your mother fled with you. With me in tow, my parents found her to warn her that it wasn't over and that they were all in trouble, but they didn't know they were being followed. Your mother left you with a friend and tried to flee, but… I don't think she made it."

"Why didn't she just leave me with your parents if they were so close?"

"Because there was a target on my parents' back too, and when they realized what had happened to Anne, they returned me to Salem. I grew up with family friends while my parents disappeared."

"I'm sorry. I didn't know." She responded, her heated cheeks and racing heart going still and cold at his story.

"Like you, I've learned to live with it."

"Then why come back to the place I lived?"

"I saw you when we were children. I knew who you were from a distance and as you got closer to being eighteen, I heard whispers that the Arcana had found you. I appeared that day to find you and see that you were okay. And then… I'll admit, I was fascinated. I watched you day after day, still searching for your mother, and I tried to be careful. I made sure you couldn't find me, that I was just a protector from afar…"

"And then I saw you."

He nodded carefully, watching her reactions.

Her heart sped, thumping in her chest as he continued.

"I caught your eye and my beast form… craved you. I shifted out of it but it was no use, I wanted to get to know you. I didn't want to rock up at your house and frighten you, but I had to know you. You didn't exactly socialize with the outside world much though. I had a stroke of luck that day when you went to the diner and I knew that was my only chance to be closer to you in person. To be around you in more than just beast form. And *you* came up to *me* and as soon as we talked, I knew I wanted you in more than just some physical sense."

She didn't know what to say, didn't know what she could say. All she knew was that her heart, as it tried to beat sporadically, was going to burst as her breath kept catching in her throat.

"I'd been watching you for so long and then finally

there you were, learning about me. The girl I'd seen with a fire only for finding her mother came alive for *me*. Your eyes met mine and they weren't filled with tears or pain, your steps were joyous when you walked through the forest with me. You enjoyed me as much as I did you, and I knew I couldn't let you go. I wasn't going to stay long –the longer I stayed, the more you were at risk of the Arcana finding you."

"So why not tell me?" she asked, interrupting, desperate to know the answer, to find out why they couldn't have just continued from where they'd left off and never had the break between them.

"Because if you had a tie to your parents, you would have run towards it, not away. The moment we kissed, it was too late to tell you the truth. If I said the words about my past and your family's after that, I knew I'd lose you and… I'm selfish. I know that."

It went quiet between them. He looked at her expectantly and she was unsure how to tell him that this was a better reunion between them than she could ever have imagined. That every word he said was an uplifting bounce to her heart, and she feared the moment it might all come clattering down.

"But I ended up in Salem anyway."

"You did, and if I'd known you were going to come running for the bear's den, I would've stayed in contact. Instead, you arrived here and by the time I realized, you were already with *him*." Kai's voice turned gruff as his eyes glazed over with the memory.

Mackenzie cringed, her lips tight as she also remembered, the spin of guilt in her stomach. She knew she'd let herself 'move on quickly', but she also hadn't been sure she'd ever seen Kai again and she had just been trying to live more openly, the way Lucy had invited her to.

She remembered the looks on both of the boy's faces, the hatred between them, and how vicious Kai had been at the party, trying to separate Teo and her because of his jealousy. It both excited and terrified her.

She'd never been the kind of girl who appreciated jealousy in a man, but how could she not be a little turned on that he was fighting to remove his competition and be with her… Was that not biological animal instinct?

Kai glanced at Mackenzie's face, seeing the way her eyes dropped to her fidgeting hands and her lips grew tight, the guilt written on her face. Reaching out, he laced his fingers with hers and waited for her eyes to return to his.

"I don't blame you. I know that you didn't think you would see me again either. I'm just annoyed that it happened the way that it did," he said softly, his voice sincere and silky, low and caring.

She nodded, not trusting her voice as he continued carefully.

"By that time though, they'd realized who you were and clearly awakened you. And now… from what I can gather… they've got their claws in you."

His eyes glanced down at the gold bracelets that still hugged her wrists, the cold metal thrumming with a power she'd never felt before. She sensed she could reach out with her awareness and focus and use them, but she wasn't sure what that would do.

She'd been ignoring them in the hopes she'd never find out. If they were as dangerous as the Major Arcana claimed, surely she shouldn't dare use them? No matter how tempting the power was.

She gave her head a shake. "They didn't *get their claws in me.* I heard what they had to say and being an organization that claimed to do good… I believed them," she said quietly. She could recognize the lies the second they spilled from her mouth.

Kai looked at her for a moment, probably tasting the lie of omission in the air before continuing with the conversation as though his magical power hadn't just told him the answer.

"You could've heard my side out," he said simply, referring to when he'd rocked up at her door and she'd tossed him away with her magic.

She cowered into the couch, embarrassed by her actions. If she'd listened to his answers, things might have turned out differently. "I could've, but I was so mad and I believed what I'd been told. I saw you at the party, so different from how you were when we met, and I… just realized that I didn't *know* you… I didn't know you well enough to tell what your everyday personality was and I couldn't make truth from lies. When they told me the story and I heard your initial answers to my questions, it just… fit."

"That my family killed yours?" he said incredulously.

"Well… Yes. My mom's friend said my father got in with the wrong people, and then Teo told me the same but claimed that the wrong people were your parents. I didn't have any other answers to go on and clearly when I interrogated you about it…" she tried to explain, fighting shakily to find words to make him forgive her naivety.

"You slotted my answers into what you already had," he finished for her, nodding as his eyes glazed over with a faraway look.

"I did," Mackenzie confirmed, picking at her fingernail cuticles as guilt chewed through her stomach. She could feel that pull of her bed, how easy it would be just to climb under her covers upstairs and never emerge. If she did that, maybe she wouldn't continue the mistakes she seemed to be making at a near-constant rate.

She didn't know what was right, wrong, truth, lie, or a mistake anymore. And in the rush of chaotic confusion, it seemed less troublesome to just do nothing.

Like a shock jolting through her, she remembered the obligations she'd been tasked with that would chase her even into her desired nothingness. *The Major Arcana.* She glanced from her cuticles to the gold bracelets, glinting in the dim light as she rocked her wrists back and forth.

"You know you can't give them over, right?" Kai said clearly, watching her fascination.

She looked up at him, seeing the seriousness in his eyes. It solidified the initial fear she'd held about the organization early on.

Lucy's mistrust had been right the first time. Mackenzie had lost sight of that.

"How bad is it?" she found herself asking as she sank back on the couch, bracing herself for what was to come.

"Are you sure you want to know?"

22: THE TIME FOR ANSWERS

"Kai, I need to know." Mackenzie sighed, her eyes pleading with his. "I need to know what I've gotten myself into."

He took a deep breath, running his hand over his head, smoothing sandy blonde hair too short to do so as he looked down at the gold bracelets.

She wanted to hide them, force him to look up at her. Instead, she clasped her hands together and waited patiently as he sat in the silence, his mouth opening and closing like a fish gulping for air.

The waiting was agony, her stomach twisted violently as her brain thought over worst-case scenarios. "At least tell me what the bracelets do?" she pushed, hoping to start him into talking about some of it. "I know that the Arcana said they were dangerous in the wrong hands, but if they're in the wrong hands, what do they do?"

A moment further of silence continued before Kai sighed again and looked up at her, no amusement in his eyes.

"What do you know about the history of the tarot powers?" he asked, catching her off-guard.

"Ahh... Only that it was started by a woman who fled persecution during the Salem Witch Trials." The name Sarah Good had been lost in the chaos of her weeks of training and learning.

"Well, it did. Sarah Good was the woman who once held all the powers of the tarot. It was a power gifted only to her initially, but as the witch trials began and she was accused, she wanted the power to continue to help those who could not help themselves, rather than use the powers to save herself. So, she split the powers up into each of the traits of the cards and gifted them to those in the community with the purest hearts, who swore together they would work in the shadows, helping the world advance for the good of all people."

It was hard to believe that not long ago this would have seemed like fairytale mythology, and now it was something she accepted as truth.

"The Major Arcana was once a mighty organization that did work in secret helping people, as I'm sure Teo has claimed they still do. Maybe he even believes that. But somewhere along the way, more recently, they've grown tainted and corrupt, serving those willing to pay the most. Those bracelets have been passed down since the first Major Arcana lines, designed for when the right individual came along to reunite all the powers in someone so pure of heart that the Arcana can be whole again," Kai continued.

The room was still and cold against Mackenzie's bare arms, goosebumps rising on her. She would have gone to search for a blanket, but his words held her in place, forcing her to breathe slowly as she stared at the bracelets, trying to see the age in their gold. The color hadn't dimmed and still glinted like it was new. "That doesn't exactly scream ultimate dangerous weapon. If it's designed to help reunite all the powers into... the best person to exist?"

"When you say it that way? No, it shouldn't be. But it can be used by someone who wants to take powers instead. Someone who isn't the pure-hearted destined one."

"Oh." The weight of the power of the bracelets flooded her with realization. That feeling she'd had of immense power, could that have been the bracelets' ability to steal other's powers away? Was she feeling the tempting taste of Kai's power on the edge of her abilities? Taking a breath, she flipped the bracelets over, searching for a clasp but finding none and seeing nothing to unhook them from her.

She could feel her heart rate taking off, and her breathing grew shallow and quick, the lack of oxygen making her frenzied. Her fingers scrambled furiously for the edges of the bracelets, pulling at them, trying to separate them from her to no avail.

Kai's hands covered her wrists as he leaned forward, his eyes locked onto hers. "Calm down. It's okay. You're not going to take anyone's powers. There's a spell that needs to be recited. So breathe…" he said, waiting and watching for her compliance.

Like meditation, and with obviousness, she inhaled through her mouth and blew the air out in a sigh on his face. She took a second breath, seeing his hesitation in relaxing his grip until she had calmed down. His eyes held hers and she knew – almost comfortingly – that all the panic and feelings she had were her own. The calm she had that was slowly overtaking the fear wasn't because of some magic, but because of how safe she felt with his hands holding her, even if they were clasped around her wrists like handcuffs. Her cheeks flooded red-hot as memories of how he'd held her wrists in the forest that day surfaced in her mind.

She could feel the calm taking over, but couldn't look away, trying to tell him with her eyes how much she didn't want to move from this position.

"All I'm saying is, don't give them the bracelets, because they will use it for bad. The Arcana's not good anymore," he said and she knew it was the truth. Beside his power, she'd had the feeling about the Arcana for a while. It was just more valuable to get information from them first.

She nodded slightly, locked in his gaze as his voice

dropped to a whisper for only the two of them. "Your parents left the organization because they found out what they were doing, and it got them killed."

The ball of lead in her stomach that she'd done so well to ignore since joining the Arcana pulled her body down, only Kai's hands kept her from escaping upstairs to her bed and never leaving. Only him sitting there kept her from falling apart. "Do you know who did it?" she couldn't help but ask, not sure she wanted the answer.

Disappointment filled her when he shook his head slightly. "All I know is it was someone with a lot of power and resources. Some of the families of the Arcana have garnered a lot of influence and are backed by some very powerful mortals who don't want the arrangements they have to end. If your father tried to leave and threatened to expose them, who knows who could have done it? There are too many people to even guess at one."

"Then I find out who and I expose them," she found herself saying, the ball of lead that weighed her down turning to steel in her gut.

"You could get yourself killed doing something like that, Kenzie. Don't!" he begged, shock taking over his face as fear swarmed his eyes.

But she wouldn't back down. "I just joined and then stole from the Major Arcana, and you just casually mentioned how powerful some of them are. I don't think they're going to let me leave with a prized artifact that they desperately want, are they?"

"No, probably not. I just…"

"What?"

"I can't stand the idea of them coming after you."

"Well, I have no choice now." She smiled, her resolve strengthening as she realized she was on the right path. Against the people of power or not, this was where her father had stood once, and she wouldn't disappoint him. It was that or cave to the needs of a corrupt organization she'd found herself in bed with, and she couldn't stoop to that level. "They'll find out I'm not with them the second I refuse to hand over the bracelets."

His lips turned up slightly as he watched her, the glint in his eye, enjoying her defiance.

"What?" she asked, smiling back at him as the mood between them changed and his fingers, which had been holding her wrists, traced circles on the inner part of her arms just above the bracelets.

"I'm just glad to have you back," he whispered as though this happiness between them would crack if he spoke too loud.

She could feel how warm he was, how close he was, and couldn't help feeling that same fluttering feeling in her chest she had when they'd met. "Oh? So this was all a ploy to get me back, was it?" she joked, leaning on her end of the couch, ignoring how her body wanted to pull him closer.

She pulled her wrists from his, crossing her arms over her chest lazily, daring him to close the distance she'd set between them. The grin on her lips grew wider as she sucked her bottom lip into her mouth and watched him physically overtaken by the sight of her. His hunger wasn't like she'd seen from Teo – Kai's was a passion that couldn't be quelled, a hunger for everything that was her, including her body. She was more than just a body to his hunger: he wanted to claim her soul.

"This wasn't a ploy at anything. I shouldn't have ever let you get away," he said quietly as a moan rose in his throat and he slid forward along the couch towards her on his hands and knees.

Her breath grew shallower as the anticipation grew between them.

He slowed purposefully, letting the tension build. It felt like a pressurized bubble between them; the closer he got, the more she yearned for it.

"I'm sorry I didn't believe—" she started as his body came over hers, his face hovering close to her lips.

"Ssshh… None of that matters now," he said with a

wanting smile.

The presence of him so close to her, his breathing tickling the nerves in her lips, made every inch of her feel alive. Goosebumps danced over her exposed skin, displaying to him what the anticipation of this moment was doing to her. The heat of his body, so achingly close to hers offset the chill of the room.

In sync, they breathed… waiting… exploring each other's faces, both keeping their eyes on the tiny gap between their lips.

The need between them grew like physical tension, a rising crescendo to the moment of touch.

Mackenzie broke, cutting into the space between, meeting his lips.

He responded furiously, unable to hold back his desire as he kissed her back. One hand held him over her, the other sliding up into her hair, fisting near her scalp tightly.

The gesture had her gasping against his mouth, feeling his tongue take advantage of her surprise to meet hers.

Her legs wrapped around his waist, tightening and pulling him down on her. The crush of their bodies only deepened their embrace as her fingernails dug into his bicep, feeling him flex against her.

He shifted against her body, his hardness pressed up in the right spot, only limited by their clothing. She moaned against him, feeling the noise reverberate through their joined lips.

His free hand trailed up her bare leg, fingertips lightly tracing the side of her thigh. It reached the hem of the dress, teasing it up further until it was above her hip. With careful, deliberate fingers, he slid her underwear down, circling the jut-out of her hip bone softly as his lips left to devour the join of her neck and shoulders. His teeth kneaded the muscle as his mouth claimed her.

He broke back from the kiss, studying her face, his

hand pausing.

"What?" Mackenzie said, suddenly reeling as her eyes widened. What had so abruptly stopped their moment? What had she done to spur it? Her racing heart no longer sped away out of desire but fear.

"Maybe we should take this upstairs?" Kai said slowly.

But despite his words, she couldn't help feeling as though she had done something wrong. "Ahh… Sure…" she said slowly, meeting his gaze, breathing hard like he was. "Is everything okay?"

His eyes dropped as he blushed and her heart leaped into her throat as though it would suffocate her. Depending on his next words, she worried it might.

"It's nothing wrong with you, it's just… The beast in me has a very sensitive nose and you still smell like *him*," he said, growling over the mention of Teo, the sound of his other form coming through at the end of his words.

She curled inward slightly as the meaning of his words hit her properly and for a moment, she didn't know what to do but feel the embarrassment claim her.

His eyes lifted to see her face, stewing in her shame, all too aware now of how quickly she'd acted these past weeks and how unlike her it all was.

"Hey…" he whispered, his hand on her hip lifting to tuck under her chin and raise her gaze to his. His eyes held no reluctance towards her, she could see that, but she knew his hate of Teo and her behavior of late had scared even her. "It's just the sensitive nose and I want you, I'm telling you I do. I don't judge you and this isn't some comment on you…"

"Okay…" she replied softly, only slightly convinced by his words. She could still feel the chewing in her gut of her self-consciousness, shaming her behavior, even if it had been for information collection.

He pulled himself off her carefully and held out his hand for her to take.

She reached up slowly and climbed off the couch.

He laced his fingers through hers lightly as her feet sunk into the soft carpet, giving her the chance to remove them if she chose.

The bracelets felt cold on her wrists, thrumming with power as she followed him warily up the stairs.

His eyes glanced back deliberately, glazing over her body, making her feel at ease as they carefully trailed it.

Once at the top of the stairs, Kai located the bathroom, leading her into the cold white-tiled room. Her face displayed her confusion loud and clear as he turned to her.

"What are we doing?" she said slowly as her hand left him and she waited for answers.

"I want you. You're the most beautiful woman I've met and there's this thing between us. A fire that I know you feel too. And I have you back, I'm not losing that. All I wanted was to wash the scent of him off so when I claim you, you're all mine. *All mine*," he said quietly, the last of his words growled in a much different manner than before as his arms slipped around her waist, pulling her close as his eyes glanced where the tight-fitting red dress ended to reveal her cleavage. "I need you."

His words removed the fear and embarrassment as she welcomed his warmth around her, sliding closer across the cold bathroom tiles towards him as he pulled her in by the small of her back.

She pressed against him, her arms slipping around his shoulders as his fingertips reached up to trace along the bare back of her shoulder blades exposed by the dress. "I need you too. And I'm all yours, I promise," she said confidently as the shivers climbed her spine in delight. "If you'll have me."

"Absolutely I will," he grinned wickedly, the shameless gleam returning to his eye as he held hers.

"So take what's yours already." She giggled teasingly, biting her lip and watching the flash of hunger in his eye again, feeling the pulse as it renewed the hard want in his body. She knew what it did to him, and she was challenging him to let loose on her.

His hands traced to the edge of her dress, one hand clasping the edge of the zipper as he slowly, teasingly trailed it down her back, feeling her body arch in response. His face was so close to hers, she could almost feel the presence of his lips on hers.

She yeaned for his touch, needing it. It was the hole Teo would never be able to fill.

It was all her own emotion and it was *real*.

Kai just wanted to protect her, he wouldn't hurt her. And she knew in return she wanted him safe, she wanted to make sure that she held him close to her as well. They would protect each other, no matter what.

With the zip fully undone, the dress slipped off easily from her body, revealing herself bared to him in a way she hadn't been before.

There had been their heat of passion and fire and they'd been so caught up in each other's bodies but here, staring into each other's eyes in the cold hallway-lit bathroom, it was a new level of vulnerability.

Goosebumps danced over her skin as his eyes devoured her. She reached forward, a sly grin on her face as she slowly undid the buttons, deliberately taking her time. She watched his impatience written plainly on his face as though she were water and he was parched.

His muscles twitched as he held himself around her, watching her fingers as they popped button by button down his shirt, Mackenzie testing how long she could take to loop each out of its hole.

Kai's Adam's apple bobbed as he swallowed deeply, his eyes shutting for a second with the motion.

Three buttons remained and she could feel him about to burst against her, his hips pressed against her stomach, pressing into her. Her lips parted as she felt his pulse against her and the small gasp that left her undid his resolve.

Kai's lips smashed against Mackenzie's as his arms tightened around her, lifting her in the air.

Her arms swept around his shoulders in an embrace as her feet left the cold tile behind. She closed her eyes, enjoying his heat pressed against hers, his naked chest boiling against her breasts where his shirt flapped open. She could feel him moving, the air brushing past her as he rushed them smoothly across the room.

The freezing cold of the shower tiles met her back.

Her gasp as he pressed her hard against it made her wet with anticipation. She gripped him tighter, keeping his fiery skin against her.

His lips never left, his tongue grazing hers over and over, teasing until she sucked his bottom lip into her mouth hard. Pulling more and more, she felt his growl deep against her. She wanted to test him, see how hard she could go as her fingernails played with his back, scraping harder and harder…

Finally, she let his lip loose and rested her hands on his back, pressing her forehead against his.

She breathed hard, staring down at their melted bodies with a smile of genuine joy.

"You know, if you want to, you can let the beast loose. I don't want you to hide anything from me ever again. *I'm yours.*"

"Would you surrender to me fully?" he rasped, his voice gravelly as he pulled her even tighter.

A shudder of excitement vibrated up her spine. There was no space between their bodies except what the clothes created as she felt his pulse trying to break free of his jeans, a driving reminder to both of them of their passion.

"I surrender. Tell me how you want me," she whispered, an edge to her voice as one of his hands cupped her bare ass. She was aware of how close his fingertips rested to her opening. "Please."

His fingers twitched closer as he cleared his throat and grinned wickedly.

She was at his mercy.

"Well, love, let's test those powers of yours then." His eyes glinted with mischief as his hands moved, gliding over her body, reaching behind his head and taking her hands from around his neck. Carefully, he glanced at the gold cuffs, watching her as his body left hers and he stepped back, her hands held carefully at her eye height between them, their fingers interlocked. "Use your magic to will them free."

Blinking as she processed his words, it took Mackenzie a moment to respond to his command. She glanced at her wrists and imagined the cuffs clicking off like they had a secret clasp. Then, reaching out with her magic, she willed it.

As though they had never been sealed, the cuffs unclasped themselves and jangled onto the floor.

Kai reached his foot and kicked them back across the tiles, out of the shower, and into the other end of the bathroom near the entryway.

"Good girl," he growled hungrily, his eyes trailing over her again. His next words came as a command, a glint of a challenge in his eye.

"Next test of your magic, you're going to make rope." He grinned, his eyes glancing at the strong frame that the shower hung on above her head.

23: THE CALM BEFORE THE WAR

Orange light glinted through Mackenzie's heavy closed eyelids as light filtered through the curtains onto her face. She was so exhausted that she barely minded it at all. The events of the night before slowly worked through the fog of sleep in her brain, pulling her lips into a smile.

She lay in the bed on her front, face turned towards the window and breathing deeply as her body slowly pulled out of sleep, the slight ache in her muscles worth it after the night of bliss.

She could feel the light trace of Kai's fingers along her naked back.

Shivers raced up her spine, heat flushed her skin and the warmth settled between her thighs. The memory of how he'd claimed her body had her biting her lip lightly.

A moan escaped her. Kai chuckled under his breath, his fingers dipping lower and lower on her back.

She flexed her fingers as the touch slipped down one of her butt cheeks to the back of her thigh. The rope burns on her wrists made her gasp. The memory of how he'd tied her up in the shower and made her squirm with delight making her wet.

I would be so happy to feel his fingers on me all day and never move. And yet I will have to get up soon.

Mackenzie shifted slightly, twisting against the

pillow, feeling her deep sleep coming to an end as her body finally accepted waking up. Her eyelids tried to open, breaking the crusty sleep in her eye creases. The light blinded her from the curtains and she ducked into the pillow, groaning.

Kai's lips kissed her spine lightly.

Goosebumps raised along the skin, spurring him on. She sighed happily, the muscles along her back twisting under his touch, unable to get enough of it. His kisses trailed up her spine as his hand slid lower between her legs.

His lips pressed against her cheek as her head returned from the depths of the pillow. "How are you feeling this morning?" he whispered as his fingers began to stroke slowly.

"Sore..." Mackenzie giggled, her cheeks growing hotter by the second. Facing him, she caught his grin as his hand halted and retreated. He placed his hand on the curve of her waist as he rolled her onto her back, moving over her. She could feel his desire hard against her, but she searched his face carefully, seeing only the softness of his features unhardened by lust.

"It's okay, love. Rest up."

"Are you sure?" she asked, reaching up to rest her hands on either side of his neck, her fingers splayed on the sides of his face.

"I'm sure. We have all the time in the world for that. I'll just conserve my energy for *later*," he said, his playfulness making her grin as he lowered his lips to hers, pressing a soft kiss against them.

He rolled off her slowly, lifting his arm and inviting her to curl into him.

Her finger traced the curve of his collarbone, feeling his body hum as he relaxed into her touch. All her sore muscles relaxed knowing she was safe and secure in his embrace.

The quiet let her mind wander and then it began to spiral with the events of the last few days that she'd been trying to ignore. All her organs weighed her down as she thought about what had happened prior to her reunion with Kai last night. "How long do you think it will take for the Arcana to realize I'm not on their side anymore?" she asked, her anxiety prickling her nerves like an uncomfortable itch along her limbs.

She fought the urge to scratch at her skin.

Have they already discovered my change of heart?

Mackenzie's free hand curled into a fist at her hip, nails biting into her palm.

Kai caught sight of her anxiety, reaching a hand to cover hers softly. Plying her fingers open away from where they threatened to break through the skin, he watched her warily.

In for 5. Out for 5, she told herself, trying to slow her frantic heart and mind. *Breathe.*

"When were you supposed to meet with Teo to give the cuffs over?" he asked, his jaw clenched as he spat out the name violently. She could see his hard swallows in his Adam's apple as the tension refused to leave his face.

"Today. Midday-ish." Mackenzie rolled to pick up her cell from the bedside table, only to return it with a groan. "So just under an hour…God, I slept in."

"It's a Saturday, it's allowed," he offered in response with a tight smile. Tension lined the muscles of his face and neck, but she could see him trying to lighten her anxiety regardless.

Her mind still continued to spiral as she returned the smile.

"Just for today, we'll hide out here. How about that?"

"Hide out? Won't he still be able to sense our emotions?"

"Not if you shield us," he said with a devilish grin as she looked up at him through her dark, thick lashes.

"If I knew how to do that, don't you think I would have done it? I've been subject to his magic for the last several weeks…" she spilled, trying to seem lighthearted until the memory of her time with Teo made her dizzy and lightheaded.

Her stomach twisted violently, robbing her of breath.

"He did *what?*" Kai growled, the volume shocking her.

She sat up quickly, flinching as her heart strangled itself.

He followed her movements, touching her shoulder softly as he hushed soothingly.

Mackenzie studied his face, seeing how he worked to calm it, unsure of how much she should reveal about the happenings with Teo, feeling at fault for some of it.

He relaxed his grinding teeth and tightened muscles that were ready to go to battle for her against Teo's manipulative powers.

Letting him in to control her emotions and sensations for sex was something she felt responsible for. *Why didn't I stop Teo when I first felt the inklings of dizziness?* Her gaze dropped to her fist, clenched once again, breaking into the skin this time with a painful lance shooting up her arm. For a moment, it helped, clearing the growing volume in her mind as she fought not to cry. *How could I have been so stupid to think I could manipulate someone who could control emotions?* She tried to focus on the blood in her hand, on the sensations seizing her arm in a flash of torment, on anything but the choice she'd made regarding the Arcana and Teo since she'd moved to Salem.

Kai sniffed at the air, and Mackenzie knew when she glanced at him that the scent of the blood had reached him, her stomach twisting up further as she thought of what to tell him. His features hardened and drew together, darkness taking over his face despite the sunshine entering the room.

Her eyes refused to meet his as she felt the near spiral of emotions send everything in her into a flurry of nervous activity.

"Kenzie," he said, waiting for her to turn back and

look at him. When she didn't, he pulled himself up and climbed in front of her, his naked body free from the blanket as he sat in front of her. His manhood was in her direct line of sight, breaking her thought-consumed stare. Looking up at him with knitted brows, she watched his eyes scan her face, as though he could read every thought that was swirling around in a mass of confusion in her head. "What did he do?"

Her insides stilled at his words, frozen as everything in her grew cold. Her mind kept running though, as though the world was paused, but she kept reeling for how to answer.

"Maybe it's something I did…" she said, dropping her eyes from his before she'd barely met them, afraid to see the hurt that would cross his face if she told him.

"Mackenzie, you can tell me anything. I mean the same thing to you that you told me last night. I want who you are, not something censored. So, tell me what has you so wound up that you're bleeding yourself?"

She could hear the waver in his growling voice as he glanced at her hand and the blood that slowly leaked from the nail marks.

"I never truly believed the Arcana and Teo were good… but I wanted answers. They stopped giving me anything after a while unless I did my initiation task. They seemed reluctant to trust me – Teo included. I wanted to make him think I was into him so he'd help get me in the ranks," she said slowly, seeing no surprise cross Kai's face as she watched all his movements carefully. "The most recent time we trained, I told him I thought I was ready for the task and I… tried to reinforce his opinion of me by flirting… He controlled my emotions and we had sex… Afterward, I just felt… sick. Like I didn't know which were really my own feelings anymore."

At this, Kai's eyes widened, glazing over as he drifted off into his own faraway thoughts. He fell silent as she waited for him to let go of her, swear or leave. He stayed though, still deep in thoughts she couldn't decipher from his face.

His hands left hers, massaging his temple.

Knives of panic drove through her heart as she anticipated the "this is over" conversation that would inevitably follow what she'd done.

"Please say *something*," she whispered. She could see the anger in his eyes, the disappointment that she was sure was meant for her.

"Kenz…" he whispered back, his mouth opening as though he had something to say before closing as it disappeared.

"Please," she begged, her voice breaking as her eyes welled with tears.

"Love, I want to kill him," he said quietly, the anger barely held back from his tone.

Her heart stopped at his words, her widening watery eyes spilling their tears. "What?"

"I don't *care* if you let him into your emotions or knew what was happening, what he did is not fucking consent!" he said harshly and with a struggling breath, she realized his rage was not meant for her at all. "He turned off your ability to say no at any further point. That's not okay."

If Teo hadn't taken control of my mind, I would've said no. I would've stopped him. My willpower might be strong and I might have been hungry for answers, but… It didn't feel right. He brought his powers into the act…

He knew I'd turn back.

He took my choice.

Her eyes widened further, staring in the nothingness of the duvet as she was robbed of breath.

Her body was shaking, but it was disjointed and numb. She had no control of it anymore. Warmth fell down her face and her gaze moved to the blood coagulating in the cut.

"I'm sorry," she mouthed, and Kai rushed forward, pulling her into his bare chest. His warmth was a comfort as everything in her shivered with cold.

"This isn't on you. It doesn't matter if you gave him an invitation, his power shouldn't have taken that awareness from you. I know what you were thinking, I get it. This isn't on you. *He* took advantage of his power and should have left you with enough self-awareness to say no at any point of the act," he said, his hand stroking her hair.

She could feel his body tighten around her, holding her together. She couldn't speak, didn't want to think, sinking against his body.

"And to make sure he can never do it again, whenever you're around him you're going to will a shield around your mind, resistant to all magic."

His command struck her, making her pull back and stare at him in confusion. It wasn't because she wouldn't take the order, but because somehow he knew exactly what she needed in that moment not to fall apart. She could hear the resolve in his voice.

"That sounds complicated…" she said.

"Sounds? Yes. It really isn't though. I imagine it was just left out of your Arcana training so they had a way of controlling you."

Cold shivers crept up her spine. Her mouth tightened, feeling her anger at the Major Arcana and Teo heat her against the cold that wanted to take her body. "What do they want from me? Why do they *need* me?" she asked, hoping he had all the answers. At the very least, he'd tell her the truth.

"Because the Major Arcana started with your family. Whatever they have planned, they must need your magic…With or without you manning it," he said, prompting her mind to return to the item she'd stolen the night before.

She met Kai's eyes, defiance solidifying inside her like stone. "Well, they can't have *it* or *me*," she said.

His frown tugged up into a boyish grin.

Her lips pulled too as his face softened, silence falling

between the two. It was only broken by words filled with so much love that she struggled to contain the warmth that filled her.

"That's my Kenzie."

24: THE GAME PLAN

"I'm still of the opinion he needs to die," Kai said severely as Mackenzie sat with him, curled together on the couch.

She leaned her back against his side, nursing a cup of hot cocoa on her lap. Hours had passed since Teo had come knocking, looking for Mackenzie, furiously on the front door and calling her phone. She'd stuck her phone on silent and shielded both her and Kai's minds from his magic as they hid away in her bedroom. When he'd finally left, they'd gone downstairs to the living area, shut the curtains, and attempted to brainstorm ideas for how to deal with the Arcana. So far nothing productive had formed.

"We're not going to kill him!" Mackenzie said again, breathlessly amazed that Kai continued to come back to it.

"After what he did, he deserves it."

"But we're not killers," she retorted, sitting forward of his touch and turning around to check his face. "Can you stop being the jealous boyfriend for like five minutes and think critically?"

"Did you just call me your boyfriend?" he asked with a grin, snapping out of his testosterone-fueled aggression.

Her mouth flopped open as she studied his complete

demeanor change. "Really? That's what you got out of that?" she asked incredulously.

Before he had time to answer, the lock in the front door clicked.

Kai jumped up quickly, his muscles readied for an attacker as he turned to the source of the noise.

Mackenzie rotated further around on the couch, sitting backward on it, still nursing her hot cocoa as she followed Kai's gaze with a growing smile.

Lucy's blonde curls bounced into view, lugging a bag as she moved inside. She shut the door behind her and caught sight of the two figures watching her. Her eyes widened, eyebrows raised as she slouched the bag off her shoulder with a heavy thump and stood tall, rolling her shoulders back at the sight of Kai. "I thought I said you couldn't have a crisis while I was gone." She met Mackenzie's eyes, flicking them quickly back and forth to Kai.

He stood still, only slightly more relaxed than before as his eyes tried not to narrow at her presence. "What are you doing here?" he asked, drawing her full attention, and earning a deep scowl in response.

"I could ask the same of you, devil boy. I think you should leave before I show your beastie ass why you don't lie to my KZ," she said ferociously, standing her ground in a way Mackenzie had never seen her friend do for her. It warmed her heart for a moment as she welcomed the support and protection of her best friend, before she caught the way Kai bristled at her words. With the anger he already possessed for Teo, being yelled at by a near stranger - even his girlfriend's best friend - was setting the animal loose inside him.

Mackenzie moved quickly, rising from the couch, leaving her cocoa mug on the table behind her. Heading straight for Kai, she placed a hand softly on the center of his chest, feeling his muscles soften under her touch. His eyes never left Lucy's, neither breaking their stare nor backing down until Mackenzie addressed them both.

"Luce, there have been some big developments and what you need to know is Kai is on our side and I'm certain of that fact now. Kai, Lucy has been my support for all of the chaos Salem has given me. Besides the last two days, she's been here the whole time. She's my rock," Mackenzie explained, trying to make eye contact with each as she lectured.

It took both parties a moment to collectively call a ceasefire as Mackenzie waited on them both to find sense.

"You're going to need to fill me in," Lucy said slowly as she stepped cautiously into the living area towards the two of them. "What happened to Teo and… training with the Arcana?"

"That's not an option anymore," Mackenzie replied quickly as Kai's torso stiffened under her fingers. Surprisingly, he stayed silent, letting Mackenzie explain as his skin heated. "The Arcana were the ones who ordered my parents killed."

She watched the uncontained shock impact her friend's features.

"What about him and his family?" Lucy pushed questioningly, her eyes flicking to Kai.

It was then he chose to speak before Mackenzie could, calm as he addressed the newcomer. "We were there in Oregon, trying to warn and protect. I should have told Kenzie about that when we met and I've apologized for that. We had nothing to do with the death of Kenzie's parents except as fellow targets," he replied, earning a wide-eyed nod of respect from Lucy as no anger touched his voice at the accusation she had put on his family.

"Fellow targets?" Lucy pushed, picking up on his word choice.

"The day Kenzie's mother disappeared, my parents sent me back to Salem to live with a family friend and now they're gone too. On the run or dead, I'm not sure."

Mackenzie turned back to him at the emotion leaking

into his voice. She wasn't sure, but it looked to her as though his eyes glistened more than usual, with tears he refused to let well. Her heart squeezed knowing they were the same, their pain was understood. The way he'd appreciated her pain and perseverance the first time they'd met officially made sense. She found herself smiling at him as he met Lucy's gaze.

As though he could feel her eyes, he turned back to her and giving her the soft smile she was sure was only reserved for her.

"I'm sorry to hear that, Kai. Given what I know about what you withheld from her… I'm going to assume that you aren't the villain here. However, as the best friend, I'm going to warn you, if you hurt her - beast or not - I will make you suffer in every way possible. Understood?" Her voice crept from sympathy to a darkness Mackenzie hadn't known Lucy capable of.

But Kai met her eyes confidently, serious and sure. "Understood." He nodded.

The sharp edges fell easily from Lucy's face as she smiled widely and bounced over to her best friend eagerly. They met each other with a tight hug.

"Hey, KZ…" she whispered in Mackenzie's ear as they embraced.

"Hey, Luce," Mackenzie whispered back with a smile unable to stay off her lips, warmed already by her presence.

"You're absolutely sure we can trust him?" Lucy asked quickly, holding her best friend still.

"I can hear you," Kai chimed in loudly as he watched the two girls.

"A hundred percent," Mackenzie replied all the same, not bothering to be quiet. "I judged too quickly before and I didn't have all the answers. The Arcana are the real villains here, we were right about them from the start."

Lucy pulled back, ready for the explanation. She moved over to the couch Mackenzie and Kai had been sitting on before, taking a seat and watching the two of them expectantly.

Mackenzie joined her and Kai took the armchair across from them.

"So what are we going to do about the Arcana?" Lucy asked.

"That's what Kai and I were trying to figure out just before you got here," Mackenzie said with a half-smile, half-grimace as she thought about how to explain to Lucy what had happened. She opened her mouth to speak, shutting it quickly as she tried to find the words, picking at her cuticles.

"And?" Lucy pushed, looking to Kai quickly as though he'd offer a solution because she was getting impatient with Mackenzie's silence.

"And I'm going to kill Teo," Kai said, leaning back in his chair, his face a calm seriousness that was sure of himself.

"No you're not!" Mackenzie snapped, turning to him quickly and watching his face scrunch up at her comments.

"What do you propose then, Mackenzie? He can't go on unpunished and I don't see a jail cell around here we could keep him in," Kai responded, a heavy, rough edge leaking into his voice as he sat forward and forgot all about Lucy's presence, his eyes focused on Mackenzie.

"I don't know! But we can't go around killing people or we're no better than the Arcana, are we?" she said, watching the words dawn on his face as they hit him. She was right. They had no intention of repeating the atrocities committed against them to someone else.

Lucy observed them, her eyes narrowing, assessing the situation before she responded. "What did Teo do?" She looked at Kai instead of Mackenzie, who turned to her as though remembering she was there. Lucy stared Kai down until he responded.

"He used his powers while they were having sex and controlled her," he said, meeting Lucy's eyes, the fire of his anger burning in his.

She caught it, not a single ounce of surprise crossing her features as her face gained an intense, hardened quality. She looked pissed. When she met Mackenzie's gaze though, there was a softness, though Mackenzie could almost hear her "I told you he was bad news" in her best friend's gaze.

"I agree with Kai," Lucy said. "He needs to be punished. Maybe not killed, but he can't just keep walking around, able to do it to others."

Mackenzie nodded. They just had to figure out how to get the best of both worlds. Her stomach twisted uncomfortably at the memory, causing her stomach to cramp and her mouth to go dry. She kept nodding as her eyes dropped and thoughts swarmed her.

I have no ideas outside of murder.

Is there even any justice for the Arcana – surely the police don't believe in magic? Even if I went to the police, would they have any connections to thwart my plan?

Did the Arcana even know that Teo had been manipulating me?

"I need some water," Mackenzie said, rising from the couch quickly, every nerve under her skin buzzing. Both Lucy and Kai glanced at her but didn't seem to notice the war of anxiety kicking off in her body. "You guys brainstorm how to stop Teo without killing him and I'll be back in a second."

Mackenzie walked out of the living room, trying to hold her composure until she made it to the kitchen. Her heart started thundering and the further she got from her friends, the less oxygen her body would let her have.

Don't let them see. You'll just worry them and there's nothing they can do.

Her bare feet touched the smooth cool tiles of the kitchen and the last of the strength gave way. It didn't matter how the ceramic tried to calm her, everything in her heated uncomfortably and shook.

Her knees gave way, and she crumpled to the floor, trying her hardest not to make noise and alarm her companions.

Sliding over so that her back pressed against the wall of the archway, she hugged her knees into her chest. Everything in her was too tight and too far from her center simultaneously.

The sick, rancid acid feeling in her stomach made her squirm in her huddled position. Her mind replayed the night with Teo, the feeling only worsening the more her mind focused on it.

Mackenzie's heart constricted, and she clutched at her breastbone uselessly, as though she could make it loosen.

This is the moment I die, right? My body is trying to kill me and no one will know.

Snippets of sentences drifted to her between the thunderous sound of her blood pumping in her ears.

Too quick. Why is everything moving so quick...

As the memory of Teo pumping inside her moved through her mind, a phantom feeling relived itself.

Her mouth opened to scream.

Surely this is the moment I die of a heart attack.

No sound escaped her throat.

Her mind spiraled further.

The buzz of her cell in the back pocket of her jeans was the only thing that jolted her from her panic.

Curiosity and confusion temporarily dulled all the sensations.

Who would be texting me?

Reaching back, she slid it out from between her butt and the floor, dizziness hitting her when she saw Teo as the sender.

HEY GORGEOUS,
HOPE YOU'RE OKAY? WE WERE SUPPOSED TO MEET TODAY BUT I HAVEN'T HEARD FROM YOU.

I HAVE NEWS. THE ARCANA GAVE ME INFORMATION ABOUT YOUR MOTHER I THINK YOU NEED TO HEAR IN PERSON.

LET ME KNOW THAT YOU'RE SAFE.

TEO

She stared at the text, simultaneously urged to call Teo and run as far and fast as she could. *It could be a trap? Maybe he already knows I've changed my mind?*

MEET YOU AT THE PARK, she texted back before she could stop herself. The answers she'd craved for so long might finally be here.

Lucy and Kai talked in soft voices in the other room, deep in conversation.

Her head tilted towards the noise as her heart raced for a whole new reason. *Answers.*

Her anxiety-ridden body buzzed with new purpose.

She couldn't alert her best friend and boyfriend to her new choice, they would definitely try to stop her.

She pushed to her feet – ignoring how weak her ankles felt – and bolted up the staircase, only slowing enough to stay quiet.

The most dangerous magical artefact I own is on the bathroom floor? Clearly I'm not mature enough to be trusted with this. Mackenzie chuckled to herself quietly as she found the gold cuffs where she'd discarded them the night before. She wasn't yet sure if she would hand them over – probably not – but she might need them as leverage for her own life if it turned out to be a trap.

She stared at them for a moment, knowing she couldn't just pack them in a bag. Shutting her eyes, holding one onto each wrist with the opposite hand, she reversed her magic, willing them to shut. With a click they responded: the cold metal circled her wrists fully and a jolt of power zapped through her system as the power in the bracelets connected with hers.

No one but me can take these off now… Perfect.

Crossing to the bed and smiling at her own genius,

she took a long-sleeved shirt from her closet and swapped it out with the one she had been wearing.

Mackenzie rushed, knowing the longer she took, the more chance she had of her companions stopping her from leaving.

Hurrying to the window, she unlocked and slid it open carefully, cautious to avoid any squeaks or grinding noises as it lifted. Pushing the screen out quickly, she heard the clunk when it hit the roof and knew she couldn't hesitate. Slipping out the window and creeping across the roof quickly, she really hoped she wasn't about to regret this.

25: THE ANSWERS

Mackenzie had run from the house before Kai or Lucy could figure out what she was up to, much less where she'd gone. As she ran along the edge of the park, she spotted the figure exiting the stone monument in the center of it.

She slowed as the figure turned its head to her in the dying afternoon light and familiar dark hair and eyes found hers.

Teo walked down the steps and she could feel the jolt as her body warned her to run away. She fought it though, staying in place, committed to however this was going to play out.

She had to fight the urge to put up her mental barrier as he sauntered over, not wanting to give away her new-found power. Her nerves vibrated with an intensity that made her feel weak, like she'd drunk ten cups of coffee and it was hitting her all at once. Her heart hammered her ribs and she lifted her hand, sliding her necklace out of its hiding place under her shirt to fiddle with it between her fingers. Tracing the engraving of her father's name in the dog tag, she forced herself to take big, heavy breaths in the hopes it would calm some part of her.

Or at the very least, stop it from getting any worse.

Teo walked up to her place at the edge of the park,

staying a few feet away as he looked her up and down, his brows furrowed in concern. Despite the bags under her eyes and the bruising around her throat, there were no other injuries to account for.

"Did you get them?" he asked as he looked at her empty hands and lack of a bag.

She dropped her gaze to the ground in her best attempt at shame, thankful she had a reason to look anywhere but at him as she responded. "I got in okay and managed to find the basement with the cuffs, but when I did, they attacked me. They were so much more powerful than I thought and I barely escaped with my life!" she exclaimed, making sure to stay as close to the truth as possible. She let the anxiety that had driven her nervous system take over as she ran forward, flinging herself into his arms. She hoped he believed it – that her anxiety was because of her terror. "I hid. I wasn't sure if they'd come looking for me even after they got the bracelets back."

His arms settled around her back, finally welcoming the embrace as her voice shook in his shoulder. She didn't have to pretend her fear. At such a closeness, Teo could use his powers for anything and without her shield, she'd be all too compliant.

"That's horrible, Kenzie. I really thought you'd be able to complete the task. Come on, let's get out of the public eye then," he suggested, squeezing her before releasing to take her hand.

She nodded for a moment as she worked to keep her hand relaxed. "Do you mind if we stay outside? I think I still need the fresh air," she said quietly as he led the way, trying not to let herself feel panicked at the idea of going into an Arcana hideout.

"No problem. I know just the place," he said, looking back at her with a soft reassuring smile as he pulled her along the darkening cold street.

Streetlamps were coming on and the population of Salem was hurrying inside – into their homes or the bars and restaurants – seeking solace. She was beginning to regret following him to a dark, private place when she roused on herself, mentally noting the reason why she'd come. *Her mother.* She needed to know what the Arcana did, given they might have been the last ones to see her alive.

They moved to an area Mackenzie hadn't visited before, walking along in silence as he led her. They didn't rush but his pace was fast enough that she knew Teo wasn't relaxed either. She wasn't sure if he believed what she'd said about the Order of Wands or if it was something else, but she followed behind obediently, trying to ignore the alarm bells going off in her head that made her skin crawl.

He stopped them in front of a granite wall with jutting-out stones and Mackenzie surveyed their destination. She stood on the dirt path, looking around at the quiet area around her. It was peaceful, the stones that stuck out next to the path adorned with a flower each and engraved with a name.

She let go of his hand to investigate further. She moved down the stones, reading the names until her body froze and her breath hitched.

'Sarah Good' was etched into the stone, a single yellow carnation below it like an underline.

She looked up at Teo, who was unsurprised by what she'd found as he followed behind her.

"Sarah Good?" she questioned, hoping the name would ask the question she meant to ask: *Where are we and what is this?*

"It's the memorial. A lot of their bodies back then weren't buried on consecrated ground because of what they were, so the bodies were lost over time. This is where they honor them and the atrocities of the past." Teo's whole demeanor had changed. He'd gone cold and calculating and she could feel the hairs on her body stand up even under her long-sleeved shirt, the cuffs on her wrist turning to ice.

"That's horrible," she said slowly, the sadness of their fates not reaching her voice.

"It is. Especially considering she was your ancestor," he replied, watching her reaction.

She widened her eyes as though this was a new revelation to her. "What?"

"Those bracelets are powerful. In the hands of the Order of Wands, it could be disastrous. They were the artifact Sarah used to separate her powers to the family lines they are with today, and in someone else's hands, could rob good people of their powers…"

Covering her mouth quickly, Mackenzie forced a gasp. He couldn't know of her existing knowledge and so she watched, wide-eyed waiting for him to continue.

"You need to finish what you started. Those bracelets could be deadly if the Wands chose to use them," he said, meeting her eyes strongly, warning her.

She held his gaze as she let her face become a mask of seriousness, nodding determinedly. "I will. I promise. I'm sorry I failed the last time," she gushed, hoping he felt the sincerity she tried to force herself to feel.

"You don't fail until it's over. Keep trying," he said, his voice growing harsh.

She continued fighting the urge to use her magic, just nodding her understanding and hoping he would notice her compliance and not push it further.

Like he could sense the growing fear in her, he softened, stepping close and reaching out to rest his hand on her upper arm. "I'm glad you're safe though."

"You said you had information about my mother?" she asked, unable to wait any longer for why she was here, her impatience taking over.

Teo sucked in air between closed teeth as his free hand ran through his hair, tousling it.

Her stomach dropped, feeling as though she'd been cheated into coming.

"Well, I had that as congratulations for when you completed the task. I'd hoped you had because what I have is strictly Arcana-only knowledge. I can't give it to you till you've completed your initiation task."

She couldn't help the way her jaw dropped. She felt like she'd been punched in the gut as she looked at him in disbelief. "That's extortion!" she yelled, unable to contain her voice or emotion as she took a step away from him, pulling herself out of physical reach.

"That's a bit much!" he said with a half-smile, as though it were a joke to him.

Her eyes widened as she pulled her agape mouth into a shocked grimace.

"It's a secret organization, Kenzie. What did you expect? You'd get all the answers and wouldn't have to give anything in return?"

Her anger at him and the Arcana flared inside her. She couldn't hide her distaste anymore. He wasn't going to give her anything. She wasn't even sure now that he knew how to be selfless, he only knew how to get what he wanted, and she refused to be a pawn in that any longer. She wasn't his to take and never would be again. "Teo, she's my *mother*. I deserve to know! And last time I checked you and the Arcana were the ones that awakened me and asked *me* to join *you*." She let loose, the anger boiling out of her. "You know what? No! That isn't how you treat people, I'm out."

She took another step backwards, finally ready to leave and be done with the Arcana and Teo forever.

He reached out, snagging her arm by the wrist, pulling as he stepped after her. His hand readjusted, clasping over the cuff, still hidden under her shirt.

She knew by the look on his face when she glanced up that he'd felt it.

His grip tightened as he tugged on her arm aggressively, bringing her fumbling back towards him.

With wide eyes and a snarl that said he'd sensed her panic, he yanked her sleeve back to reveal the gold, glinting even in the dim lighting of dusk.

She fought to pull her wrist away, struggling against

his vice grip.

It was no use fighting him.

He pulled her even closer, taking her other wrist in his hand before she could realize what he was doing.

Thrashing her body, trying to be free, she watched the anger take over his face and body.

As she was about to focus her magic to block him, the dizziness hit her.

Pain, unlike any she'd ever felt, shot through every part of her skull as well as a tiredness in her muscles that had her knees crumbling under the weight of her body. With a severe crash, she fell to the ground, Teo crouching over her as he held her wrists above her head.

The overwhelming dizziness was so harsh, she felt like she'd been drugged.

She struggled uselessly to find the tie to her magic.

Realizing her mental efforts weren't working, she fought against the wrists that held her.

Turning her head to the side, stomach acid burned its way up her esophagus and out her mouth.

She turned her face to Teo, hoping she might be able to plead for release, but the moment she caught his gaze she knew it was impossible.

Teo watched her with cold rage, not an ounce of pity in his expression. "Give me the bracelets and this stops!" he said, his rough voice so low it nearly sounded like a growl.

She considered it for a moment before reminding herself that it could still be lies. With the bracelets, he could take her power and then kill her.

I am not yours to control, a defiant voice in her screamed.

"Not a chance in hell!" she yelled, using the last reserves of her energy to kick at his ankles. She felt his unsuspecting body give way and he teetered away from her.

He fell backward, releasing her wrists to catch

himself before he smacked backwards into the ground.

She fought his power quickly, sure this might be her only chance.

Acting on the first thing that came to mind, she climbed onto him as his backside touched the ground.

She punched his face as hard as she could. The satisfying crack it made was trumped by the pain that exploded in her knuckles and thumb in response. She cried out, drawing her magic to her, feeling his lessen in her mind.

It still lingered, but finally she was starting to find clarity.

Willing her mental shield, she pushed it into existence.

Teo's influence didn't disappear as she expected, slowly growing as he came back to his senses, a hand holding his nose, broken and gushing blood.

She was finally feeling some of her own emotions, but knew that would be short lived if she didn't act again.

Mackenzie looked down at the bracelets he wanted so badly, biting into her skin like a bitter cold, and could feel the answer pull on her like instinct.

The bracelets had belonged to *her* family and she could feel the power brimming inside them, mixing with her own.

Teo came to enough sense to pull her close and roll them both over until her head hit the dirt.

Focusing on her magic instead of struggling, she shut her eyes, finding the strand within her magic that felt cold in her soul - different from everything else inside her. Pulling on it, she welcomed the magic from the cuffs like it had always belonged as a part of hers.

It felt as though it was always meant to be.

When she opened her eyes, she could feel the power surging inside her.

Awakened.

26: THE FINAL SAY

Mackenzie's eyes opened, staring directly into Teo's. Hot flashes of power spun through her head and she could see the glimpses of purple lightning flashing in the reflectiveness of his cornea.

Teo had taken hold of Mackenzie's burning cold wrists, gasping at the change in her. Still, he held on.

She hated the feeling of his touch on her and in her mind. She let the intertwined power loose.

It was a duality that balanced perfectly in her soul; her power wanted to create and the cuffs wanted to destroy.

With her own power, she manifested the invisible wall in the air between them. Only Mackenzie could see the little purple glints that flickered in the space between. She could feel Teo's magic moving around in her emotions, making her dizzy as he worked to mute it, but with her newfound strength, she didn't care for it anymore.

Pushing the wall out from its place, straight in his face, she heard the howl when it made contact.

Teo pulled away, giving Mackenzie the chance to get to her feet and stand her ground.

He struggled to his feet shakily, the blood from his nose running anew, trickling through his fingers. He looked even more angry, feral even, as the blood rushed over and into his mouth, dripping off his chin. He looked up at her with bloodstained teeth, watering lashes, hunched over himself. Rage-filled focus overcame him.

Like a bomb had gone off in her head, the pain made her knees buckle again. She fought to stay standing and keep the tie to her magic.

Focus. Will it, she ordered herself even as she cried out.

"Get out of my head!" she screamed, and finally gave in to the instincts of the cuffs' magic, which was easier to grasp with her faltering focus.

She pulled.

Like a magic tug of war, she yanked on Teo's magic messing with her mind.

His face blanched at the gesture. His eyes flickered wildly as though there was someone around to assist as she pulled at his rope again and again, harder each time.

She could feel a dark part of her revel at his fear, knowing he was paying for what he had put her through.

Comforted by the fact that he would never be able to control her again.

He cried out, clutching at his chest as though the pain came from his heart, crumbling to his knees.

The heavy thud of his kneecaps against the gravel made her pause. She wasn't actually sure what this would do to him, but she had to remind herself that if she returned the magic, there was no guarantee he wouldn't do it all again.

Taking a deep breath, she pulled hard on the tether – if only to make his suffering as quick as possible – feeling it go taut. With one final yank, she heard the blood-curdling scream from Teo before he passed out, slumping to the ground.

Teo's magic collected in her, awakening a new sense of noisy awareness.

Foreign emotions all came at her at once, ones that

she knew didn't belong to her from all different directions. She felt like she was in a loud room, but as she frantically glanced around, she found no one around her except Teo and herself. With a deep breath, she hunched over, hands bracing on her knees as she focused on the new power in hopes of quieting it, breathing hard to try and steady herself.

Telling herself again and again that it was over, she closed her eyes. Teo lay unconscious and unmoving in front of her, proof that she'd done it – she'd removed the current threat.

The more attention she paid to the emotions that yelled at her, the more she could isolate and quieten them, able to determine how far each was from her one by one. And as she quietened the ones belonging to the houses nearby, she noticed one emotion mere feet from her, terrified.

Straightening up quickly, she turned around, meeting dark brown eyes that peered around the tree. She could feel the power and heat inside her simmer down as she watched Amari emerge slowly.

Walking over and stopping a few feet away from Mackenzie, Amari surveyed her as though her appearance could give her answers to her questions.

Blood from Teo's nose spattered Mackenzie's blue shirt, she knew the bruises around her neck had deepened in color with the flush of exercise and she was brushed all over with dirt from the path. Most of the pain had been mental for her thankfully.

Unlike Teo, who drew Amari's eyes to his place resting on the grass beside the path, his limbs splayed haphazardly around his body. Despite his unconscious bloody state, it looked extremely uncomfortable.

"How much of that did you see?" Mackenzie asked quietly as she felt Amari's fear through the air between them. She didn't know what the emotion was directed at and ached to ask but wasn't sure how the information about her new power would be received.

"I followed along but stayed back… So all of it. Were you so unhappy with us, Kenzie? I thought you were enjoying yourself. He trained you, and we welcomed you as our *friend*. Why would you do this?" she asked, a sadness leaking into her fear as well as a hint of confusion. She took a step towards Mackenzie, hands out defensively as though she might be attacked for moving close too quickly.

"You don't understand, Amari," Mackenzie said quietly as her heart squeezed painfully, her gut twisting as she realized the fear was of her. Her first friend in Salem *feared* her. She hadn't seen what had been going on – what Teo had done to her – or heard about any of it. Perhaps he had acted alone, not on the orders of the Arcana. She questioned her memories, wondering if once again she had got it all wrong.

"Then help us understand!" Amari pleaded, her eyes swimming with tears.

"He controlled me. He pushed into my emotions again and again, making me feel things that weren't mine. I asked him not to and then when we… The other night… He controlled it, he took away everything except what he wanted me to feel. Amari, he…" She faltered, unable to bring herself to say the words as her voice broke and tears slipped from her eyes before she could hold them back.

Amari glanced down at Teo for a moment, before she turned back to Mackenzie with a pale horror on her face that was echoed in her broadcasted feelings. "I had no idea, Mackenzie. I'm so sorry. I really thought you two were just hitting it off. I never even considered…I'm sorry," she said, rushing forward to wrap her arms around Mackenzie.

Mackenzie welcomed the embrace, slowly closing her arms around Amari in return.

"We're not all bad though…"

"I know you're not," Mackenzie whispered, squeezing Amari's warmth closer before releasing, wiping the tears from her cheeks as she found the comfort of her friend's presence. "I just had no idea what to do. No one person is willing to give me all the answers for nothing. That's what my parents should be here to do, but…"

"The Major Arcana might be able to help you still. You can give them the bracelets and get all the information you need," Amari reasoned frantically, glancing at Mackenzie's wrists.

A shiver crept up Mackenzie's spine as she heard the words, her instincts snapping to alert. "I think I'll hold on to them for the moment, thanks," she said slowly, feeling her legs tighten, urging her to back up and run as Amari's emotions and expression changed so quickly it was like a curtain of truth being pulled back.

Amari's features tightened as a flare of annoyance flashed through her emotional aura.

Before Mackenzie had time to move, Amari rushed her, coming in close. Fire exploded in her stomach.

Mackenzie gaped as the excruciating pain engulfed her, a warm wet flowing over her hands as they reflexively went to the source of the pain to find a metal dagger protruding from her abdomen. Her legs didn't hold her long as weakness took over her body. Her brain began to numb, the world around her going fuzzy as the pain grew too much.

Everything else faded into the background of her awareness.

She dropped beside Teo, feeling the harsh gravel meet her back too quickly. The impact sent a fresh wave of pain through her and she yelped.

Amari smiled down at her, leaning over to gloat to her. "You didn't think he'd bring me along without telling me the whole story, did you? How *naive!* But I'm feeling merciful, so I'll do you a favor. I'll tell you what he should've about your mother."

Mackenzie stopped in her tracks as she fought to grasp at her magic.

Amari closed in excitedly, her mouth a breath away from Mackenzie's ear. She whispered just loud enough for her to hear.

The revelation froze Mackenzie, all the breath rushing from her.

Amari leaned back, seeing how pale Mackenzie's face had become and how still her body was as she tried to process the words.

She was shaken and numb, not only from the knife wound that now consumed her stomach but at the news Amari had delivered.

"Want to give me the bracelets now?" Amari asked sweetly, but before Mackenzie could begin to consider it, a noise erupted through the area.

A mix between a growl and a roar came from the black-furred beast that prowled up behind Amari. She turned quickly to view the newcomer, and Kai's beast form issued a warning as his body sank lower to the ground, ready to pounce.

Amari smiled between the creature and Mackenzie before lifting herself to her feet and backing away from the both of them. "Well, it's been nice but I have to go."

Mackenzie's vision blurred and darkened as Amari ran off. She spotted Kai and Lucy appearing above her as her eyelids pulled heavily and she surrendered to the darkness that overcame her.

27: THE AMAZING KENZINI

The first thing Mackenzie became aware of as she returned from the darkness was the smell. It was bitter with an artificial aspect to it that made her scrunch her nose up in disgust. The smell was too clean, trying to mask any and all other scents.

The beeping came next, a recognizable sound intruding upon Mackenzie's rest that told her exactly what to expect as she opened her eyes.

The dim, lukewarm air of the hospital room greeted Mackenzie as she blinked away the tiredness in her heavy eyelids. The room was small and quiet except for the machine she was attached to. Her gaze was drawn to the armchair beside her bed where Lucy curled, knees up near her chest, her feet pressing on the seat of the cushion, and her phone up in front of her face, colors flashing across her skin as she watched a video on mute.

"Hey…" Mackenzie said quietly, her voice gravelly and hoarse.

Lucy's head whipped up, eyes wide as her phone dropped into her lap. "Hey! Oh my gosh, you're awake!" She sat up and leaned towards Mackenzie's bed, taking her hand. "I'm so glad you're okay!"

"I'm okay? How long was I out?" Mackenzie asked, double-checking as she looked down at where the blanket covered her stomach, aware of the stiffness of her body.

"Only a few hours, but you'll stay here a few days because of the stitches and things. You're very lucky she missed any vital organs. You lost a bit of blood but they managed to sort you out once we got you here." Lucy squeezed her hand.

Mackenzie nodded but couldn't help feeling like she had been unlucky. She'd made it out alive but had been attacked twice, totaling in a stab wound.

"But I'm tempted to kill you myself after what you pulled!"

"I'm sorry," Mackenzie said, feeling the use of her voice finally bring it back to normal as the pangs of guilt radiated through her gut.

"What were you thinking running off to meet with Teo and Amari without help?"

"They had information about my mother," she said weakly, knowing it didn't make her case for why she went alone, and from the raised eyebrow look Lucy gave her, Lucy knew it too.

Lucy's face softened though, after a few moments looking at each other. "I know you want answers." She sighed. "I get it, I do. But one day you'll find the information and you won't need the Arcana to do it. Just promise me you'll stop doing stupid things that could get you killed."

"I promise," Mackenzie lied, meeting Lucy's hazel eyes. Her stomach twisted viciously as she thought about Amari's words, knowing that she was bound to do something stupid soon.

The door to her hospital room opened quietly, drawing the two girls' attention as Kai slid through the entryway, surveying the room. His eyes were framed with dark circles as though he hadn't slept, and he still wore the same clothing she'd left him in at the house. His face, which was hardened into a frown, softened as he caught sight of her awake and alert in the bed, looking up at him. With an easy smile, he let his back sink against the door and relaxed. "I'm glad you're safe now," he said quietly.

She smiled back, meeting his eyes and feeling her heart squeeze guiltily as she remembered leaving them in the house and disappearing. "Thanks. How did you two find me?" she asked, looking between the two of them and seeing their shared smiling glance.

"He used the beast's nose," Lucy said with a grin, flicking her eyes to Kai with waggling eyebrows.

Mackenzie laughed breathily at Lucy's expression for a moment but it didn't touch her eyes as she met Kai's again. "Thank you," she said softly, knowing even at his distance by the door he had heard her.

He nodded, his jaw tightening only slightly as he glanced at the blanket and where her wound was bandaged up out of sight.

Waves of guilt hit her from Kai's place by the door, reminding her of the power she'd taken and letting her feel how truly horrid she'd made him feel. "Lucy already made me promise never to do something like that again."

"Good," he said, nodding, meeting her best friend's gaze and saving an approving nod for her.

Mackenzie watched the two of them, surprised at the agreement they had somehow come to.

Silence fell between the three of them; the only noise filling the room was the sound of Mackenzie's strong heartbeat beeping out clearly from the machine. She waited for someone to say something, feeling Amari's news begin to hit her again as she recalled the conversation, making her numb. She wasn't sure how she was going to tell Lucy or Kai, but figured she couldn't keep it to herself.

It was her best friend's words that broke through her numb thought spiral, bringing her back to reality for a moment.

"Oh hey, I found this in my old stuff in New York and thought you should have it," Lucy said excitedly, reaching into her clutch and pulling out an old photograph. Handing it to Mackenzie, whose eyes went wide, watering with happy tears. "You remember it, don't you? Guess it has a whole different meaning given recent events…"

Kai pushed off the door to look at the photograph from Mackenzie's other side, intrigued.

Lucy and Mackenzie smiled down at their six-year-old selves in the photo. Lucy had a red sparkly leotard on with a top hat, midway through a curtsy as her curly blonde hair flopped around uncontrollably. It was younger Mackenzie's appearance that made them linger with their eyes. She also wore a top hat but had worn a white button-up shirt that was too big for her, black pants, and a large black cape with a purple underside. In her hand was a black-and-white wand.

"It's the day *KZ* was born!" Lucy exclaimed as though the two girls didn't already know it.

"KZ?" Kai echoed, questioning the childhood nickname.

"My mom used to dress us up and we'd try to put magic shows on for her. We were never any good but she used to call me 'The Amazing Kenzini: Magician Extraordinaire'."

"And her lovely assistant," Lucy chimed in with a smile. "Your mom wanted you to have these powers KZ, she just hadn't been able to tell you yet when she disappeared."

The two girls shared a look, remembering, and as Mackenzie thought about her mother and the world of magic she was now in, she ached. The nostalgic watery smile faltered on her face, long enough for Lucy to see.

"What's wrong?"

"I got the information about my mother," Mackenzie said flatly. "After I took Teo's powers."

"Wait? You what?" Kai interrupted, a flash of worry reaching her from his emotions.

"I went there, intending to lie and say that I didn't get

the bracelets to see if they'd believe me. Teo declined to give me the information he'd lured me there with; he wanted the bracelets in exchange for the information. He found out I was lying when I tried to leave, found the bracelets hidden under my shirt and got angry. He attacked and climbed into my emotions before I could stop him and I had no other choice. I wanted him punished and I knew I could do both things so I used the bracelets on him," she recounted, watching both Kai and Lucy's eyes widen at her words, but they stayed silent, allowing her to continue.

"When it was over, I relaxed. Amari appeared, scared and worried, and I trusted her. I couldn't believe she might be corrupted by the Arcana too. She stabbed me before I could see it coming, and… right before you both got there, she told me the information about my mother."

Lucy and Kai both went rigid with bated breaths as they waited to hear the information Mackenzie had suffered to get.

"My mother's alive and the Major Arcana has her," she whispered, hearing the collective gasp in response.

Lucy reached to take her hand, skin warm against hers as Kai spoke softly. "Whatever happens, we're here. You don't need to do this alone. We do it together and we don't rush it."

Lucy adamantly nodded her agreement.

"You'll help me get her back?"

"Of course, love," he replied, leaning down to press a soft kiss to her forehead.

And for the first time in a long time, as Lucy held her hand and Kai rested his chin against the top of her head, an arm around her, she finally felt at home.

WANT TO KNOW MORE?

This story is far from over! Stay tuned for further updates by following along with Harley Jane Rose's social media and website.

ACKNOWLEDGMENTS

Honestly, there are so many people to thank on this written journey and it's hard to know where to start.

This project was one I needed when I was dealing with a lot of chaotic mental health struggles of my own and helped me process my feelings around belonging and relationships (of varying kinds).

Firstly, thank you to the amazing women I dance with. You are all a family I am so lucky I have found. I was just looking to get my physical health back and found so much more.

In particular, thank you to *Steph & Tanele*, who saw me through a lot of pain when this project was being created. You were both there as a solid support and an honest voice of reason every single time I needed it. I am so much better for it.

To *Renee & Lissa* (Laura), it's hard to imagine how I'd get on without you. I'm not sure my creative process would survive without your helpful curbing of my chaos and you are lights in my life that let me be my authentic self.

Thank you to *Tahlia* for being my Monday night rock, putting up with the ebbs and flows of my life, the writing process, the weird ideas I get and the questions I throw your way. The heavy stress I was dealing with when this project came about hit me hard and you are one of the reasons I didn't crumble.

And finally, the biggest thank you to *Amy Laurens*.

You have been a mentor, an adopted sister, and a guide when I've wanted to quit on my writing dream.

You are why this has become real.

ABOUT THE AUTHOR

Current topics of interest are; psychology, folklore, and the dark parts of history to tell stories that hopefully will make you hope, love and cry with the characters all too real in her head.

Harley Jane Rose in the capital of Australia. Proud of her life abundant with travel, she has used her home to experience the world through travel and extensive education.

The light and dark of history, folklore, and the human psyche have always inspired Harley's writing, and the more she discovers, the more detailed those ties become in her writing.

She grew up inspired by what she read, and always making up stories. You would be hard-pressed to find her without a notebook and a book on hand, just in case. She loves the feelings that are all too real when a writer does the job right, and hopes one day to make readers laugh, love and cry the way she has with her own tales.